WOLFEBITE

A Medieval Romance

By Kathryn Le Veque

Part of the de Wolfe Pack Generations Series

WWW.KATHRYNLEVEQUE.COM

ARE YOU SIGNED UP FOR KATHRYN'S BLOG?

You'll get the latest news and information on exclusive giveaways, exclusive excerpts, coming releases, sales, free books, cover reveals and more.

Kathryn's blog followers get it all first. No spam, no junk.

Get the latest info from the reigning Queen of English Medieval Romance!

Sign Up Here

kathrynleveque.com

De Wolfe Motto: *Fortis in arduis*

Strength in times of trouble

Leonidas de Wolfe is the son of a diplomat… but every inch the grandson of William de Wolfe.

This wolfe is going to BITE!

As the son of Edward de Wolfe, Henry III and Edward I's greatest diplomat, Leonidas has been in the heart of England's politics since the beginning of his career. An elite knight, Blackchurch trained and Kenilworth educated, he is the pinnacle of the de Wolfe stable of knights, sons, grandsons, and great-grandsons of the greatest knight of his generation, William de Wolfe.

But what Leonidas is about to face will put that education and training to the test.

He has to keep a young French princess alive long enough to marry the next King of England.

The future queen comes with a nurse and governess in the fair Christelle de Lorrain, but the truth is that Christelle is a trained spy and bodyguard sent to protect the young royal. Leonidas may be tasked with guarding the queen, but Christelle has been tasked with the same thing—and what she says goes. It isn't long before the battle of the wills begins.

So does the attraction.

Leonidas isn't thrilled with the young princess's nurse. The woman seems to have more involvement than a nurse should have, but she's brilliant at pretending to be submissive when she's really doing exactly what she wants to do. Leonidas is used to men obeying his commands without question, but the fair-haired Frenchwoman clearly never got that memo. Leonidas is so busy being irritated with her that he doesn't even realize when he's fallen in love with her.

That brings an entirely new set of problems.

Christelle, however, is a little slower to come around. She finds Leonidas quite handsome and virile, but she has no intention of falling for an English warlord. Her life has been carefully planned out by her de Lorrain family, one of the ruling families of France, and that life does not include a de Wolfe.

… does it?

Join Leonidas and Christelle in an enemies-to-sort-of-lovers trope that takes them from the dangers of Edward III's early reign to the halls of Woodstock Palace, where the young king and his young queen finally take their vows. Will their marriage finally separate the great *Le Morsure* and the French bodyguard known as the *la protecteur de la reine?*

It's another exciting de Wolfe Pack Generations adventure!

AUTHOR'S NOTE

When I'm not writing de Wolfe Pack books, I find that I really miss them!

Here we are, with the latest and greatest de Wolfe Pack Generations novel, *WolfeBite*. Leonidas de Wolfe is our hero, son of Edward de Wolfe and Cassiopeia de Norville, which gives Leonidas a very unique mix of William and Paris in his bloodlines. We've had others—Will and Tor among them—but Leonidas, I think, has more of Paris in him than those two did. He's got William's looks, but his personality has Paris' vivaciousness (arrogance?? Lol). He's a standout knight in a family of standout knights, the son of a diplomat and Paris' only living daughter. I can't wait to introduce you to him!

So, let's talk a little about the year this book is set in and who is still alive in the original de Wolfe Pack. With each successive book, the years are getting further and further away from the mid-thirteenth century, which is when *The Wolfe* and many of the Sons of de Wolfe books take place. We know when Kieran died (*A Wolfe Among Dragons*), but we never see when William or Paris pass away. Thankfully, you won't see it in this book, either, but in this novel, they are long gone. Let me show you the notes I work off so you know who's alive and who's not:

Ages based on Year of Our Lord 1327

Scott 86

Troy 86

Patrick 84

James/Blayth 82

Katheryn 82

Evelyn 79

Edward 75

Thomas 72

Penelope 64

As you can see, the children of William and Jordan are quite elderly, but keep in mind that William lived until he was ninety-two, so their longevity is reasonable. Plus, de Wolfe men are ageless and they fight until they can no longer hold a sword, so don't be surprised if you see an elderly Patrick (my beloved Atty) showing up in battle in some future book. Speaking of which, I get this question a lot—how tall is Atty? If you've read *Nighthawk*, then you know he's the tallest de Wolfe sibling. Patrick de Wolfe is six foot eight. The man is a giant. Not that any of them make an appearance in this book, but this is the most "recently" set book (meaning the timeline is advanced far beyond the usual de Wolfe Pack books), so I thought you'd like to know who's still around.

Now, away from the Sons of de Wolfe, we have an appearance of a group we haven't seen in other books. Shockingly, they've never appeared elsewhere, which is odd, considering I named a publishing company after them. The Dragonblade knights play a significant role in this novel because, as we discover, Leonidas is involved in the whole Roger Mortimer-Edward III issue that Tate de Lara, Kenneth St. Hever, and Stephen of Pembury are involved in. I love that I've been able to incorporate the trio into this tale. They are one of my first loves, so I'm delighted to be writing about them again.

Let me set this up a little for those who haven't read the Dragonblade series—in the initial novel, *Dragonblade*, a major plot point is Tate, Kenneth, and Stephen protecting Edward III from Roger Mortimer. In reality, that period of time was really dicey—for lack of a better word—because young Edward was growing up, he married (at fourteen by some accounts), and Mortimer and Isabella, Edward's mother, were ruling as "regents" for the adolescent king. Well, Edward didn't want them to rule as he grew older, and there were plots, by Mortimer, to supplant Edward. I mean, the guy (allegedly) already killed Edward's father, so it was only a matter of time before he went after the young king.

And that's where our book starts, three years after the book *Dragonblade*, only Leonidas is involved now. And not even Mortimer is going to mess with the entire de Wolfe empire.

One more thing I want to mention is that Phillipa of Hainault plays a significant role in this tale. She was the wife of Edward III. Historians differ on just how old she was when she married the king, but some think she was only fourteen years old when she was crowned Queen of England. She was very, very young. Most agree, however, that she was one of England's most cherished queens—kind and compassionate and genuinely loved by the English people. Quite a change from queens like Eleanor of Aquitaine and even Isabella of France, who was Phillipa's mother-in-law. To be clear, in this book, she's anywhere between fourteen and sixteen years of age and Edward is just a couple of years older. Teenagers ruling a country, folks. It's also very true that Roger Mortimer hoped to gain control of Edward and Phillipa's firstborn child, which happened to be Edward, the Black Prince.

And now, the usual pronunciation guide:

Christelle: Not like "Crystal." It's more like "criss-TELL."

De Lorrain/Lorraine: Not the American pronunciation of lor-RAINE. It's more like "Loren."

Happy Reading!

"Fair son, have pity on the gentle Mortimer..." ~ Isabella of France to her son, Edward III, upon the capture of Roger Mortimer

October, Year of Our Lord 1330

PROLOGUE

Year of Our Lord 1330
Farringdon House, London

"THERE IS A plot to murder Edward and place Mortimer and Isabella's child upon the throne."

The words hung in the air, the impact of which resonated like an explosion. But the truth was that they'd heard the rumor before. The winds of gossip, true or not, blew heavily in the highest halls of England as the young king, Edward III, grappled for the throne with his mother's lover, Roger Mortimer.

But these words were different. They were spoken to a chamber full of the greatest spies in the land—men known as the Executioner Knights—and they had more of a grip on what was actually happening as the maelstrom of politics threatened the very foundation they believed in. Therefore, these words were not simply conjecture.

Now, the rumors were transformed into reality.

There is a plot to murder Edward!

"And you are certain of this?" An enormous man with piercing blue eyes and a mane of full, dark hair spoke. "There is no doubt in your mind?"

"None," replied a man who was a third-generation Executioner Knight. Gideon of Loxbeare was one of the very best, like his father and his father before him, and he did not speak empty words. "Lest you forget, Leo, that my family is still allied with Mortimer. I heard this from his own lips not a fortnight ago after the man had too much to drink. He is convinced that Isabella is pregnant, and he intends to put his own son upon the throne."

Sir Leonidas de Wolfe stared at Gideon a moment longer before letting out a long, deep sigh of regret. Turning away, he let his gaze fell on the other men in the chamber, men who were in various stages of acceptance and outrage over the news.

Tate de Lara.

Stephen of Pembury.

Kenneth St. Hever.

Men who had been more involved in the situation between Edward III and Roger Mortimer than anyone else in England, Leonidas included.

Now, they were facing a crisis of historic proportions.

"So you have gathered us in de Lohr's London home, the very heart of the Executioner Knights' lair, to give us this terrible news," Leonidas muttered. Then he turned to face Gideon. "While you and your underworld brethren have been keeping this country from tearing itself apart, Tate and Stephen and Kenneth and I have been trying to keep Edward and his wife from falling victim to Mortimer's greed. We work in concert with you."

Gideon nodded patiently. "I know."

"*We* keep this monarchy alive."

"I *know*," Gideon stressed. "Leo, I realize this is not what you wanted to hear, but now that I have heard it from Mortimer's own lips, we can at least form a plan to keep Edward from his grasp."

Leonidas snorted softly. "Plan, indeed," he said. "Because it is worse than you think, Gideon."

"How?"

Leonidas glanced at Tate and Stephen and Kenneth before continuing. They were men who had been in the trenches ever since the issue between Edward II and Roger Mortimer arose. Highly trained veterans who tended to act as a group more than individuals. Everyone knew that de Lara and St. Hever and Pembury were an inseparable trio. From Tate's level head to Kenneth's quiet strength to Pembury's willingness to be the first man into a fight and the last man out, they were a formidable line that stood between the monarchy and death.

They were honor personified.

"There was a time when the knights you see before you kept our young king out of the reach of his mother and her lover," Leonidas finally said. "We could not help his father, God rest his soul, so we had to focus on the son who is now the king. A young king who is trying to rule this country with the help of many advisors and allies, Marcus de Lohr included. The Earl of Ludlow, like his father and his father before him, have been in command of the Executioner Knights since William Marshal's sons passed on the responsibility to the House of de Lohr. Farringdon House used to be a Marshal property, in fact."

"What is your point?"

Leonidas' gaze was intense. "The point is that the names may change, but the core of what we do remains the same," he said in a low voice. "Men like William Marshal and Christopher de Lohr and others formed this foundation. We are merely continuing what they started. I was recruited by Marcus de Lohr for the Executioner Knights because he wanted a de Wolfe. He wanted *me*. I am a knight from a family of knights, grandson of the greatest knight England has ever seen in William de Wolfe. When I tell you there is trouble more than you know, it is because I know what I am talking about because I am not one to sound an alarm when there is no need. There *is* great need, Gideon."

"Then what is it?"

"Edward's wife, Phillipa, is pregnant with their firstborn."

Gideon, who was a man trained to keep his composure, couldn't help the brief flash of shock that crossed his face. "My God," he breathed. "Mortimer must not know. He's not made mention of it."

Leonidas lifted his dark brows. "The child is due in the summer," he said. "She is about midway through the pregnancy, but you can see the danger. If Mortimer knows she is pregnant…"

"Then that puts a price on her head as well," Gideon finished for him. "And Phillipa is a daughter of Holland, so her death would bring the wrath of the Holy Roman Empire on a scale that might tear this country to shreds."

Leonidas tapped himself on the head. "Now you understand," he said. "We have allowed Edward and Phillipa relative freedom at Woodstock Palace because Mortimer remains either at his properties or in London. He hasn't paid a tremendous amount of attention to Phillipa, but he has to Edward. And the fear is that Isabella will be unable to truly prevent Mortimer from eliminating her son if he is determined to, but now… now we have the next heir to the English throne to be concerned with."

"My concern is for Edward," Tate spoke up. "I mean no disrespect to Phillipa or the child she carries, but my concerned has always been for Edward. I do not want him to end up like his father."

All eyes turned to the big man with black hair and blue eyes. He had a special concern in this situation and they all knew it. Sir Tate de Lara had the distinction of being a royal bastard, the firstborn son of Edward I, the result of young Prince Edward having a liaison with a Welsh princess many years ago. Tate's Welsh name was Tatilian, given to him by his mother, but his father gave the infant over to the House of de Lara to raise, great marcher lords, and Tatilian became Tate. He was the man who should have been king, but instead, he'd been forced to watch his half-brother assume the throne—and now, he was charged with protecting his nephew. As the Earl of Carlisle, he wielded much power in England.

Therefore, when Tate spoke, they all listened.

"Then Edward must be removed from Woodstock," Leonidas said. "I know you hid Edward from Mortimer while his father was still alive, but it is my sense that he must, once again, go into hiding. Phillipa most especially now that there is an impending child that could quash whatever plans Mortimer has for his own offspring."

Tate couldn't disagree. "We did not have to worry about Phillipa a few years ago when Edward traveled with us, disguised as my squire," he said, indicating Kenneth and Stephen. "It was easy to keep his identity concealed. But he married, and now we must contend with a young queen who is carrying the next king."

Leonidas nodded. "Edward is not going to like this, but I believe he and his wife should be separated," he said. "It will be much more difficult for Mortimer to get his hands on both of them if they are not together."

"Agreed," Tate said. "We have been discussing this possibility ever since we learned of Phillipa's condition, but now it has come time to act. If Mortimer finds out, and he will at some point, then both Edward and Phillipa will be in great danger."

Leonidas knew that. This was the moment they'd been anticipating for quite some time, ever since Edward had been crowned king and married his very young wife. They were both children, really, children who had been thrust into a world of greedy and dangerous men. They had powerful warlords around them, but the problem was that Roger Mortimer did, too. He and Isabella had been acting regents for Edward, but the boy was becoming a man. He didn't want regents any longer.

And Roger Mortimer knew it.

"Then I would suggest you take Edward to Carlisle Castle immediately and keep him there," Leonidas said. "I will take Phillipa to Ashendon. The place is impenetrable."

"But for how long?" Gideon wanted to know. "So you separate them and take them to safety, but for how long? When does this all end, Leo?"

Leonidas looked at a man he'd worked with for years, a man who had asked a very valid question. When *did* it all end?

"When we rid ourselves of Mortimer," he muttered. "That is something Edward has been speaking of. Roger Mortimer will not willingly give up his power. Now he speaks of supplanting Edward with a child that Isabella is allegedly carrying. This ends when Mortimer has been neutralized."

"But that is Edward's decision," Tate said quietly. "This is his fight. We have made enough decisions for him throughout his life, decisions that he was forced to go along with, and we have just made another one in separating him from his wife. Let the decision to rid himself of Mortimer be Edward's. He is the king. Let him be one."

Leonidas knew that, but it was difficult to see a fourteen-year-old boy as a king sometimes. Leonidas had stepchildren Edward's age, so it was difficult to see the young boy as a man able to assume the mantle of king.

"He is a king who must share his kingdom with a power-hungry bastard," he muttered. "And Phillipa—she was only just crowned queen even though she has been Edward's wife for two years. Isabella was loath to surrender her crown to the young woman."

"Isabella had no choice," Tate said. "But that does not mean she is no longer the queen. She sees herself as the only true queen."

Leonidas grunted. "And Mortimer sees himself as the king," he said. "What a pair."

"A pair we have been dealing with for years," Kenneth spoke up. He was usually the silent type, but in the company of men he was close to, he tended to be more confident to voice his opinions. "We know their tactics. We have the advantage. But we will not keep the advantage if we do not move the young queen out of Woodstock and into hiding. Leo, I can go with you to Ashendon. Tate and Stephen can take Edward on to Carlisle dressed as me. Edward is tall enough to wear my clothing—and what does not fit him, we can stuff with cloth because I am considerably bulkier than he is."

That brought snorts of laughter from Stephen, who tended to be the most comically inclined out of the trio. "You have the build of a bull, Ken," he said.

Kenneth, born without a keen sense of humor, cocked a blond eyebrow at his closest friend. "And you have the wit of an ass, so I would be cautious when making light of others," he said, watching Tate and Leonidas grin. "As I was saying—let anyone who sees Tate and Stephen think the third knight is me. That will help Edward move freely until he reaches Carlisle. Meanwhile, I will go with Leo to Ashendon with the young queen. She'll need the protection."

Tate lifted his dark eyebrows in a knowing expression. "Do not forget that she has her own protection," he said. "That Frenchwoman she keeps with her, the one she tells everyone is her lady-in-waiting."

Leonidas rolled his eyes. "That woman is no more a lady-in-waiting than I am," he said. "She may look like a flower, but she stings like a wasp. I saw her break a servant's hand once when the man touched the queen's sleeve. She did it so quickly that it was over before anyone could draw a sword."

Tate nodded as he headed over to a table upon which sat a half-filled pitcher of wine and a few dirty cups. "I remember," he said. "But the servant should have known better."

"The man was trying to hand the queen a kerchief, Tate."

"Imagine if he hadn't been? Imagine if he'd been raising a dagger?"

Leonidas shrugged, conceding the point. "That woman is fearsome, in any case," he said. "She only came about a year ago, when her father became aware of the trouble with Mortimer and Isabella. I've not had much contact with her, but Marcus de Lohr told me she was Blackchurch trained."

That brought the men in the chamber to a halt. Even Gideon, who had been converging on Tate for some of that stale wine.

"Blackchurch?" Gideon repeated. "*Who* is this woman we are speaking of?"

Leonidas found the most comfortable chair in the chamber and sat wearily. The chair itself was cold and dusty, near the dark and ashy hearth, but it was the first time he'd sat down all day. "A woman who is Phillipa's constant companion," he said. "She told everyone that she was her lady-in-waiting, and she still stays to the story, but the reality is much different. The woman is a personal guard and, from what I've seen, lives up to the Blackchurch reputation."

"You're Blackchurch trained, are you not?" Gideon asked.

Leonidas nodded. "Me, and Tate, and Ken," he said. Then he grinned at Stephen. "Pembury's father would not let him train at Blackchurch, fearful that the only Pembury son might hurt himself somehow. You know how nasty and dangerous Blackchurch is."

That was true, in fact, though he'd meant it as a taunt against Stephen. The Blackchurch Guild was the premier knight training school in England, if not the world. Fully fledged knights, farm boys, and more were allowed to apply for Blackchurch's training. Men and women alike. A man's background didn't matter at Blackchurch. If he, or she, was tough enough to get through the initiation, then they were accepted into the training, but one failure on the part of the recruit at any point during the time of their years-long training would see them expelled. That was the high standard set by the Lords of Exmoor, the family who controlled Blackchurch. It was a standard that made Blackchurch graduates the very best warriors in the known world.

And Queen Phillipa had one by her side.

Soon, she would have two.

"I can still train at Blackchurch should I so decide," Stephen said with a hint of defensiveness. "But why? I've been a knight for twenty years. What more could they possibly teach me?"

Leonidas chuckled softly. "You would be surprised."

As Stephen shrugged, Tate brought Leonidas a cup of the flat wine. "Stephen doesn't need the training," he said. "He's better than most who come out of the guild, me included. Speaking of Blackchurch, don't you have a brother going through the training now?"

Leonidas sipped on the awful wine. "My youngest brother, Pallas," he said. "He's two years into the program and hasn't failed yet, so there is hope for the big dolt. My father thinks so, anyway."

Tate sat down opposite Leonidas. "And how does your father fare these days?" he asked. "The great Edward de Wolfe. He has been a source of great guidance to me, more times than I can count."

Leonidas smiled faintly, thinking of the man he looked up to most in the world. "He is doing very well, thank you for asking," he said. "In fact, all of his siblings are doing well."

"Are they all alive, still?"

"Still," Leonidas said. "My oldest uncles, Scott and Troy, have seen more than eighty summers. In fact, the eldest five siblings have all seen eighty summers and more, but they are still healthy and solid of mind, thankfully. All except Uncle Blayth, that is. He had a severe head injury as a younger man and the damage has become worse as he's grown older. He does not remember much these days, and I do not think he even knows who his wife is sometimes, but that does not matter. He can still jump on a table and sing a song better than anyone I know."

Tate smiled. "He is a legend," he said reverently. "All of your uncles are. Sons of the great William de Wolfe. He has left a great legacy."

"Aye, he has."

"Did you ever really know him, Leo?"

Leonidas finished off the last of the wine. "I was only four years of age when he passed away," he said. "I do not remember him well, truthfully. All I remember is a feeling. He was a very big man and I remember his lifting me up and putting me on his shoulder. I felt as if I was on top of the world when Poppy lifted me up."

He used the name that all of the de Wolfe grandchildren and great-grandchildren called William, and Tate nodded in understanding. "You have good memories of him, then," he said, his smile fading. "I have none of my grandfather. I never knew him."

"But you knew your father."

"I did," Tate said. "I do not look like him, as I take after my mother's Welsh side, but I fight like him. Edward's blood is in my veins. Mayhap that is why I feel so strongly about preserving our young king. My father would want me to. He would want me to fight at his side, no matter what the cause, but he would not want me to fight his battles for him."

"Understandable," Leonidas said, his gaze lingering on Tate as the others joined them with cups of stale wine. "You are an inspiration to us all, you know. The man who should have been king. You live your life with such dignity and honor."

Tate averted his gaze. It wasn't necessarily a sensitive subject, because the general consensus was that he would have made a legendary king, greater than any of his ancestors, and that praise tended to embarrass him.

"If I was, then we would not be having this discussion," Tate said, trying to make light of the subject. "We would not be having these troubles, in fact. Mortimer would be in a cage, there would be no Isabella, and life would be good."

Leonidas quietly slapped his thigh a couple of times. "Hear, hear," he said in agreement. "But, unfortunately, there are tribulations we must deal with, so mayhap we should get on with it. Gideon? Is there anything else we should know?"

Gideon had the pitcher of wine in his hand because there were no more cups left. "Nay," he said. "I will return to the marches and keep watch over Mortimer. But when you hide Edward and Phillipa..."

He left the sentence hanging in the air until Leonidas looked at him. "What is it?"

Gideon sighed heavily. "Hide them well," he said. "Mortimer is not jesting and he is no fool. If he can get to them, he will."

Tate was still looking at the ground, slumped back in the chair he was sitting in. "Gideon?"

"Aye, Tate?"

There was a long pause before Tate answered. "If you have the opportunity to dispatch Mortimer, so that no one suspects his death was not an accident, would you take it?"

Gideon's expression almost became one of amusement. "De Lohr asked me the same question, once."

"What did you tell him?"

Gideon took that moment to drain what was left in the pitcher and set it back down, wiping his mouth with the back of his hand.

"That I am my father, and grandfather's, son," he said, dark eyes glimmering. "Of course I would take it. And I would be doing us all a favor."

With that, he quit the elaborate chamber, the room where Executioner Knights had been meeting for well over one hundred years. The very walls themselves were saturated with intrigue and righteousness, put there by the voices of men who had shaped the course of a nation. At this moment, the men in the chamber, even three and four generations later, were still trying to do the same.

England was a complicated vessel.

"Amen," Leonidas whispered after a moment. "That he would."

No one disputed him.

Within the hour, all four of them were riding hard for Oxfordshire and Woodstock Palace.

CHAPTER ONE

"DO NOT LEAVE, Christy, please. Stay and talk to me."

It was a soft plea, a tender plea, and one that had Lady Christelle de Lorrain pausing at the door to the queen's chamber. The plea had, in fact, come from Phillipa as she sat in her bed, surrounded by furs and silks, resplendent as a queen should be, but there was one problem.

She didn't like to be alone.

Christelle smiled.

"Lonely, your grace?" she said. "Truly, you should be used to sleeping alone by now. Your husband has been gone several days."

Phillipa frowned. A slight young woman with long, dark hair and big brown eyes, she was a petite, pretty woman. She had seen seventeen summers, the same as her husband, and there was a grace and maturity about her that well exceeded her chronological age. But physically, she still looked childlike, young and innocent and slight, and sometimes that immaturity bled over into her manner like it did tonight.

"He goes hunting and I am left alone," she said, standing up from the bed. Dressed in an elaborate robe of red silk, she moved to the polished bronze mirror to inspect her reflection. "Mayhap it is because he does not wish to stay here with me. Mayhap he thinks I am too fat!"

She emphasized her statement by pulling the robe tight to reveal a very small belly bulge. It was hardly noticeable. Christelle fought off a smirk as she came away from the door and back into the chamber.

"You know he is so proud of your coming child that he is about to burst," she said. "And he went hunting because he enjoys it and for no other reason than that. This hunt has been planned for some time."

Phillipa rubbed the tiny bump. "He told me I could not come."

"Do you truly want to go in your condition, your grace?"

Phillipa turned to Christelle, brow furrowed. "I can ride a horse, still," she said with some indignance. "I did not want to hunt. I simply wanted to go with him."

With that, she turned away from the mirror, hurt and lonely. Christelle wasn't unsympathetic, but the truth was that her role as *la protecteur de la reine* had become something more than simple protection. Somewhere over the past year, she'd become the big sister and Mother Confessor as well, nurturing the young queen through some of the most difficult days of her life.

That was something Christelle had not been taught at Blackchurch.

As she watched Phillipa head back to her bed, Christelle knew that there wasn't anything more she could say or do to give the young woman comfort. She'd learned that long ago.

Phillipa was very attached to her husband, a young man who was finally coming into his own as a king but also as a man. He had a good head on his shoulders. The truth was that Phillipa and Edward had practically grown up together because they had been betrothed at such a young age. Even though the marriage had been by proxy, Phillipa had come to the shores of England shortly thereafter so she and her new husband could grow to at least like one another.

Phillipa's father had hoped for that, at the very least.

The truth was that her father, a powerful count, had been so desperate for his daughter to become a queen that he had agreed to a marriage that put his daughter in a good deal of danger. It wasn't any secret that Edward's mother, Isabella, permitted her lover to rule England in her son's stead. The excuse had always been that Edward was too young to rule as king and, therefore, Isabella and Roger Mortimer were forced to be the lad's regents. Mortimer's involvement in the Crown of England had long roots, starting back in the days of Isabella's husband, Edward II, when Edward and the Despensers practically ruled England as a trio and Isabella was demeaned and humiliated by her husband's actions, including the terrible act of having her own children taken away.

To Isabella, Roger Mortimer had been a godsend.

The entire situation of Edward, Isabella's husband, and Edward, Isabella's son, was incredibly complicated. Christelle was all too aware of it because before she returned to England to attend Phillipa, she had been schooled in the situation by French courtiers, who understood the circumstances as well as an Englishman could. The French, too, had been involved in the situation because Isabella was French.

And so was Christelle's family.

La Maison Lorrain.

A very powerful house that would like nothing more than to see the collapse of the English Crown.

Therefore, Christelle's presence at Phillipa's side was complicated as well. She had the mission that Phillipa and young Edward knew about, as an attendant and protector. She also had a mission they didn't know about. She had been specially trained, by her own father and his allies, as a spy of the most nuanced kind. Christelle was always meant to be a weapon.

That was the mission Phillipa didn't know about.

Not until the time was right.

"It would not have been enjoyable for you to go on a hunt, your grace," Christelle said after a moment, watching Phillipa pace. "It would have been cold and uncomfortable, and a lady in your delicate condition requires warmth and a soft bed to sleep in. Your husband will be home soon enough, I promise."

Phillipa shrugged. "I suppose," she said. Then she came to a halt and sighed sharply. "I cannot sleep, Christy. Will you read to me?"

Christelle nodded. "Of course, your grace," she said. "What is your wish?"

"Anything."

That meant any one of the manuscripts and books Phillipa proudly collected. She had hundreds of them, most of them left behind at her childhood home, but her most valuable ones had made it to England and were neatly stacked on shelves far away from the window and far away from the hearth. As Phillipa explained, the heat or the cold affected the vellum and the leather, so they were kept away from everything.

Christelle was well acquainted with the books because she often read aloud to Phillipa, who would gaze from the windows and daydream about the world that was being spun through Christelle's words. Her favorite stories were those of romance, but she also loved myths and religious stories. Christelle was thinking about continuing a book about ancient Welsh legends, written in Latin that had been translated from oral stories about three hundred years earlier, when she passed by the large window that overlooked the ward of Woodstock Palace. A cold breeze caught her attention, so she paused to close the oilcloth windows.

Woodstock Palace was really nothing more than a large manor house with a big bailey and an enormous wall with a central gatehouse. The manor house, however, had two entrances—one for the king's set of chambers and another for the queen's. Both monarchs had their own halls, antechambers, bedchambers, privies, and the like, so it was like two households in one structure. Christelle was used to seeing people going into the king's hall, with an enormous flight of stairs leading up to it, but tonight everything was still and quiet. It had been ever since Edward went away to hunt. She was about to close the curtains for the night when she saw figures coming in through the gatehouse, dark shapes on horseback that were moving for the manor.

Curious, Christelle looked around to see if she could spot any of the royal guards that roamed the grounds and walls of Woodstock, but she didn't see anyone. Not a soul. More than that, the usual torches weren't lit on the walls or at the gatehouse, and as she watched, the four men approached the entrance to the queen's hall, which was usually well guarded. Given the fact that she didn't see any guards about the grounds, however, she was coming to wonder where all of the guards had gone. Perhaps purposely gone. When the shadows down in the bailey dismounted their horses and unsheathed their swords, realization hit her.

A lone queen… her king away on a hunting trip… would be a perfect target for enemies.

Damn!

Swiftly, she moved away from the window.

"Quickly," she said to Phillipa. "Douse the lights. Hurry!"

Startled by the tone of Christelle's voice, Phillipa slid off the bed and hurriedly doused the taper next to the bed.

"Why?" she asked fearfully. "Whatever is the matter?"

Christelle grasped the woman by the hand and quickly pulled her from her bedchamber and into the privy chamber. It was a chamber full of wardrobes, a tub, and other things for the queen's toilette, but it also contained a hidden chamber for moments just like this. Tucked in behind one of the wardrobes was a panel that opened. Christelle rushed for it and hit the secret lever that swung the door open.

"Get inside," she whispered urgently. "Bolt the door and do not come out until I tell you to."

Phillipa was terrified but did as she was told. The panel shut and Christelle heard the bolt thrown. Only then did she swing into action.

Her things were in what was called the queen's withdrawing chamber, but it was simply a chamber where Christelle slept behind a painted wooden screen, a chamber that guarded the door to the queen's bedchamber. Anyone wanting to get to the queen had to pass by Christelle first, so she rushed into the chamber and grabbed her sword and a club she had tucked under her bed. It was all she had time for. After quickly fastening the scabbard around her hips, she shoved the sword into its sheath and picked up the club, heading for the queen's hall and the antechamber that was next to it. If anyone came into the hall, they'd have to enter the antechamber before they were able to move any further into the palace.

And she was going to be waiting for them.

Truthfully, Christelle didn't even know if the door to the queen's hall was locked. The servants usually bolted it after dark, but sometimes the guards moved in and out, so she couldn't be sure it was bolted. As she rushed into the antechamber and sank back into the shadows, she listened for the hall door to open. It was still and dark in the queen's hall, and the antechamber, so the only sound she eventually heard was that of the entry door opening. Her heart sank when she realized it hadn't been bolted yet for the night.

Footsteps.

Heavy footsteps.

The men were in the hall.

Sneaking up to the door to the antechamber, Christelle positioned herself well.

And then, she waited.

℃

"Where is everyone?" Stephen wondered, looking around the darkened bailey. "I do not even see the sentries, who should be on duty."

Tate and Leonidas dismounted their steeds, looking around too. "There were men at the gatehouse," Tate said. "But it does seem oddly quiet."

Leonidas removed his helm and propped it on his saddle. "Are the king and queen even here?" he asked. "Did they move to another residence?"

"Where?" Tate said, looking at him. "There are no royal

residences nearby, unless you want to include that hunting lodge about a day's ride to the west."

Leonidas just stood there, looking around, wondering why everything felt so strange. "I do not like this," he said after a moment. "The sooner we find Edward and Phillipa, the better."

Kenneth, who had pulled his horse next to Leonidas, slid off his saddle. "What's wrong, Leo?"

Leonidas shook his head. "I do not know," he said. "But Tate is right—it seems oddly quiet."

The realization of stone-cold surroundings seemed to put them all on heightened alert. Leonidas was the first one to draw his broadsword, quickly followed by the others. He pointed toward the queen's hall because that was a small, less-traveled entry point, and Stephen took the lead. He was the tallest out of the four of them, at least a head taller than those around him, and he was also the one who usually insisted on being on point. He'd take the lead and open the way, letting Leonidas and Tate and Kenneth take on the heavy fighting. Heading right for the door, he tried the latch to see that it was unlocked. Silently, he lifted his hand to the others, telling them to be prepared, as he opened the panel and stepped through.

Whack!

Because Stephen was so tall, the weapon flying at him in the darkness hit him in the throat rather than the face or the head, which was where it was probably aimed. Startled by the blow, and very nearly choking on the impact, he stumbled sideways as Tate charged in, pushing Stephen aside as the man fell to his knees. But Tate immediately took a blow to his left wrist and hand, not enough to crush but certain enough to hurt like the blazes. He faltered as a result, and the figure in the darkness with the club rushed toward the rear of the hall, back into the shadows, as Leonidas and Kenneth entered. As Kenneth went to make sure Stephen wasn't choking to death, Leonidas fanned out into the corner near the door, watching the hall closely, as Tate shook out the stinging in his hand.

"Whoever you are, we will find you," Leonidas said loudly. "Surrender now and we may show mercy."

There was no answer. Motioning to Tate and Kenneth, and even Stephen now that the man could at least catch his breath, Leonidas and the knights began to move in a line, from one end of the hall to the other, sweeping forward in slow, methodical steps. Swords were leveled defensively because it was very dark and the queen's hall was somewhat elaborate. There were several opportunities to hide behind chairs or even a great curtain that was draped at the far end, concealing the door to the next chamber. They were halfway across the hall when the shadow suddenly appeared again and something went flying out at them.

Whatever it was happened to be metal. It flew into the hall, clipped a chair, and ricocheted right into Leonidas' head. He saw stars as a metal cup, a heavy one, hit him in in the forehead, and he staggered as he came to a halt. But the pause was only momentary. When he realized the cup had cut him, his fury took over.

He charged.

The figure was trying to make it to the door behind the curtain, but Leonidas was on them. The figure was armed and a sword came out, though it was low, at about Leonidas' hip. Because it was so dark, he almost saw it too late, but he caught the movement and was able to lower his sword to deflect it. Tate, Kenneth, and Stephen were right behind him and managed to chase the figure away from the door and into a small alcove used by servants.

That was when things really started to fly.

The figure began to throw anything and everything at them—cups, bowls, and cutlery. A spoon nearly put Kenneth's eye out. Leonidas, in the lead, had his arm up, deflecting the flying dinnerware, but he crowded the figure too much and ended up being kicked in the knee. In fact, feet were flying at him and he caught kicks in the thigh and lower belly as well, but he managed to grab the foot and yank, trying to pull the figure out of the shadows. It didn't work immediately because whoever it was put up a hell of a fight. Tate tried to help him and got kicked in the face for his efforts. Enraged, Leonidas grabbed whatever he could on the figure and pulled as hard as he could, sending the person onto the ground. Then he managed to get a hold of the head, which had masses of long hair that he painfully wound his hand into.

The sword that the figure was holding clattered to the ground.

"You'll never find what you are looking for, you bastards," the figure grunted. "The guards will kill you when they realize you are here!"

Leonidas suddenly came to a halt. He recognized that voice. He'd heard it over the past year as he'd kept guard over the young king and queen and, very quickly, he realized who was within his grasp.

"Lady Christelle?" he said, incredulous.

It was so dark that no one could see much of anything and certainly not enough for identification, but the figure in his arms slowed her struggles.

"Christelle?" Leonidas said again. "Is it you?"

There was hesitation. "Who is it?" she demanded.

Leonidas' suspicion was confirmed and he immediately released her. As Christelle fell to the ground, he put a hand to his bloodied forehead.

"It is de Wolfe," he said, unhappy with all of the wetness he was feeling. "I'm with de Lara and Pembury and St. Hever."

Christelle scrambled to her feet. "Leonidas?" she gasped. "But… what are you doing here? What are you *all* doing here? You are supposed to be in London."

The knights made their way out of the alcove and Kenneth managed to find a taper, using flint and stone to light it. A soft, warm glow emerged, making faces clear.

Leonidas still had his hand against his forehead. "We *were* in London," he said, irritated. "Now, we are here. Where are all of the guards? Why is this place so dark and empty?"

Christelle peered at him in the dim light. "You know the guards," she said, pulling his hand away to get a look at his forehead. "They are lazy when Edward is not here. They're probably all in the troop house, drinking and gambling."

Leonidas snorted unhappily. "I am not surprised."

"You had better let me tend your wound."

He scowled at her. "You'd *better* tend it," he said, jabbing a finger at the rest of them. "And Stephen's throat. And Ken's eye. And Tate's face. You probably broke the man's nose with that kick."

Christelle looked at the four knights she'd managed to wound. Four of the most powerful knights in the realm and men she'd been acquainted with for the past year. Not friendly with, but acquainted with. They mostly served Edward and she exclusively served Phillipa, so their paths were parallel rather than crossing.

With Leonidas, sometimes she wished they *would* cross.

It was true that she was here on a mission, and that mission was only regarding the queen. It did not involve English knights or warlords or any number of people that Edward sometimes surrounded himself with. Though she did keep an ear to what the king was doing, and what was being said, she never got involved. That wasn't her place. Nor was it her place to particularly interact with the knights.

But that didn't stop her from thinking one, in particular, was rather comely.

All of the de Wolfes were. Or, at least, that was what she'd heard. Leonidas de Wolfe was the eldest son of Edward de Wolfe, a man who had been Henry III's chief diplomat. He'd served Edward I in the same capacity, but Edward's son, Edward II, had relegated de Wolfe to the background in favor of his most cherished companions, the Despensers. If anyone should take issue with the Despenser father and son, it would be Edward de Wolfe. An experienced and well-loved diplomat, he'd not been treated well by the former king. But Leonidas' devotion to Edward III had shown no animosity or reserve. Leonidas de Wolfe, according to some, was the most powerful and clever knight of his generation. He did his grandfather's legacy proud.

Christelle thought he was all those things and more.

But she'd never let him know it.

As Kenneth and Stephen, nursing a sore neck, went to harass the sentries who had shirked their guard duties, Christelle took Leonidas and Tate into the queen's antechamber and released Phillipa from the concealed room. As Phillipa fussed over Tate and his slightly bloodied nose, Christelle forced Leonidas to sit down on a cushioned bench so she could take a look at the cut on his forehead. The man was so tall that even sitting down, his forehead was about at her eye level. The wound had bled a lot, so the man had blood all over him, and as he tried to clean up his hands with a wet rag, Christelle inspected the cut she'd given him.

"I think you will need a stitch or two," she finally said, taking the rag out of his hand as he was in the middle of wiping. "But I must stop the bleeding first."

He frowned that she'd taken his rag and pressed it against his forehead. She pushed so hard that she pushed his head backward, irritated when he didn't hold steady.

"Do not move so much," she told him.

He rolled his eyes. "I would not move at all if you did not push so hard," he said. "Stop using your brute strength on me."

She grunted. "You'll know when I use my brute strength on you," she said. "I would do more than push your head backward."

"I've seen your brute strength. It tried to take my head off with a bowl."

He was referring to the cut, and Christelle fought off a grin. "You complain much."

"You give me much to complain about."

"I imagine you were an annoying child."

"I was the *perfect* child."

Christelle simply shook her head, putting her hand against the back of his skull while she pushed the rag against the cut at the same time to help hold his head still.

"There, darling," she said with mock sweetness. "Is that better?"

He eyed her. "Careful, love," he muttered. "Next time, I may not be so forgiving if you throw a bowl at me."

"Next time, don't sneak in like an assassin."

"Next time, I will catch you, string you up by your thumbs, and beat you like the incorrigible child you are."

She peeled back her lips to display a very fake, and quite sassy, smile. He did the same thing, and it looked as if they were baring their teeth at each other. Christelle was forced to turn away lest he see her smile, because he really was annoyed with her and she found it hilarious. And charming.

Damn the man!

"Here," she said, slapping the bloodied rag back into his hand. "Hold this against your forehead. I must collect the needle and thread."

He put the cloth against the wound. "Find a color that blends in with my skin," he said. "No need to flash around your handiwork."

Christelle cocked an unhappy eyebrow at him as she went to find what she needed and Leonidas watched her go. That fiery woman who wasn't afraid to stand up to him, taunt him, and generally annoy him.

That beautiful little minx.

Stop thinking like that, you fool.

He *was* a fool—a stupid, idiotic fool—to let thoughts like that into his head, but when Christelle was around, he couldn't help it. It was her appearance that first caught his attention; she was a stunningly beautiful woman with long spirals of auburn hair, rather wild at times, and a face that would make any man take a second look. She had a square jaw, pert nose, eyes the color of the sea, and a smile that was brighter than anything he'd ever seen. A very rare smile, if he thought on it. The woman was tough and focused, not leaning into her femininity like most women did, but rather more toward the life of vigilance and the training that she'd endured. If she brushed her hair once in a while or wore something other than breeches and a broadcloth surcoat over them, she could outshine the sun.

Or so he thought.

But he'd die before he'd say such a thing.

A timid privy chamber servant joined them, an older woman who had heard all of the fighting and yelling, and she went running for hot water and other items at the queen's request. Meanwhile, Phillipa made a poultice for Tate to hold on his nose as Christelle gathered her lady's sewing kit and some wine, returning to Leonidas, who was trying not to look at her. He had the rag still pressed against his forehead, but his focus was on Tate as Phillipa tried to help the man.

Christelle pulled the rag out of his hand and set it aside.

"Here," she said, handing him a cup with some wine in it. "Drink this while I do this. I'll be quick."

He drained the cup and set it down. "Have you done this kind of thing before?"

"I have."

"Did they live?"

"Nay, none of them."

He did look at her then. He could see the mirth in her eyes as she focused on the cut, antagonistic little chit that she was, and couldn't decide if he was irritated or amused. He settled on closing his eyes because he didn't want to see the enormous needle she was going to use on his forehead, undoubtedly just to be cruel to him.

He wouldn't have been surprised.

"Hopefully I shall not be among them," he said after a moment. "Remember—I told you to use thread that will not be obvious against my skin. No black thread."

Christelle glanced at him, seeing that his eyes were closed, and her lips twitched with a dastardly smile.

"No black thread, I promise," she said. "Be strong, de Wolfe. This may sting a little."

He grunted in response, and she took some of the wine she'd brought over to cleanse the wound, pouring it onto his forehead and letting it dribble down onto his nose and eyes. But Leonidas didn't flinch. He sat stock-still as she swiftly put five rather big stitches in his forehead, into the cut which was oddly shaped like a cross.

"You are finished," she said, taking the bloodied rag and using a clean corner to clean the wine that had dripped onto his eyes. *Such nice eyes.* "I would continue to put wine on the cut every morning and every evening until it begins to heal. You do not want poison taking hold."

He stood up, towering over her. "I have had wounds before," he said. "I know how to tend them. But I thank you for your kind attention."

"My pleasure, my lord."

"Even if you did cause it."

"You should not have been moving in the dark like a phantom."

They were verging on an argument, and he eyed her with displeasure before moving over to where Tate was holding an arnica poultice over his nose. Phillipa and Christelle quit the chamber, heading back to the queen's bedchamber, as Leonidas bent over Tate and pulled the poultice back to get a look at the damage.

"Well," he said, replacing the poultice. "It is not too bad. It looks as if she mostly got you under the eye. You'll have a bruise."

Tate, seated on a stool, was looking up at Leonidas but not

looking the man in the eye. He was looking at his forehead.

"Christ," he muttered. "Leo, have you looked at your forehead?"

"What about it?"

Tate gestured to the mirror on the other side of the chamber, near the wardrobe. "You'd better go look."

Puzzled, Leonidas went to the mirror, peering closely in the dim light to see what Tate was referring to. Not only did he have a cross-shaped wound on his forehead, but it was a cross-stitched with bright red thread. There it was, sticking out like a sore thumb, right in the middle of his brow. He looked like a damn flagellant, cutting crosses on his head to prove his devotion to God.

He'd told her no black thread.

He should have said no red thread, either.

CHAPTER TWO

Two Days Later

"TATE, YOU KNOW I will do anything you ask, but *must* we be separated?"

Tate could hear the sorrow in the young king's voice. Having just returned from his hunting trip that morning, Edward, King of England, had been thrilled to see his uncle and mentor back at Woodstock. He was also thrilled to see his wife, whom he affectionately embraced beneath clear skies and soft winds. The hunt had been a success, and the young couple was reunited again, but according to Tate, that wasn't going to last long.

Truly, Tate felt bad for him.

"I'm afraid so," he said. "Mortimer has confided in a source I trust that he believes your mother to be pregnant with his child. It is his intention to supplant you with his own offspring, and we do not believe your mother will have the power to stop him, so until we can arrest Mortimer once and for all, you and the queen must be taken to separate locations of safety. It is for your own good, Edward, truly. You know I would not tell you this were it not so."

Fair and lanky as he grew into manhood, Edward was genuinely disappointed. "I know," he said. "And… and you believe this is credible?"

"I do."

"But I am certain my mother would not agree to such a thing."

Tate cocked a dark eyebrow, over the eye that was black and blue from the kick he'd received two days earlier. "We have discussed this," he said, lowering his voice further. "Your mother is engaging in a difficult dance at this time. Mortimer has done things for her that she believes to have been helpful, and she feels that she is in his debt. Does she love the man? Or has he hypnotized her? No one can say but your mother, but the truth is that she has acquiesced to Mortimer before. Even in matters of your safety, so I do not trust her, I am sorry to say. Once again, you must go into hiding. I do not take pleasure in this, but if you want to live, it must be done."

Edward trusted Tate more than anyone in the world because the man had nearly single-handedly kept him alive all these years, but he was still indecisive about splitting him from his wife.

"But Phillipa—" he began.

Tate cut him off, though not harshly. "Your wife carries the next heir to the throne," he said in a tone that suggested the subject matter wasn't up for debate. "Given what happened to your father, and what could possibly happen to you if we are not careful, the child your wife carries is the biggest threat of all to Mortimer's quest for power. Do you understand me?"

"But why?"

"Roger Mortimer would kill your wife, and your child, and

take pleasure in it. Is that plain enough?"

After that, Edward shut his mouth. There was no more time for protest, no more angles to play on this sickening situation. Tate had told him about Gideon of Loxbeare's conversation, so he knew that Mortimer had plans for him. What Mortimer didn't know was that Phillipa was pregnant.

With a child that would change everything.

"It is plain enough," he finally said. "But you will listen to me, Tate. I am finished running from Mortimer. I am finished fearing him. The man must be stopped for good and I intend to do it. Your king has spoken."

Tate dipped his head. "Aye, your grace," he said. "The king has spoken, indeed, but what has he said other than he intends to stop Mortimer? *How* does he intend to do so?"

Edward's jaw twitched. "That is something we shall discuss while sequestered at Carlisle," he said. "The plans will be laid."

"Good," Tate said, approval in his eyes. "It is time."

"But I still do not want to be separated from Phillipa."

"I'm afraid you have no choice," Tate said. "Think on a scenario where we rush you both off to hide and Mortimer discovers you. If he discovers you, he discovers her. Would you truly put her in such danger? But if you are separated, it will take much more work on Mortimer's part to locate you. Even if he does, he may decide it is not worth the risk to lay siege to Carlisle or Ashendon."

"Ashendon?"

"Seat of the Earl of Hull," Tate said. "That is Leo's seat."

Edward nodded quickly as he was reminded of what he already knew. "I've not seen Ashendon but I hear it is a massive place," he said. "And I remember that the previous earl was loyal to my father. What was his name? Ned or Nolan de

Cottingham?"

"Edmund de Cottingham," Tate corrected him. "He was a good man, loyal to the Crown. That is why your father arranged the marriage between his widow and Leo when Edmund passed away. It was to stabilize the Hull earldom, but also to link them to de Wolfe. You know they control the entire northern border. Marrying Leo to Lady Hull not only gave Leo the earldom, but it brought three thousand soldiers to support the de Wolfe empire. It was a wise political move."

Edward's memory was refreshed as Tate spoke. "I heard about Lady Hull's death last year," he said. "And there are children now?"

Tate nodded. "They were her children from her marriage to Edmund," he said. "She died giving birth to Leo's daughter, who also died."

"Was he sad about that?"

Tate eyed him. Edward may have been barely a man, and he was mature in some ways, but he was immature in others, including empathy. "I will tell you so that you do not ask him," he said. "Aye, he was sad. He and Lady Hull had a good marriage. That is why he came to Woodstock so quickly when Marcus de Lohr summoned him into your protection detail. I think he wanted to leave the sad memories behind."

Edward pondered that. "Phillipa likes him," he said. "She says he behaves like her father."

Tate smiled faintly. "Leo's stepchildren are about your age, I think," he said. "At least, the older one is. A daughter, I believe. Then there are younger twins, a boy and a girl. He's had to assume the fatherly role in their lives, so I'm not surprised he's that way with Phillipa."

Edward averted his gaze for a moment, thinking on what

was to come. They were in a small antechamber next to the king's hall, a room that was much more private and secure than the gaping hall. It was just him and Tate because Tate wanted to speak with him privately about the situation, and Edward could understand why.

But he still wasn't happy about it.

"Very well," he finally said. "When do we leave?"

"As soon as Phillipa can pack a satchel," Tate said. "The sooner we leave, the better. We must get to Carlisle before Mortimer catches on to the fact that we are moving you out of Woodstock."

"He would try to stop us," Edward said. "He would block the roads. He would know me on sight."

Tate smiled ironically. "Not really," he said. "Ken is going with Leo to Ashendon, so we are going to dress you in his armor and tunic. It will only be you, me, and Stephen. If men see us, they will think you are St. Hever."

Edward looked at him as if he'd lost his mind. "Are you mad?" he said. "Kenneth is considerably bigger than I am. The man has arms the size of tree branches."

Tate chuckled. "We will stuff the tunic, have no doubt," he said, but quickly sobered. "I know you do not want to go, Edward, but it must be this way. If you truly want to protect your wife and child, then it must be this way."

Edward understood. He'd had it drilled into him. He slumped a little, thinking of the wife he would soon be separated from.

"Does Phillipa know?" he finally asked.

Tate shook his head. "I thought I would leave that to you," he said. "No matter how much she begs, you must be strong. Convince her that it is only temporary."

Edward mulled over the suggestion. "I thought to tell her that I am going on a great mission," he said. "One that will secure our future. If she thinks I am doing something with the knights, then she will not ask to come."

Tate's lips twitched with a smile. "It's sweet that you think so," he said wryly. "She asks to go everywhere you go, including hunting. What makes you think she'll not want to go on a military mission?"

Edward shrugged, fighting off a grin. "She will listen to me."

"Again, it's sweet that you think so."

"Does your wife not listen to you?"

Tate looked at him incredulously. "Toby?" he said. "You *know* her. How well do you think she obeys me?"

That gave Edward pause. "My wife is more obedient."

Tate broke down into soft laughter. "Every wife in England is more obedient than mine," he said. "But she is mine and I would not trade her away for all the gold in the world."

Edward reluctantly grinned. "I understand," he said. "I like Toby. You are deserving of her."

"She is deserving of *me*," Tate said, putting his hand on the young man's shoulder. "Come along, now. Let us see if you can convince your obedient wife not to come on a mission of significant importance."

Edward stood up. "I cannot make it sound too dangerous," he said. "I do not want to worry her."

They headed for the door. "Just dangerous enough," Tate said.

"Precisely. Just dangerous enough."

They reached the door that led to the queen's suite of rooms, but Edward came to a pause before they passed through, facing the knight who was his uncle, his mentor, and his friend.

Tate de Lara was all those things to Edward, the man who had been the steadiest male figure in his life.

A role model, even.

The young king caught a glimpse of the sword at Tate's side.

"Dragonblade," he muttered, indicating the sword when Tate looked at him questioningly. "The sword that gave you your name. Will you pass it on to your son, I wonder, or will you be buried with it?"

Tate looked down at the heavy sword with the dragon-head hilt in its scabbard at his side. Edward referred to the moniker that he had acquired a long time ago as a young knight. That distinctive sword had defined him in battle, but his prowess had firmly cemented his reputation as an elite knight and fearless warrior.

Llafn y Ddraig was what the Welsh had called him.

Dragonblade.

He put his hand on the sword.

"I will not be buried anytime soon," he said. "Nor will you. But in answer to your question, you do realize that this is a Welsh sword, forged by my mother's ancestors because Wales is the land of dragons. The sword did not start with me, nor does it end with me. Is Roman, my son, worthy of it? He will be a great knight someday. He will be the Earl of Carlisle after I am gone. But during my lifetime, he will have to prove himself to me worthy of the sword. If he is not, then mayhap I know a young king who is."

Edward's eyes widened as he looked up at him. "Me?"

With a smile, Tate opened the door and stepped through, leaving Edward to follow. They headed over to the panel leading to the queen's antechamber, and the moment they opened it, they ran into Leonidas. He'd just come from the stables, selecting the mount that would take the queen into East Yorkshire, so he had entered the antechamber the same time Tate and Edward did, only Edward hadn't seen Leonidas since his return from hunting.

One look at the man and he burst into laughter.

Leonidas knew why.

"Laugh if you must, your grace," he said, sighing sharply. "I've just endured servants and soldiers alike doing the same thing, but this will be the last of it. There will be no more laughter in an hour."

Tate was struggling to keep a straight face. "What do you intend to do?"

Cocking an eyebrow, Leonidas lifted a hand and pounded on the door leading to the queen's privy chamber. Edward, hands over his mouth, could see that Leonidas was quite annoyed, but he couldn't stop laughing.

"What happened?" he asked between snorts. "Who did that to you?"

Leonidas' eyes narrowed. "Someone who will pay, your grace," he said. He pounded again and shouted, "Open the door! The king has arrived!"

The door abruptly swung open, straight into Leonidas, bashing him squarely in the face because he'd been unprepared for it to open so swiftly. Christelle stood in the doorway, her eyes wide as she realized she'd hit the man, who was standing there with a hand over his nose and mouth.

"*You*," he growled. "I should have known it would be you."

Christelle was genuinely contrite. "I did not mean to do it," she said, moving to inspect the damage. "Let me see what I've done."

"This!" Leonidas hissed, pointing at the red cross on his

forehead. "You did this and now I am a laughingstock, so if you do not remove this thread, I am going to do it myself and probably tear a hole in my forehead."

Tate and Edward slipped into the privy room, grinning, as Christelle faced Leonidas apologetically.

"It was the only thread I could find," she lied. "It needed to be stitched up quickly and that was all I could find at the moment."

He sighed sharply, with great disapproval. "Take it out."

She hesitated. "Removing it may pull the wound apart again," she said. "I do not think enough time has passed to allow it to heal properly."

He frowned. "I do not care," he said. "Remove it or I will."

"Do you want me to replace it with thread of another color?"

He shook his head. "Nay," he said. "I do not trust you. I will have Stephen sew it up. He used to be a Hospitaller and, I'm sure, will do a far better job than you did."

Christelle nodded. "As you wish," she said, turning for the privy chamber. "Come inside and I will do it."

He followed her into that cluttered chamber that was now moist with humidity because the queen had taken a bath earlier. Christelle indicated for him to sit on the same stool he'd sat on before while she went to find a sewing kit.

Leonidas watched her closely, making sure she wasn't grabbing a hammer to use on the wound instead of a needle and thread. What he wanted to do was put her over his knee and spank her because he'd endured almost three days of men snickering at him as he'd walked by, knowing that red cross on his forehead looked ridiculous. He was certain she'd meant it as a joke, but what it had done was undermine men's respect for him.

That was something he wouldn't tolerate.

Spanking her, however, was out of the question. The Black-church-trained warrior in her would not stand still for that, and he could find himself in more of a fight than he had intended. Nay, Christelle was different from the annoying women he knew, mostly because she was far more dangerous. That lovely, fiery woman wasn't just something pleasing to the eye.

She was also deadly.

Therefore, he had to tread carefully in his quest for revenge.

But make no mistake… revenge *would* come.

Christelle returned with a sewing kit that had at least a dozen different colors of silk thread. Leonidas could see it as she set it down on the table next to him. Amidst the moist air of the chamber and the faint smell of lavender, he sat still as she silently and swiftly remove the red thread from his forehead. Leonidas kept his eyes closed because if he opened them, she would have been six inches away and he didn't want to study the woman and her perfection more than he already had. If he didn't focus on his annoyance with her, he might actually feel some attraction, so it was important that he didn't. Therefore, he kept his eyes closed. Even so, he could still feel her touch.

And that would have to be enough.

❧

HERE SHE WAS, close to him again.

This wasn't how she'd expected her day to go. Christelle had been helping Phillipa mix some paint colors because Phillipa liked to paint from time to time, but here Christelle was, standing a few inches away from Leonidas and dragging out removing those stitches because she didn't want to be finished too soon. She liked standing next to the man who was more than twice her size, even if she did make a game out of annoying him. She especially liked it when he smiled because he had a beautiful smile, with straight teeth, and big canines that protruded slightly, enough to give him a rather fang-like appearance. She'd heard the soldiers whisper about Leonidas—

Le Morsure

The Bite.

In battle, that was a terrifying expression, or so she'd heard. Soldiers talked and, over the past year, she'd listened. Leonidas used that fanged smile to frighten his enemies because he had a helm designed in the image of a wolf so that when he smiled, his teeth were fully visible. She knew that he had dozens of cousins and four brothers. She'd heard him tell Phillipa about his family once, and he had four older sisters and four younger brothers, born to a diplomat and his lady wife, whose father was the captain of the army at Northwood Castle, far to the north.

In fact, Leonidas had been born in the north and spent a good deal of time there until he fostered at Kenilworth and Warwick Castles before enduring the rigorous training at Blackchurch. Christelle had endured it as well, only years after he had, but the truth was that she had failed at an exercise in her third year, which had drummed her out of the guild. Blackchurch only allowed one mistake from its recruits in the five years it took to train there, and she'd made her one mistake. But it didn't really matter because she was still highly trained at that point. However, it was an embarrassment for her to admit she hadn't finished the training.

But she'd finished enough.

But Leonidas…

He was a warrior beyond anything she could ever hope to

be.

As Christelle was removing the last stitch, they began to hear voices from the queen's chamber. The voices grew louder until they could hear Phillipa shrieking about something. They could only hear the tone, not the words, and Christelle looked at the door with concern. Setting down the tiny scissors she'd been using to remove Leonidas' stitches, she started to move toward the panel, but Leonidas grasped her by the wrist.

"Nay," he said quietly. "Leave them alone."

Christelle frowned. "But my lady is upset," she said. "Should I—"

He cut her off, but softly. "You needn't do anything," he said. "Finish my forehead."

"It is finished," she said. Then she gestured toward the chamber door. "What is going on in there?"

Leonidas let go of her wrist. "What does my forehead look like?" he said, ignoring her question. "Do you need to replace the stitches?"

Christelle's gaze lingered on him for a moment before she looked back at the wound, studying it. "I do not think it is necessary unless you want your scar to be minimal," she said. "It will heal, but without stitches, the scar will be bigger. The skin will stretch a little."

Behind the door, Phillipa began weeping. They could both hear it. Christelle took a step toward the door again, but Leonidas grasped her wrist one more time and stopped her.

"Leave them alone," he muttered again. "This is not a situation for you. Stay out of it."

She looked at him again. "*What* is happening?"

Leonidas inhaled, taking a deep breath of contemplation. "Edward and Tate are telling her that she and her husband must be separated for a while," he said quietly. "She is reacting to it."

Christelle's brow furrowed. "Separated?" she said. "Why?"

Leonidas was still holding on to her wrist as he gazed up at her. "What I tell you will not leave this room," he said. "Do you understand me?"

She nodded without hesitation. "If you ask, I will comply," she said. "But what is it all about?"

He tugged on her wrist, directing her toward a chair that was a few feet away from him. "Sit down," he said. "I will tell you, but this is for your ears only."

Christelle promptly took her seat and looked at him expectantly. "Has something happened?"

Leonidas still seemed hesitant to tell her. "I realize that you and I have not worked closely together even though we both serve the king and queen, so I've not built any trust in you," he said. "Know that my trust is given, but if broken, you will never have it again."

"The same can be said for me," Christelle said. "I do not abide liars, and if I tell you that I will not repeat anything, I will not. Now, can you tell me what has happened?"

Leonidas didn't insult her by delaying further. They understood one another, so there would be no mistake if she broke her word.

"We have it on good authority that Isabella may be pregnant with Mortimer's child," he said in a low voice. "It is Mortimer's intention to supplant Edward with his own offspring. There was a time, in the past, when de Lara and St. Hever and Pembury took Edward into hiding to protect him from Mortimer and, unfortunately, we are going to have to do the same thing again, only it is more important now that Phillipa is with child. That will make her Mortimer's target, as well."

It was shocking news. Since Leonidas had never shared information with Christelle, she took it very seriously. Gone was, perhaps, the flippant attitude toward him, the one always daring him to take her challenge so she could verbally best him. Or stitch a red cross in his forehead.

For once, she took him seriously.

With Phillipa involved, she had little choice.

"That is not welcome news," she said after a moment. "Roger Mortimer seems to have been quiet over the last several months. Now we see that he was, mayhap, not so quiet."

Leonidas shook his head. "Nay," he said. "Therefore, the plan is to send Edward to Carlisle Castle with Tate and Stephen, while Ken and I will take Phillipa to Ashendon Castle."

"Where is that?"

"East Yorkshire."

"You were born there?"

"Nay," he said. "But it belongs to me through marriage."

She cocked her head. "I did not know you were married."

He eyed her. "How much do you know about me?"

Christelle shook her head. "I know you are a knight who used to serve Henry's father," she said. "I know your father was a great diplomat and that you are from a powerful northern family. Truthfully, you and I have not had much contact other than what was completely necessary, so I do not know much about you."

"Not even rumor?"

Again, Christelle shook her head. "Not really," she said. "The queen only speaks of Edward and her family in Brabant. Sometimes she speaks of Tate. He is Edward's uncle."

"He is."

She shrugged. "Then I know you are knights in Edward's service and that he trusts you completely," she said. "That is all I really need to know. Why do you ask?"

"Because Ashendon Castle is my seat, as the Earl of Hull," he said. "I obtained the title when I married the widow of the former Earl of Hull—and, nay, I am no longer married. My wife died last year."

Christelle was a bit taken aback by his frankness and his story. "I see," she said, with perhaps a hint of remorse. "I did not know that you were an earl, my lord. And I am very sorry about your wife. My sympathies to you."

His gaze lingered on her a moment before he stood up and looked for the big, polished mirror that Phillipa kept in the chamber. It was in the corner and he made his way to it, inspecting his forehead once he could see his reflection.

"It is healed enough," he said. "It does not need further stitches."

"It might," she said, peering over at him. "If it pulls apart, it will bleed again."

He grunted and turned away from the mirror. "That should be a source of pride for you," he said. "I am going to tell everyone who will listen how you tried to kill me. You can gloat."

She smiled faintly. "I do not think so," she said. "Gloating is in such bad taste."

He let out a guffaw, those famous canines making an appearance as he grinned. "You think so?" he said. "If it were me, I would gloat. I suppose that means I have bad taste."

"You probably do," she said. "But I shall not hold it against you because when you take the queen to Ashendon, I go with her. And I should not like to be looking over my shoulder for the duration."

He conceded the point. "Wise," he said as he wandered back in her direction, listening to more crying in the queen's chamber. "It sounds as if Edward has his hands full with his wife. I do not envy him."

Christelle watched him as he sat down on the stool again. "You speak from experience, of course."

"Of course."

"Do you have children?"

"Do you?"

He deflected the question right back at her and she looked surprised. "Of course not," she said. "I am not married, nor have I ever been. I do not ever expect to be."

His brow furrowed. "Why not?"

She looked at him as if he were daft. "Who would want a wife like me?" she said. "I'm not a fine lady, trained in a fine household, but rather a woman trained in a way most women aren't. And do not make jokes about it. I do not find them humorous."

"I was not attempting to be humorous," he said. "You are relatively young and if you would brush your hair once in a while, you would be quite comely. Do you not have a dowry? Is that it?"

She looked at him, rage on her features. "I told you not to jest about it," she growled. "Do not talk to me anymore."

With that, she stomped off toward the door leading into the queen's chamber, leaving Leonidas puzzled.

Puzzled and intrigued.

"Come back over here," he commanded softly. "Come along—turn around and come back over here."

"Why? So you can make jokes about me?"

"I was not joking when I said you were comely," he said. "We may not know each other well, but I suspect that you know me well enough to know that I do not say anything that is not the truth. Now, come back here and sit down."

"I won't."

"Don't make me come over there and get you."

There was a threat in that, and Christelle eyed him with a frown. But he was waving a hand at her, gesturing for her to return, so she did. Reluctantly, she did. Truthfully, she didn't want him dragging her back to the chair, which he was pointing at.

"Sit down," he said. "I think you and I must have a discussion."

"Why?"

"Because you know about me but I do not know about you, and if we are to work closely together with the queen, then we should remedy that."

Christelle considered that. She'd admired de Wolfe from afar for so long that the thought of actually having a conversation with the man that didn't involve insults or relaying the queen's wishes seemed… interesting.

Unnerving, even.

"Very well," she said, still not particularly happy with him. "What do you want to know?"

Leonidas sat back down on his stool, facing her. "Start from the beginning," he said. "You were not born in England."

She shook her head. "I was born in Metz."

Leonidas nodded. "That is the duchy of Lorraine," he said. "Your family is not ruled by France."

"Nay," Christelle replied. "My father and the queen's father are old friends. That is how I came into her service."

"As a woman protector?"

"Can you think of anyone better to protect the queen and remain close to her at all times?"

Leonidas shook his head. "Probably not," he said. "But the truth is that we all thought it was mad when you first came to serve Phillipa. That is, we thought it was until we saw you in action for the first time. Then we did not think it was so mad."

"The servant who tried to touch her?"

"The man whose arm you broke."

"He should not have tried to touch her."

Leonidas couldn't argue with that, but he was getting the distinct feeling that she didn't want to talk about herself. Christelle had always come across as professional and guarded, and even now in this situation, she remained wary. If she wasn't insulting him or taunting him, she was wary of him. He'd seen her with Phillipa and knew she could be easy with her laughter and quick with a smile, but she'd never been that way with him.

Given his attraction to her, perhaps that was a good thing.

But he had to make things clear.

"Agreed," he said. Then he fixed her in the eye. "Lady, we are to spend a good deal of time together in the future, so the only purpose of this conversation is so we'll be more at ease with one another. You will be in my home, around my children and around me, so I am asking you politely—be respectful and show restraint. No more red crosses on my forehead. By doing that, you imply a lack of respect for me and you try to undermine the respect my men have for me, so I do not want to be the butt of any further jokes from you. Do you understand me?"

She eyed him as if debating whether or not to agree. "In my defense, the truth is that I did not know you were an earl," she said. "I thought you were simply a knight like the others. I thought…"

He held up a hand to stop her from continuing. "Tate is the Earl of Carlisle," he said. "Kenneth is a widely respected knight and Stephen will assume the Culpepper barony on the death of his father, so we are not simply 'knights.' We are knights of the highest order and, I might remind you, Tate and I are also Blackchurch trained. That should invite respect immediately."

Christelle knew she didn't have a point to argue so she simply nodded her head. "I understand," she said. "No more red crosses. But it really was the only thread I could find in a hurry."

"And no more lying."

"I am *not* lying."

He knew it wasn't the truth, but it wasn't a topic he chose to fight about. Scratching his chin, he studied her. "So you say," he muttered. "Tell me where you fostered."

"Foix Castle."

"How did you come to Blackchurch?"

Christelle sighed sharply. "This is *not* a conversation," she said. "This is an interrogation. You want to know about me? Then let me tell you. I am the only child of Bernard de Lorrain. My father is of the House of Lorraine and he serves Louis IV."

"The Holy Roman Emperor?"

"Indeed," she said, rather clipped. "My father's mother was a de Hapsburg, which makes me related to several royal families. When my father was young, he spent a few years with the King of France because France held him as a hostage against his own family's disobedience against the French throne, so when I was born, my father made a vow."

"What vow?"

She calmed a little. "Isabella is French," she said. "My father has no love for the French. Given the fact that Phillipa's father and my father are childhood friends and distant cousins, it was agreed when Phillipa was betrothed to Edward that I should go with her as her lady-in-waiting, only my father wanted to make sure that I could protect Phillipa adequately. He did not want me to be a weak lady. He wanted me to be strong and sure. When I fostered at Foix, I was trained by their sword master, and when I came of age, my father sent me to Blackchurch. He told me that if I failed to be accepted into their training, then I was not to come home."

That diatribe explained quite a bit about Christelle's background, and Leonidas acknowledged that. "Thank you for telling me," he said. "Now I know a little about you and you know a little about me. We will be more comfortable comrades in the future."

The crying on the other side of the door ceased and the panel abruptly opened, effectively ending their conversation. Tate spilled forth, looking straight at Leonidas.

"We leave at dawn," he said. "Have you selected an appropriate palfrey for the queen?"

Leonidas stood up from the stool. "I have," he said. "But wouldn't it be better for the queen to ride in a wagon, given her condition?"

Tate shook his head. "You're not traveling on horseback all the way home," he said. "You are going to London where you shall take a cog and travel by sea. It should be easier on her and also keep her away from Mortimer and his supporters. Less chance of her falling into his hands if she is on the ocean."

Leonidas understood. "Have arrangements already been made for the cog?"

"I'm sending Ken ahead to do precisely that," Tate said.

"You will meet him in London and then all of you will continue on to Hull. Come—we shall find Ken and make plans."

His manner was weary and sharp, unusual for him, but that told Leonidas that there had been quite a battle in the queen's chamber. Tate was eager to move on. With preparations to make for the coming journey, Tate and Leonidas headed out of the manor, leaving Christelle watching them go. Of course, when she told Leonidas of her relationship to the Crown, and her duties to Phillipa, she'd left out one very major point—that she was still in touch with her father, sending him missives of any and all developments between Mortimer and Edward, and splitting up the royal couple and sending them into hiding was, indeed, a major development.

One could always find messengers in London willing to delivery missives for a price.

And she had one to send.

CHAPTER THREE

S HE'D NEVER BEEN so sick.

After three weeks of travel from Woodstock, one of those weeks on land and two at sea because of the prevailing winds while traveling north, Christelle had to admit that she was more than relieved to see the shores of East Yorkshire and, more particularly, of the mouth of the Humber as it opened up into the North Sea.

If she never saw a wave, gull, or fish ever again, she would be quite happy.

Fish and onions.

That was all the captain of their cog fed them, morning and night. At least for the nooning meal they had a chance of eating bread and cheese that they'd brought along in their provisions, but otherwise, the captain and his men were catching big fish off the sides of the vessel, throwing them into an iron pot with onions that they brought up from the hold, and they'd boil them or steam them or fry them and then distribute the fish and onions among the crew and passengers.

The mere smell had Christelle upheaving.

This morning was no different. They had traveled by hugging the eastern coast of England, travel made very slow because the headwinds were coming down from the north. The smell of fish and onions lay on the deck of the boat—Christelle would swear that—made worse by the fact that the fog had rolled in and that seemed to keep the greasy smell trapped.

So, as she did every morning, she made sure Phillipa was well tended before making her way up to the railing to hang over the side and try to breathe in the salt air to keep from vomiting. She'd tried to hide her condition, of course, but it hadn't gone unnoticed by either Leonidas or Kenneth, who would sit with Phillipa when Christelle was up on deck. Christelle was strong and she'd muscled through some genuine sickness and weakness, but in moments like this, she simply couldn't stand it any longer and went to gulp down fresh air.

That was where Leonidas found her.

"We'll be entering the mouth of the river within the hour," he said, coming up behind her. "You will be off this boat before the nooning hour."

Christelle heard his voice, standing tall and trying desperately to pretend nothing was amiss. Not a thing. But when she turned to face him, her face was pale, maybe even a little green, and over the past three weeks, she'd lost a bit of weight because she couldn't keep anything down. Her face was drawn and there were rings around her eyes. She couldn't see it, but Leonidas could. They all could.

Still, she wasn't going to admit it.

"Good," she said. "For Phillipa's sake, I am glad. We have been caged on this vessel long enough."

Leonidas simply nodded, coming up to stand next to her on the rail. He was looking at the mouth of the Humber to the north. The way the fog was sitting, it was as if it were a blanket in the sky, hanging over the land. The land itself was clear, but the sky wasn't. Because Leonidas was looking at the distant shores, Christelle turned to look also. The boat hit a particularly rolling wave and she held on as hard as she could, swallowing the bile that rose in her throat.

Leonidas could see her white-knuckled grip on the rail.

"I've brought you something," he said after a moment. "I know this journey has not been easy for you, so I brought something to ease your stomach."

Christelle stiffened. "Why should I need something to ease my stomach?"

He leaned into her and lowered his voice. "I do not know if you are aware of this, but some people become ill whilst on seagoing vessels," he murmured. "It can happen to anyone and it is most assuredly nothing to be ashamed of, but some people might be embarrassed by it. Not that you would be. But some people might."

She was looking at him, fully prepared to refute everything he said and, if the mood struck her, become angry with him, but she couldn't seem to manage it. He knew she had been ill. The whole damn boat probably knew it. She'd be a fool to deny it.

"I know it's obvious," she muttered, bracing herself on the rail. "I've never been on a boat this long before. The most I've ever traveled by such a conveyance has been two or three days at most. And the seas were calm. It was nothing like this."

He looked at her, seeing her eyes filling with tears. She was exhausted and probably starving because she hadn't been able to eat anything. He felt a good deal of sympathy for her, in truth, so he fought off a smile as he put his big arm around her shoulders and produced the small earthenware phial he'd brought along. She almost reacted violently to his arm around her shoulders until he put the phial in front of her face.

"Here," he said, putting it under her nose. "The captain keeps this as a delicacy, but he says it will help your stomach. Eat one."

She wasn't so sure. Her hands came up and she took the phial from him, sniffing at the contents. It looked like strips of leather, long and thin, but there was a coating on them.

"What is it?" she asked.

"Ginger cooked in honey," he said. "Very sweet and quite delicious."

"Did you try one?"

"I did. And I am not dead, so it will not kill you."

Timidly, she pulled forth a strip. The boat hit a big wave and she would have staggered had Leonidas not been holding on to her. He was big and strong and warm and he completely threw her off guard, which she didn't like. She yanked herself away from him.

"I do not want you to touch me," she said, frowning. "You will never do that again."

He shook his head at her stubbornness. "I did it to give you some comfort, you silly wench," he said. "You looked as if you needed for someone to be kind to you."

"Not you," she said, handing back the phial with the ginger. "Take it back. I do not want it."

He rolled his eyes. "Why?" he said. "Because I brought it?"

"Because I don't need your help. I don't want it."

"You make it difficult to be kind to you."

"I didn't ask you to."

The mirth in his eyes faded. "Someday you are going to regret being such a stubborn goose," he said. "No one is trying to hurt you or insult you. You have been sick the entire time we've been on this boat and I am quite sure you've hardly eaten enough to keep a bird alive, so I went out of my way to find something to soothe you. You do not have to thank me, but you also do not have to be rude. If you want this to be the last kindness I ever show you, that can be arranged."

He started to turn away, but as he did so, the tears in her eyes spilled over and she lowered her head. He was almost all the way turned around, preparing to go in the other direction, when she broke down in sobs.

"I am sorry," she murmured. "I'm… I'm so tired. I cannot keep anything down, but I'm hungry. I cannot even drink because it comes back up again. I've never felt so terrible in my entire life."

He couldn't very well walk away from her now. With a sigh of regret, he went to her, put his arm around her again, and began leading her over to some wooden benches that were built around the hole that brought light and air into the ship decks below. He set her down, pulled out a piece of the candied ginger, and put it against her lips.

"Chew it," he said in a soft, low purr. "That's a good lass. Chew it slowly. Let it trickle into your stomach. Do that until we dock and as soon as we are on land, I will find you something to eat, I promise."

She was still weeping, but at least she was chewing on the ginger, which was mild and delicious and sweet.

"I am sincerely sorry to have been so rude," she said, wiping her eyes with the back of her dirty hand, leaving streaks across her face. "I did not mean it."

"I know."

"Will you do something for me?"

"If I can."

"Will you kill that captain if he cooks fish and onions again?"

Leonidas started to laugh, revealing those big canines. "Do you really want me to?"

"I do. I swear, I do."

He shrugged. "Very well," he said. "But let me confiscate all of his sweet ginger first and then I will kill him. Fair enough?"

She nodded, managing to swallow the ginger and picking up another piece. "That is fair," she said, knowing that neither one of them were really serious about a murder. "This is quite good. It's spicy."

"If you cannot eat it, at least suck on it. That should help."

She nodded, timidly chewing a corner. "Boats do not make you ill?"

He shook his head. "Nay," he said. "They never have. I think I might have made a good pirate."

"Did you ever consider it?"

"Of course I did, but my mother would not let me."

He said it with some humor, causing Christelle to smile weakly. "You are a good son to listen to your mother," she said. But her gaze moved beyond him, to the approaching shore, and she gestured toward it. "Once we stop at Hull, how long will it take to reach Ashendon?"

"Less than an hour," he said, looking over his shoulder at the looming land. "My castle sits on a rise overlooking the town. We will see it once we get upriver."

"Do you miss it?"

He looked in the direction of the land, which was looming closer now. "I do," he said. "It is mine. The only property I've ever had that belongs to me, so I do miss it."

"Is it big?"

"Quite big."

"You must have a big army."

He nodded as he turned around to look at her. "Big enough," he said. "Mostly de Cottingham troops, which I inherited when I married the earl's widow. But my brother and a couple of cousins are in command, with some de Wolfe men mixed in with the de Cottingham men, so the army is under control."

She choked down the piece she'd been chewing on and pulled forth another. "You have more than one brother, do you not?"

"I have four," Leonidas said. "Dayne is one of my younger brothers. You will get to meet him."

"And your cousins?"

He flashed a grin. "I have many," he said. "My grandparents had nine children and each of them has had many children, so I literally have dozens of cousins, both male and female. The cousins who serve at Ashendon are Lesander de Norville, son of my Aunt Evelyn and Uncle Hector, and Talan de Shera, son of my Aunt Penelope and her husband, the Earl of Coventry. Talan is a Welsh princeling, in fact."

Christelle seemed to show some interest in that. "Truly?" she said. "How is that possible?"

"Because his father is the hereditary King of Anglesey," he said. "Bhrodi's mother was a Welsh princess and his father was English. My grandfather, William de Wolfe, married Penelope to Bhrodi many years ago to secure peace. Fortunately for them, it turned out to be a love match."

He was talking quite a bit about himself, Christelle noticed, more than he'd spoken about himself since she'd known him. He kept turning to look at the approaching mouth of the

Humber, and she was coming to think that he was in a good mood because he was returning home. He was friendlier than she'd ever seen him.

And she had to admit that the offering of the ginger was quite kind.

That handsome knight seemed to be getting more handsome.

"You seem close to your family," she said. "That must be nice."

He folded his big arms across his chest, his attention moving between her and the approaching shoreline. "We are a very big family and quite devoted to one another," he said. "Not simply out of duty, but because we actually like one another. Well, mostly. My cousins, Atreus and Hermes, can be quite annoying, but they're good at heart. And my Uncle Tommy can be loud and spoiled. He's the youngest of my father's brothers, you know. It seems strange to say that, since they're all quite elderly."

She finished the ginger and decided she'd had enough. Standing up, she extended the phial back to Leonidas.

"You were right," she said. "My stomach does feel a little better, thank you."

He wouldn't take it. "Keep it," he said. "You may need it when we get on land."

She frowned. "Why is that?"

He lifted his eyebrows in a way that gave her some apprehension. "You'll see."

Unfortunately, she did.

❧

"SHE CANNOT WALK, Leo," Kenneth said. "She staggers around

like she has been on a drinking binge and I'm leery to put her on a horse because her balance is so off."

As Leonidas had predicted, Christelle's experience on the boat got worse when she was on land. The ground was rocking around as if she were still on the boat, and as Leonidas and Kenneth waited for their horses to be brought out of the hold, Phillipa and Christelle sat over near the banks of the river because neither one of them were feeling very well. Phillipa had been a little ill during the trip as well, but not nearly what Christelle had been. Now, they were sitting on the ground, eating strips of ginger and trying not to get sick.

"See if Phillipa can ride," Leonidas said. "If she can, well and good, but take Christelle with you on your horse. She'll need something to hold on to."

But Kenneth shook his head. "My horse does not appreciate more than one rider," he said. "He'll try to buck. You must take her with you."

Leonidas grunted in displeasure, but he nodded. The truth was that he didn't want to take Christelle because he didn't want her that close to him. Or perhaps he did. He'd just spent three weeks traveling with the woman, watching every move she made, listening to her speak, watching her become ill and wanting to do something to help her until he was bristling with frustration. The more time he spent with her, the more he transitioned from being mildly attracted to her to full-blown interest.

But he didn't want to be.

A romantic entanglement wasn't part of his plan.

A plan that included keeping a young queen alive until something could be done about Mortimer. A plan that included living at Ashendon, permanently, and establishing himself as one of the more powerful warlords in England. He was a de Wolfe, after all, and that kind of thing was expected, most certainly in Northumberland, but he was down in East Yorkshire. He was far from his family's empire.

His plans included forging an empire of his own.

But the queen's personal guard didn't figure into any of it. He'd been nice to her about the ginger. He'd done his part. But now, he was going to have to hold that firm, young body next to his on the back of a horse and try to pretend that he didn't care.

I don't care.

I don't care!

The horses were brought to the deck of the ship at that point and Kenneth broke away from him, heading over to collect his beast. Leonidas followed, noting that his big black-and-white spotted warhorse was giving the ship's crew some trouble. He leapt up onto the deck and took the horse from the frightened crewman, coaxing it to jump over the side and into about two feet of water. The horse, young and strong, hurled itself off the boat and into the water, splashing about as Leonidas led it up onto the shore. Kenneth was right behind them with his big gray steed.

With the horses on the shore, the process of saddling them up commenced. With each knight attending his own horse, the animals were wiped and brushed down before the saddle blanket and saddle went on. Soon enough, the animals were completely prepared and ready to move out, and as Kenneth held on to them, Leonidas went down to the river's edge where the women were sitting.

"Your grace?" he said to Phillipa. "We are ready to continue. It will be a short ride into town and to the castle."

Wearily, Phillipa stood up. "Thank you, Leo," she said. "I

am eager to be done with travel and I believe Christy is, as well."

Christy.

That was what Phillipa called Christelle. Leonidas had heard it before, many times, but it never seemed to suit her. Christelle was strong and bold and beautiful, and the nickname implied something weak and fragile to him. But the moment she looked up at him from her seated position, he could see how bad she truly felt.

He could see vulnerability in her eyes.

"And you," he said. "The castle is a short ride away and then you can rest. I promised I would find you food when we arrived and I shall, but first, we must get you to the castle."

With effort, Christelle stood up. Then she teetered. Both Phillipa and Leonidas reached out to steady her, assistance she shrugged off. Politely in Phillipa's case, not-so-politely in Leonidas'.

"I can walk," she said.

Leonidas watched her as she tried to take a few straight steps. "Unfortunately, my lady, you are experiencing what many people experience when they have been on a boat for some time," he said. "It will go away, eventually, but please let me take you on my horse to the castle. It will be safer for you that way."

Christelle came to an unsteady halt, preparing to retort, but Phillipa stepped in.

"Please, Christy," she said softly. "I need to rest on something that is not rolling like a leaf in the wind, so the sooner we can make it to the castle, the better for me. Please?"

"It will be a short ride to the castle, I promise," Leonidas said, holding down a hand to her and encouraging her to take it. "I will take you and the queen to the most comfortable room in the keep, where you may both rest while I ensure a meal is prepared for you. You'll feel better soon, my lady. Please trust me."

She was reluctant to take his hand. He could see it. But she was more reluctant to fall over and make a fool of herself, so she took his hand and he pulled her carefully to her feet. She teetered a little, but managed to steady herself. Leonidas tucked Phillipa's hand into the crook of his elbow before doing the same with Christelle, who fought him on it at first. But then she tried to walk on her own and thought better of it. Sheepishly, she held on to him.

Leonidas led them over to Kenneth.

"Your grace," Kenneth said, reaching out to take Phillipa. "You may ride with me."

Phillipa went with him, but Leonidas' brow furrowed with concern. "You said your horse does not like a passenger," he said. "You cannot transport the queen on a disagreeable mount."

Kenneth didn't look at him as he lifted the small queen onto his saddle. "I lied," he said. "You seem better with the shield maiden over there, so you can take her. We need to get them into the safety of the castle."

With that, he heaved himself onto the saddle as Leonidas watched in disbelief, then outrage. Grumbling to himself, he turned for his horse and mounted first. Then he extended a hand to Christelle.

"Come, my lady," he said quietly. "Ashendon awaits."

With a deep breath, Christelle took his hand, and he easily pulled her on behind him. His horse fidgeted a little, so she was forced to throw her arms around his torso to steady herself as Leonidas gently spurred his steed forward. Alongside Kenneth, they made their way up the main road.

As Leonidas had told her, the castle was indeed visible from the inlet. Ashendon Castle sat on a rise next to the River Hull, dominating the city around it. Make no mistake, Hull was indeed a city and not the dirty little village that Christelle had expected.

Far from it.

They'd happened to come into town as the fishermen were pulling in their hauls, and the fish market alone was enormous. The main street of the town was wide and muddy, with big gutters on either side that drained back to the river. But the smell was something Christelle would never forget—it reeked of fish. She was having a difficult enough time on the swaying back of a horse without the added delight of a heavily fishy smell. Exhausted, and near tears again because she felt like retching, she buried her face in Leonidas' back.

There was more comfort there than she wanted to admit.

The man was wearing a mail coat, but fortunately, he had a de Wolfe tunic over it, so her face was buried in the fabric. It smelled a little stale, as wool always did, but it was better than the fish smell. Arms wrapped tightly around his torso so she wouldn't fall off, Christelle closed her eyes and prayed their short journey to the castle would end soon.

She was halfway through her prayers when she dozed off.

Leonidas felt her go limp. It was a gradual sort of limpness, starting with her leaning heavily against his back, and then her arms went slack. He thought she might actually fall off the horse, so he clasped her hands against his belly as they made their way through the town and up the rise to the castle. When their ship had docked on the shore, he'd sent a messenger up to the castle to announce his arrival, so the gatehouse was open and men were spilling forth from inside. A couple of them waved to him. But with Christelle exhaustedly slumped against him, he didn't dare spare a hand to wave back.

But he mostly didn't care.

Here he was, in the middle of the town he presided over, with dozens of villagers coming out to greet him as he and Kenneth rode toward the castle, but all he could think about was the woman collapsed against his back. Her arms around his torso made his heart race. It had been a very long time since he'd had a woman this close to him.

Thoughts of Christelle shifted to thoughts of Juliette. Juliette Paignton de Cottingham de Wolfe, to be clear. The woman his father forced him to marry, but he couldn't have picked a nicer woman to bind him to. Juliette had been red-haired, short, a little round in the hips and bum, but he didn't care. She was absolutely delightful, like a spark, so bright and warm that it hadn't taken him long to realize he liked her. She had a sense of humor that made him laugh. She was always making him laugh. The truth was that he'd been fond of her.

And then she was gone.

The spark had been doused, and even now, a couple of years later, he was still struggling with that to a certain degree. It still made him sad to think about it, but more than that, it made him guilty. Horribly guilty. Juliette—little Juliette—had been pregnant with a very big baby that she had delighted in. A child she had been convinced was a girl, and she already had a name—Seraphina. Juliette had given birth twice, including to a set of twins, and she'd done so easily, according to her. But the day came for Seraphina's birth and Leonidas' world fell apart.

Three days of trying to bring forth a baby that refused to be born. Three days of waiting, three days of agony. Juliette developed a fever on the second day, and by the third day, her body began to shut down. Leonidas was forced to sit by and watch her suffer until he finally demanded they cut the child out of her, which the physic did, but by that time it was too late. Juliette's body surrendered to the fever, and to childbirth, and the baby was already dead. No one knew how long it had been dead, but she was dead and perfect, and Leonidas had sat there with the child in his arms, weeping silent tears for his red-headed daughter. She was buried in her mother's arms, wrapped in a silken shroud that Leonidas' parents had supplied.

That was a time he didn't like to think about, but clutching Christelle against him brought it all back.

The mere touch of human to human.

It had been a long time for him, indeed.

Lost to his morose thoughts, he didn't even realize when they reached the drawbridge leading to the castle. He'd been staring at the castle the entire time, fighting off thoughts of Juliette, and he nearly fell off his horse when he thought she was rushing out of the gatehouse toward him.

It took him a moment to realize it was his eldest stepdaughter.

"Leo!" she squealed, waving her hands wildly. "You've come home!"

Leonidas smiled weakly at the sight of Catherine de Cottingham, who had grown in the year he'd been away. She'd grown up and filled out, and now looked shockingly like her mother.

"Who is this glorious young woman?" he boomed, feeling Christelle jolt against him at the sound of his voice. "Can this possibly be Lady Catherine?"

Catherine giggled. She had a bright smile, sparkling brown

eyes, and a round face that positively glowed. "Of course it is me!" she said happily. "Who else would it be?"

Leonidas' smile grew. "A fae princess, mayhap?" he said. "Surely the most beautiful, grown-up lady in all the land."

Catherine puffed up proudly. "I've grown while you were away."

Against him, Leonidas could feel Christelle moving. She loosened her grip on him and sat up, but he kept hold of one of her arms because she seemed to be swaying around.

"That is an understatement," he said as Catherine came up and put her hand on his leg as she walked beside him. "Look how lovely you are. How many young men must I chase away these days? And do not lie to me because Uncle Dayne will tell me the truth. Hundreds? Thousands?"

Catherine laughed in delight, noticing that there was someone on the horse behind Leonidas for the first time. Her smile faded as she focused on Christelle, who was awake if a bit groggy.

"Greetings," Catherine said politely. "Who are you?"

"Catie." Leonidas captured Catherine's attention before Christelle could answer. "Where are Gabriel and Georgiana? Bring them to me at once, please."

Catherine nodded, pleased to do his bidding, but her gaze lingered on Christelle before she darted off. Both Leonidas and Christelle watched her go.

"Who is that?" Christelle asked.

"My daughter," he said without hesitation. "My wife's daughter, actually. There are two more children."

Christelle still had her eye on the yellow dress as it disappeared into the gatehouse. "She's lovely," she said. "I asked you if you had children and you did not answer me."

"Does it matter?" he said. "I have three, all children of the former Earl of Hull and his wife, whom I married. They are delightful children and you will treat them with all due respect, please."

Christelle couldn't tell if he was offended by her statement or if he simply didn't want to discuss his children with her, but he seemed short about it.

"Of course I will," she said. "I would not treat them any other way, my lord."

"Thank you."

"Leo!" A knight with blond hair and a big build was waving at them as they crossed through the gatehouse. "It's about time you have returned, brother. I was about to steal your castle out from under you."

Leonidas snorted at his youngest brother, Dayne de Wolfe, one of the rare de Wolfes who was blond and fair. "Is that so?" he said, reining his horse to a halt in the bailey and sliding off. "You always were incorrigible. Mother should have drowned you at birth, you little whelp."

Dayne grinned broadly in a gesture highly reminiscent of his maternal grandfather, Paris de Norville, and threw his arms around his big brother. "I am her favorite, so she would not do such a thing," he said, kissing Leonidas loudly on the cheek before releasing him. "Welcome home. It is good to see you."

Leonidas patted the man on the cheek. "And you," he said. "Have you been well?"

Dayne's smile turned soft. "My dear eldest brother," he said. "Always concerned for your family. Even me. I have been very well, thank you for asking."

"Good," Leonidas said. "Then gather the knights and meet me in the solar. There is much to tell."

Dayne nodded. "Immediately, Leo," he said, but he noticed the women now being helped from the horses. His expression turned to one of approval. "You brought companionship with you? Well done, Leo."

Leonidas cast him a long look. "I brought Queen Phillipa and her lady," he muttered. "Don't be stupid. And do as I say. *Go.*"

Dayne was off to summon the others while Leonidas went to take hold of Christelle and a servant led his horse away. Kenneth had charge of Phillipa, who was looking weak and pale, enough so that Leonidas was concerned.

"Come," he said, forcibly tucking Christelle's hand into the crook of his elbow. "It is time to take you to that restful place I promised you."

Christelle didn't say a word. She was exhausted, and trying to walk in a straight line took all of her concentration. But she paused, turning to Phillipa to make sure the young queen was moving well enough, even taking the woman by the arm even though she herself was feeling so poorly. In the process she let go of Leonidas, who simply went toward the keep.

But something at the top of the steps leading into the keep stopped him.

A severe-looking woman in dark robes stood there with two small children. Twins Gabriel and Georgiana de Cottingham stood side by side, now around six years of age, as they faced their stepfather. They weren't nearly as happy to see him as Catherine had been, and Leonidas paused at the bottom of the steps, motioning for everyone to come down and greet him.

The woman led the children down in a line, like ducklings following their mother.

"Lord Hull," the woman greeted him. "Surely you remember me. I am Lady Maria de Santos. You left me in charge of your children."

Leonidas nodded, hardly looking at her. He was more interested in the little ones in front of him. "They are looking well enough," he said. Then he addressed the pair. "Greetings, Gabriel and Georgiana. It is good to see you again."

The children were looking up at him with curiosity but also with what he thought might be fear. They were little tykes with Juliette's red hair, although Gabriel's was a little bushy and Georgiana's was positively wild, swept back with a ribbon around her head. Before they could answer him, however, Phillipa stepped forward, bending over to get a better look at the children.

She'd always been drawn to children, and given that she was pregnant, that mothering instinct had only intensified. Two little children right in front of her had her interest and her concern, so she smiled sweetly at the pair as she waved her fingers in greeting.

"I am so pleased to see you, little angels," she said. "How old are you?"

The children were stiff, with arms straight down by their sides. They seemed almost wooden the way they were standing, and neither one answered until Leonidas spoke in a low tone.

"Answer her," he said. "How old are you?"

The children looked at him, startled by the command, before looking to Lady Maria, who nodded her head shortly. That gesture evidently allowed Gabriel to reply.

"We have seen six summers," he said.

Phillipa smiled, reaching out in an attempt to gently cup Gabriel's chin, but Lady Maria barked at her.

"Do not touch him," she snapped, swatting Phillipa's hand

away. "The children are not to be touched."

Leonidas looked at the woman, shocked and outraged, but he didn't move fast enough. Suddenly, Christelle was standing between him and the tightly wimpled woman, and before Leonidas could stop her, she reached out and grabbed Lady Maria by the throat, shoving her away from Phillipa.

"You have brought death upon yourself, woman," she hissed, hand moving to the dagger she always kept at her side. "Your strike against the queen shall not be tolerated."

Lady Maria was older, but she was wiry and evidently strong. She began resisting Christelle, reaching out clawed hands that caught Christelle on the chin, scratching her. Christelle shoved the woman back, so hard that she fell to the ground, and her dagger was unsheathed. With the children screaming at the startling confrontation—including Catherine, who had just emerged from the keep—Christelle moved in for the kill as Leonidas came up behind her and grabbed her wrist before she could lower it.

"Nay, lady," he muttered in her ear. "Not in front of the children. Lower your weapon. That is not a request."

Christelle was furious, but she understood the command. As she reluctantly lowered the dagger with Leonidas still holding her wrist, Lady Maria scrambled to her feet and prepared to run, but Leonidas stopped her.

"Halt, woman," he boomed. "Take another step and I will let Lady Christelle have her way with you. Do not move if you value your life."

By now, the commotion had drawn the attention of a few of the men near the keep, including two knights heading in that direction. Dayne was bringing Sir Talan de Shera with him, and when they saw the skirmish, Dayne quickly made his way to his brother.

"A word, Leo," he muttered. "Now, please."

Leonidas didn't want to release Christelle because he knew what she was capable of, but he had little choice. He couldn't restrain her forever, though he considered her actions completely justified.

Still, it wouldn't do to have a murder committed his first few minutes at Ashendon.

"Go back with the queen," he said quietly. "Go back and stay there. Please."

Glaring daggers at Lady Maria, Christelle did as she was told. Leonidas watched her stagger her way back to Phillipa before turning to Dayne.

"What is it?" he asked impatiently.

By this time, Talan had joined Dayne, and he smiled at his cousin, putting a hand on the man's arm in greeting. Leonidas acknowledged him, but barely. He was more interested in what his brother had to say.

"Well?" he demanded. "Speak, Dayne."

Dayne complied. "We were going to wait to tell you, but it seems you have discovered our problem," he said quietly. "Lady Maria. She must be sent away, Leo. She has done terrible things to the children."

Leonidas frowned. "What things?"

Dayne sighed sharply. "Where to start?" he said, eyeing the woman who was standing with her back to them, quivering. "She insists the children call her 'mother.' She bathes them once a week in icy water from the river. She makes them sit for hours on end, and if they move, she beats them. She will not let anyone speak to them or be kind to them. Shall I go on?"

Leonidas was looking at him in horror. "*All* of them?"

Dayne shook his head. "We've managed to save Catherine from her," he said. "She is too old to be dictated to so severely, but the little ones… I fear she may have damaged them. We could not dismiss her, you understand, because you engaged her. It was not our right. But please, brother… send her away now. Save your children."

Still scowling, Leonidas let his gaze linger on his brother for a moment before turning to Lady Maria in disbelief. "Lady Maria," he said. "Come here."

She turned toward him and stiffly walked in his direction, all the while keeping her eyes on the ground.

"Lord Hull," she said. "Please forgive me for my actions toward the queen. I did not realize who she was. I beg for mercy, my lord."

"Shut your lips," Leonidas snapped quietly. "I will do the talking. Do you understand?"

"Aye, my lord."

Leonidas pointed to the keep. "Go inside," he said. "Go into the solar and wait for me there. If you deviate from this order in any way, my punishment shall be severe."

"Aye, my lord."

Trembling, the woman gathered her skirts and quickly headed toward the keep. When the two little tots tried to follow, she waved them off and kept going. That had Catherine coming off the stairs, unable to make eye contact with the woman as she passed by. As Lady Maria entered the keep, Catherine dropped to her knees beside the children and pulled them into her arms.

Leonidas could see that they were weeping, still.

Already, he could see that much had gone on in his absence.

"I will settle the situation with Lady Maria, but you will be there when I do," he said to his brother. "You and Talan and

Zander go to the solar and remain there until I come. I must settle the queen first."

The mention of royalty had Dayne and Talan looking over at the small woman with the reddish-blonde hair, wrapped up in an elaborate, if messy, braid. The woman who had defended her was standing close by, watching everything around her, including the knights, with great suspicion.

"That is truly Phillipa?" Dayne said quietly, awe in his tone.

"It is," Leonidas said.

"Who is the woman who protected her?"

"Her personal guard," Leonidas said. "And watch yourself with her. She is Blackchurch trained and tolerates no non-sense."

The knights looked at him in shock. "Blackchurch?" they said. "*Her?*"

"Her," Leonidas confirmed. "Her name is Christelle de Lorrain, from the House of Lorrain, and if you annoy the woman, you take your life in your hands. Understood?"

The knights nodded to varying degrees.

"Good," Leonidas said. "Now, go to the solar and I will meet you there and explain everything."

Dayne and Talan did. That left Leonidas alone as he headed over where Christelle and Phillipa and Kenneth were standing. When their attention turned to him, he swept his arm in the direction of the keep.

"If you please, your grace," he said.

The group headed into the structure without further delay.

CHAPTER FOUR

"WE ARE BEING watched, your grace."

Phillipa was lying upon a very big, and very lumpy, bed. It was Leonidas' bed, in fact, and before that it had been the bed to the former Earl and Countess of Hull. Four big posters were elaborately carved with flowers and vines and it was quite a lovely bed. It was comfortable enough. But when Christelle muttered those words, Phillipa's eyes slowly opened.

"By whom?" she asked.

Christelle was sitting beside the bed. Leonidas had given her the chamber next to the great chamber, a smaller alcove where servants slept, but she wouldn't leave Phillipa's side, at least not at the moment. As exhausted as she was and as sick as she was, she wouldn't shirk her duty. She remained at her post, sitting next to the bed, as Phillipa tried to sleep.

But they had visitors.

Christelle tipped her head in the direction of the door.

"There," she said quietly. "They opened the door and evidently do not think we can see them, but there is movement out there. I've seen little fingers curling over the side of the door, trying to peek at us."

Phillipa smiled. "How is that possible if Kenneth is watching our door?"

"They must have overwhelmed him," Christelle said. "He is probably bound and gagged."

Phillipa started to laugh. With Kenneth's size, such a thing would have been impossible, in any case. "Good heavens," she exclaimed softly. "Then they have gone through a great effort. Should we let them in?"

"You are supposed to rest, your grace," Christelle said. "How much rest would you get with children jumping on your bed?"

Phillipa laughed softly. "Not much, but it would be a joyful interruption."

"Shall I open the door?"

Phillipa nodded as she sat up, wearily, but the prospect of children made the matter of sleep seem insignificant. With a smile playing on her lips, Christelle stood up from her chair and tiptoed over to the door, which was only open about an inch. She could hear whispering and even giggling on the other side.

"Would you like to come in and visit?" she asked, rather loudly.

The giggling and whispering stopped. Reaching out, she carefully pulled the door open to reveal the twins standing outside, looking up at her with big blue eyes. Kenneth, who had been guarding the door, was standing across the landing, leaning against the wall with a smile tugging at his lips. At least, as much as Kenneth was capable of smiling, which wasn't much. The man was like stone. Frankly, Christelle was surprised he hadn't chased the children away.

"Do come in," she said to the children. "The queen would very much like to meet you."

Gabriel was standing slightly behind Georgiana, and as he began to move, he automatically pushed his sister forward, so they were both walking into the chamber, hands clasped in front of them, shuffling as if unsure about the entire situation. They were as stiff and wooden as they'd been before in the bailey.

Phillipa waved them over to the bed.

"Please come to me," she said. "It has been a very long journey here and I have been hoping for someone to talk to. Will you talk to me?"

The children looked at her as if they didn't understand a word she was saying. They looked similar, both of them with reddish-blond hair and pale eyes, but the boy was a slightly taller than the girl and had a round little belly, while the girl was rather thin. When Phillipa didn't get a response from them, she glanced at Christelle before continuing.

"What are your names?" she asked. "Surely you have names?"

More staring. More looking uncertain. Christelle crouched down near them so she would be on their level when she spoke to them.

"Do you know who this lady is?" she said, pointing to Phillipa. "This is the queen. The queen of the entire land. That means you can speak to her and she'll be very nice to you. Please tell her your names."

That seemed to jolt the children out of their catatonic state. The little girl took a couple of steps forward, standing at the end of the bed.

"I'm learning to sing," she declared.

Phillipa feigned utter delight. "Is that so?" she said. "What do you like to sing?"

The little girl cocked her head. "Songs," she said. "I sing like this."

She proceeded to trill notes that weren't exactly on key, nor did they create a tune that Phillipa or Christelle recognized, but she was singing it the best way she could. When she was finished, Phillipa and Christelle clapped loudly for her, telling her how wonderful she was. That made her rather pleased and she grinned, looking at her brother as if to make sure he just saw the praise heaped upon her. He did, but he didn't want to acknowledge it.

The little girl returned her attention to Phillipa.

"I'm Georgiana," she said. "Are you truly the queen?"

Phillipa nodded. "I am," she said. "Georgiana is a pretty name."

"Who says you are the queen?"

Phillipa looked surprised before chuckling. "I married the king," she said. "That makes me the queen."

"Where is the king?"

Phillipa's smile faded. "Far away, I think," she said. "I hope."

"Did he run away, then?"

"Nay," she said, shaking her head. "He has a battle to fight. I could not go with him."

"Why not?"

Phillipa shrugged. "Because I do not know how to fight," she said. "Now, let's speak on something else. Do you like to play games?"

"I like to!" The little boy suddenly found his voice. "I like to play Pulley."

The tyke had a loud voice, and Phillipa focused on him. "Is that so?" she said. "And what is your name?"

"Gabriel."

"Tell me what Pulley is, Gabriel."

He made gestures with his hands, like pulling apart a loaf of bread. "Like this," he said, grunting with the effort of the demonstration. "Will you play with me?"

Phillipa looked at Christelle for a clue as to what the boy meant, but Christelle had no idea. She shrugged as the little boy started to walk around the chamber, clearly hunting for something. The women didn't know what it was, but the boy came across a wardrobe and opened the doors, digging around in the laundry inside. He pulled forth something, which turned out to be a sash of some kind, and came back over to the bed.

"Here," he said, giving Phillipa one end while he took the other. "Now, you pull as hard as you can and I'll pull as hard as I can. Whoever pulls the hardest wins."

Phillipa was willing. She was barely more than a child herself and things like games struck her fancy, especially with an eager little boy. Still holding the sash, she moved to the edge of the bed, swinging her legs over the side so she'd have some leverage.

"Very well," she said. "Pull!"

Gabriel did. He was surprisingly strong, but Phillipa had him beat. She let the boy grunt and yank for a minute or two before giving a big tug and pulling the child down to his knees. She fell back on the bed and pretended to be exhausted.

"You are very strong, Gabriel," she said. "I think you will win the next time we play."

The little boy stood up, brushing off his knees. "I am the strongest one here."

"I believe you are."

"I'm stronger than Lady Maria."

"Do you play this game with her?"

He shook his head and, suddenly, the light mood faded. Both the little boy and his sister seemed to grow stiff again, almost fearful. It was the strangest reaction, and one not missed by either Phillipa or Christelle. The mere mention of their nurse had the children rigid.

Odd, indeed.

The women passed glances between them, suggesting they both saw the reaction. Not wanting to dampen the mood, Phillipa lifted the sash she held to the little boy.

"Let's try again," she suggested. "I'm sure you will win this time."

Gabriel hesitated, but the lure of playing tug-of-war was too great. He picked up the end of the sash, lying on the ground, and when Phillipa told him to pull, he did.

Phillipa feigned slipping right off the bed, much to Gabriel's delight. She slithered onto the floor, leaning against the bed as she pretended to be exhausted from the pull.

"Well done, Gabriel," she said. "You are so strong that you pulled me off the bed."

Gabriel was puffed up with pride. "I can do it again."

Phillipa held up her hand. "Let me recover first," she said. "But in the meantime, will you sit beside me and tell me about yourself? Your sister can sing and you like to play games, but what else do you like to do? Do you like to ride horses?"

Gabriel sat beside her, leaning against the bed just as she was. "I do not know about horses," he said. "Lady Maria does not let us get near them."

"Do you play in the garden, then?"

"We are not allowed to go there."

"Then what do you do all day?"

He shrugged, looking at his lap, as Georgiana came to sit on Phillipa's free side. Phillipa turned her attention to the little girl, who reached out to touch Phillipa's long, braided hair.

"You are not as old as Lady Maria," she said.

Phillipa shook her head. "Nay, I am not."

"How old are you?"

"Old enough to be a queen," Phillipa said, smiling. She put her hand on her rounded belly. "Old enough to bear a child. I will have my own playmate soon."

Georgiana looked at Phillipa's stomach. "My mother had a baby in her belly," she said. "She went away and took the baby with her."

"Where did she go?"

Georgiana pointed to the ceiling. "To heaven," she said. "Catie says that Mama went to live with Papa because he missed her and wanted her to come live with him."

Phillipa's smile faded. She'd heard about Leonidas' wife and child from Edward, but she realized that the same woman was the mother of these children. It reminded her of what a situation Leonidas had left when he'd gone to Woodstock to serve Edward, and now he'd returned to what was surely still an upsetting circumstance. Reaching out, she put a gentle hand on Georgiana's head.

"I am certain your mother misses you very much," she said. "But imagine how happy she must be to be with your papa. Now he is no longer lonely and they must have great adventures together."

Georgiana thought on that. "What about the baby?"

"The baby has adventures with them, too."

That seemed to make sense to her little mind. "I think she should have stayed with us, though," she said. "I did not want her to go."

Phillipa sighed faintly, glancing at Christelle, who was watching the scene closely. But Phillipa had something Christelle didn't have, and that was a vast capacity for compassion. Christelle was still trying to develop hers, but Phillipa's came naturally. She patted Georgiana on the head.

"I think she knew that you would have Gabriel and your older sister to keep you company," she said. "Catherine is your sister, is she not? She will take care of you until you see your mother again."

Georgiana shrugged, leaning back against the bed so far that she ended up leaning against Phillipa. Gabriel, who had been listening, somehow ended up with his head on Phillipa's lap, and before she knew it, she had one twin dozing against her right arm while the other slept on her lap.

Christelle, of course, had watched it all. When she realized that Phillipa was effectively pinned, she moved toward the bed.

"I can put them on the bed if you wish," she said softly. "It must be uncomfortable for you on the ground."

Phillipa stopped her. "No need," she murmured. "Truthfully, this is exactly what I needed."

"What do you mean?"

Phillipa looked at the boy sleeping on her lap. "I did not wish to leave Edward," she said quietly. "I did not know where we were going and what we would find when we got there, but if this is what our destination is to be—two lonely children in search of friendship—then I am where I need to be. I am content."

Christelle knew that she meant it, too. The young queen loved children, and that was never more evident as it was as the woman leaned her head back against the bed, remaining still so the small, confused pair could gain a few moments of peaceful sleep.

Somehow in the midst of it, Phillipa found a few moments of peaceful sleep, too.

❦

"I WANT YOU to tell me how you have been raising my children," Leonidas said. "And do not lie, because I have knights I trust more than you who will also tell me what they have observed, so you will tell me the truth."

Lady Maria was sitting in a stiff wooden chair in the center of the solar that she had practically taken over during Leonidas' absence. In fact, she'd taken over the keep in general and dictated everything from the children's daily tasks to the food served in the great hall. There had been a great power tussle going on between her and the knights that the Earl of Hull had left behind, including his own brother, whom Lady Maria had deemed young and foolish. There was no respect there, for any of the knights.

Now, she was going to have to face the consequences of her power grab.

She knew the knights would speak against her, so her only hope was to make her behavior seem as normal and unthreatening as possible. The knights—all three of them—were in the solar, out of her line of vision. Also out of her line of vision was Catherine, who had joined them in the solar at Leonidas' request. Pretty, sweet, and red haired, Catherine had grown tremendously during the year Leonidas had been away, and even in his short time at Ashendon, he'd seen how Talan looked at her.

That told him that other things had been going on in his

absence, too.

But for now, he was focused on Lady Maria.

"You gave me the position of tending your children, my lord," she said, trying to sound as if she were in control of herself and not terrified. "It is my duty to tend them the best way I know how."

"And how is that?"

"Discipline, my lord," the woman said. "Discipline creates strong character."

Leonidas leaned against the large table in the room, one that was despicably neat and tidy and not at all like the table he'd left last year. In fact, the entire chamber seemed to be neat and tidy—some of the shelves were empty when he knew for a fact there had been books or other valuables on them. He was so distracted by the empty shelves around him that he stood up from the table, looking around and gesturing to the walls.

"Where are all of my books?" he asked. "This room is far barer than when I left it. What happened?"

Lady Maria looked around, too, but she was struggling for words. It was Dayne who answered.

"Ask her where she sold them," he said, his gaze on Lady Maria. "She took over this chamber, Leo. She put the books into sacks, and when we questioned her, she ordered us out of the keep or threatened to write to you and tell you that we were being intrusive and dangerous to her and the children. But those sacks made their way to clergy who would visit Ashendon at her request, and they gave her money for them. I saw the exchange myself."

"So did I," Talan said. "We all did. But when we questioned her, we were told to mind our own business."

Leonidas looked at Lady Maria, who suddenly didn't appear

so calm or arrogant. She was looking at Leonidas with genuine fear.

"Where," he said slowly, "are my books, woman?"

Lady Maria began to visibly quiver. "I… I donated them to the church, of course," she said. "They were in great need, my lord, and I did not think you would mind, since it was to the church. God will reward you greatly."

Leonidas frowned. "That may be, but they were *my* books," he said. "What made you decide to sell my things?"

"I… The money was not for the books, my lord, but…"

"She's lying," Dayne said, loudly. "Christ, Leo, the woman sold your possessions and kept the money. She mistreated and starved your children and took over the keep as if it were her own private castle. What more proof do you need than the word of me and Talan and Zander? Ask Catherine. She'll tell you the same thing."

Leonidas didn't doubt his brother for a minute, but he at least wanted to pretend to be fair in this matter. He'd been gone a year and there was some guilt in that, leaving the command of his castle to others, while he followed the king around. But there had been reasons for that. Memories of Juliette, mostly. But it was odd… Returning to Ashendon hadn't been the avalanche of emotions he'd thought it would be. There had been no real sorrow in returning, even now as he stood in the solar where he and Juliette used to have pleasant conversations. All he could feel was relief that he'd made it home, drawing strength from these old walls that belonged to him. The place he wanted to establish his legacy.

But first, he had to settle a few things.

"Where is the money, Lady Maria?" he finally asked. "I will not tolerate any denials, so you may as well tell me."

Lady Maria seemed to be slipping further and further into fear. "I have no money, my lord."

Dayne snorted rudely, looking at Leonidas to emphasize just how much the woman was lying. Leonidas took the hint.

"Catherine?" he said, still looking at Lady Maria. "Can you confirm what Dayne is telling me?"

Catherine came forward from her position at the back of the chamber. She was timid, wearing that same fearful expression the twins had when looking at Lady Maria, but she came to stand next to Leonidas and focused on the woman who had terrorized the entire castle for a solid year.

"Aye," she said. "She has been terrible to the twins. Cruel and terrible. She starved Georgiana, giving her food to Gabriel, and then I would take food to Georgiana in secret. She tried to starve me, at first, but I could see that she was trying to hurt me. The knights took up my defense. But you had engaged her to tend the twins and she wielded that dictum over us like… like a sword of vengeance. Truly, Leonidas, she was terrifying. She only meant to harm all of us."

Catherine was being rather dramatic, but it underscored to Leonidas that, indeed, there had been something unsavory happening in his absence. He was angry to hear what had happened, but more than that, he felt stupid. Stupid that he had engaged a woman who had come with a recommendation document from the Earl of Carnforth, so she had said, and he had taken her at her word. He'd been so desperate for someone to take care of the younger children that he'd failed to do his due diligence. For a man who strove for perfection in all things, that had been a rare mistake.

To realize he'd been duped was a bitter pill to swallow.

"Lady Maria," he said after a moment, "do you have anything to say about these accusations before I decide what is to be done?"

Lady Maria stood up from her chair and tried to back away from him, out of arm's length so he couldn't grab her. "They… they were all against me from the start," she hissed, pointing to the knights. "Hatred and jealousy because of the trust you placed in me, my lord."

"Then you are telling me that none of this is true?"

"I am beyond reproach, my lord!"

Leonidas was well aware that she hadn't give him an answer. "Since you cannot give me a straight answer, I am forced to make decisions without your advice," he said. "Dayne, put her in the vault until I decide what's to be done with her."

That was an order Dayne and the others had been waiting for. But Lady Maria was still backing away from Leonidas and ended up colliding with a chair she didn't see. Dayne went to grab the woman by the arm to escort her out of the solar, but she didn't take kindly to being touched and slashed her nails across his hand. He didn't loosen his grip, but that action brought Talan as well, and between the two of them, they easily whisked the struggling woman out of the chamber.

"Chain her to the wall," Leonidas called after them. "She is to be suitably restrained until I decide otherwise."

He said it loudly enough that Lady Maria heard him and began to wail. She wailed all the way out of the keep, and they could hear her as she was forcibly escorted across the bailey. Catherine, who had been standing well away from the woman out of fear, wandered over to the windows that overlooked the ward as she watched Lady Maria being taken to the subterranean vault beneath the gatehouse.

"I do not think she spent the money," she said softly. "She

never left Ashendon. There was no way for her to spend it."

Leonidas came to stand beside her, his gaze on the gatehouse and the collection of soldiers now watching Lady Maria being dragged to her doom.

"That means it is somewhere in her chamber," he said. "Unless you think she hid it?"

Catherine turned to look at him. "If she did, it would be in this chamber, somewhere," she said. "She took this over, you know. No one could go into the solar but her."

He sighed heavily. "Why did no one send word to me that this was going on?" he said. "I would have come back immediately."

Catherine shrugged. "Because we knew you were with the king," she said. "Dayne did not wish to bother you. He felt that he should be able to deal with the situation, and I heard him and the knights speak about it a great deal. The only thing preventing their sending her away, I think, was the fact that you had engaged Lady Maria. Dayne did not feel it was his right to relieve her of her post without your permission."

Leonidas scratched his head. "Under normal circumstances I would agree, but in this case…" He trailed off, pondering how to end that sentence, but it was obvious. The knights should have sent her packing but hadn't because of the fear of usurping Leonidas' authority in his own home. That had set up misery for the children. His gaze lingered on Catherine for a moment. "I'm very sorry, Catie. You should not have had to deal with this after everything you have been through. All I can say is that I thought was doing the right thing by engaging a woman to tend the younger children."

She forced a smile. "I know," she said. "It was not your fault."

"You are kind to say so, but we both know the truth," he said. "I brought her in and her actions are my fault. But I have dealt with it swiftly, I hope, and I will continue to make it up to you and your brother and sister, I promise."

"That is kind of you," she said. "But now that she is gone, it is enough. We will recover."

Her words stabbed at him, painfully. "You were already recovering from your mother's death," he muttered. "You should not have to recover from an opportunistic nurse who caused far more harm than good."

Catherine looked at him until the gesture became excessive, and he lifted his eyebrows questioningly at her. That brought a smile from the young woman.

"I was thinking that most men would not care how children that are not their own are treated, but you always have," she said. "You have always shown us such regard, and we are very fortunate. I am grateful."

His gaze lingered on her for a moment. "You really *have* grown up since I was gone," he said, his eyes twinkling weakly. "You have never said that to me. That speaks of maturity."

"I hope so," she said. "I am no longer a child."

"I can see that," he said. "Now, may we speak on more pleasant things?"

"Of course, Leonidas."

He smiled, without humor or warmth. She had always called him Leonidas—never Papa or even *sir* or *my lord*. Juliette had called him Leonidas, and because Catherine had known, and loved, her real father, her mother had never forced her to address Leonidas in any fashion she was uncomfortable with. That meant she called him by his name, which truly didn't bother him, but she sounded much like her mother had when she said it.

Perhaps that was why the smile was without humor.

It brought back some memories he'd fled Ashendon to avoid.

"It seems to me that you are now chatelaine," he said. "Would you not agree with that?"

Catherine nodded. "I would."

"Then I will ask you to make the ladies I brought with me very comfortable," he said. "One of them is your queen. She is about your age and she has been traveling a very long time, so I am sure she would like food and a bath and anything else you can bring her that would make her comfortable. Will you do this?"

Catherine's eyes were wide. "I will," she said earnestly. "I saw what happened with Lady Maria when the women were first brought to the keep. I saw the fight."

"That was the queen's protector, Lady Christelle."

"She is fierce."

His smile grew genuine. "That is an understatement," he said. "She is a strong lady, and fearless, but I will also tell you that she has been ill during most of the journey."

"The poor woman," Catherine gasped. "Why?"

Leonidas waggled his eyebrows. "Because we spent two weeks at sea," he said. "A very rough sea, and she was ill because of it."

"How terrible for her."

"It was," Leonidas agreed. "And because of that, I want you to be particularly kind to her and bring her all manner of food that might help her belly settle. Bread, milk, and broth. Anything that will help her regain her strength."

Catherine took his orders seriously. "I will," she said. "May I go now?"

He nodded, and she darted for the door. "And you will be in charge of the twins from now on," he said loudly, "Catie? Do you understand?"

She was at the door, waving him off. "Gladly," she said. "I must go and help the ladies."

She was gone before he could say another word, and he grinned at her enthusiasm. That left him alone in the chamber with Zander, who had thus far remained in the shadows, observing everything from his perch on an old oak table. When Catherine vacated, Leonidas let out a heavy sigh and raked his hands through his hair as he eyed his cousin.

"Was this place really such a madhouse while I was away, Zan?" he asked.

Lesander de Norville, known as Zander since infancy, grinned. He was the youngest son of Evelyn de Wolfe de Norville and her husband, Hector de Norville, and he had the unique bloodlines that Leonidas and his siblings had—their parents had married siblings. Leonidas' father, Edward, had married Hector's youngest sister, and Hector had married Edward's older sister, so both Zander and Leonidas had de Wolfe and de Norville blood.

That was where they found out what the dominant bloodlines were.

William de Wolfe and Paris de Norville had been the best of friends since they were children. They had grown up together, endured many adventures together, and ended up serving together at Northwood Castle on the Scots border. When they both married and had children, and they happened to marry women who were cousins to one another, the big joke between them was who had the stronger bloodlines. Paris, a man of supreme ego and annoying overconfidence, insisted that that the de Norville bloodlines would show their worth. The truth, however, was that out of two dozen grandchildren that William and Paris shared, the vast majority had William's dark hair and strong features.

Paris, by contrast, had blond hair and blue eyes, and his wife had red hair. Any of the grandchildren who favored the de Norville side usually ended up with Caladora's red hair. Only a couple of them had Paris' blond hair, and that included Zander. He was nearly the spitting image of his grandfather with his blond, brawny good looks, but what he didn't share with his grandfather was an overinflated self-worth or an annoying personality.

Zander was quite the opposite.

He was, by all accounts, hell on the field of battle. His skill was beyond compare, and in a family full of knights, Zander was one of the better warriors that they had produced. But his personality was passive and even quiet; he was a gentle man who had been born into a warring family. If anything, he took after Leonidas' father, Edward, because Zander had a more diplomatic personality about him. If there were any kind of negotiations or bargaining to be had, Zander was the man for the job. Not only was he genuinely likable, but he was also one of the more sought-after men in England because of his comely good looks and the de Norville fortune behind him.

Zander de Norville was a family favorite and given that he had two elder brothers in Atreus and Hermes de Norville, who had often been considered the family idiots when they were young, the advent of a genuinely kind and loveable de Norville brother had somehow redeemed all of Evelyn and Hector's children.

At least they weren't *all* idiots.

Leonidas considered himself fortunate to have Zander in his fold.

"Unfortunately, when you left, Lady Maria decided that she was in charge," Zander said in answer to his question. "Dayne was constantly in a battle with that woman, every single day. It wasn't only that she took over the keep, but he was concerned for the children. Especially Georgiana. We would all feed her, but we had to do it in secret because she caught us feeding her once and kept the child inside the keep for a month where we could not get to her. For some reason, she seemed to have a vendetta against the little girl."

Leonidas shook his head sadly. "I truly wish you had sent me a missive about all of this," he said. "I would have come back immediately."

"We know," Zander said. "And that is why we did not do it."

"Zan, I—"

"You had just lost your wife, Leo," Zander interrupted him quietly. "We all saw how sad you were after her passing, and when Tate de Lara sent word to you about assisting him with Edward's struggles, you had something new to focus on. We didn't want to call you back to this place where your memories were still raw."

Leonidas understood, even if he didn't agree. "It was noble to try to protect me," he said. "But the children were involved. Juliette would not have been happy with a threat to her children."

Zander shrugged. "They were never in any real danger, I suppose," he said. "Uncomfortable? Aye. Cruel? At times, there was cruelty. But none of us have raised children, Leo. Lady

Maria acted as if she'd done it a thousand times, so who were we to challenge her, especially when you engaged her? All we could do was keep watch on the situation, and if it got too terrible…"

He didn't finish, and Leonidas encouraged him to continue. "Then… *what*?"

Zander shrugged, but he was looking him straight in the eye. "Then Lady Maria would have an accident and we would send you word that she was dead," he said quietly. "You should know that we made a pact to protect the children, Leo. If it looked as if they were in genuine mortal danger, then we would do what needed to be done."

That made Leonidas feel a little better, but not much. "I appreciate that," he said. "I truly do. And I appreciate that it must have been difficult to decide just when to intervene and when not to. It was a complicated situation."

"It was," Zander said. "But I can assure you that we always made sure to feed Lady Georgiana when the opportunity arose. She was never truly starved even if Lady Maria wanted her to be."

Leonidas pondered the nurse a few moments longer—but that was all he could manage because he didn't want to expend more energy over her than he already had. "Then I am comforted," he said. "The woman is in the vault and things will return to normal now that I have returned, and that is the best outcome of this situation. Now, what else can you tell me about the past year? What else went on here that did not have to do with Lady Maria?"

Zander thought on the question. "Truthfully, Ashendon is rather quiet," he said. "Not at all like the alert status we have always had to adhere to on the Scots border, although I have been told by some of the town's folk that Northmen come to Hull once in a while. Usually, they come to trade, although one old man told me that he remembers when they would raid the countryside."

"Christ," Leonidas said, frowning. "We do not want that."

"Nay, we do not."

"But I'm glad to hear it has been quiet."

Zander nodded as he stood up from the table he'd been leaning against. "I suspect that is about to change," he said, heading for the chamber door. "You've brought royalty into our midst. I'm curious to know why."

Leonidas watched him open the door and call to a servant for food and drink. Zander was considerate that way, knowing Leonidas had just arrived from a long journey and was sent head-on into a crisis without any refreshment or sustenance. But he waited until Zander shut the door before answering.

"I'll wait until Dayne and Talan return before I tell you," he said. "I want them to hear it."

"Are we in for a battle, Leo?"

Leonidas shrugged his shoulders. "If Mortimer decides to lay siege to Ashendon to get to Phillipa, it is possible," he said. "You may be sorry you told me that everything had been quiet around here. Let us hope you have not cursed us."

Zander laughed softly. "Let us hope," he said, but he quickly sobered. "Speaking of curses, I fear I should tell you something that is not my business, but I feel you should at least be forewarned."

Leonidas was hunting for a comfortable chair to sit in. "What do you mean?" he said. "What is not your business?"

"Lady Catherine."

"What about her?"

"She is… fond of someone."

That had Leonidas' attention. "Oh?" he said. "Who?"

Zander held out a hand to beg for the man's patience while he explained. "Before I tell you, I will stress to you that nothing inappropriate has happened," he said. "Nothing even close. Everything has been quite proper. I do not even think they have kissed."

Leonidas' face scrunched into a scowl. "Kissed?" he repeated. "Catie?"

"She is a young woman now, Leo," Zander said as if the man needed reminding. "She is pretty and vivacious and much loved at Ashendon. It was only a matter of time before she had suitors."

"She is only sixteen years of age!"

"Seventeen," Zander said. "Her day of birth was last month."

Leonidas looked stricken. "God's Bones," he muttered. "You are correct. It was. And I completely forgot."

Zander shook his head. "Do not tell her that I reminded you," he said. "She believes you know everything, so keep up the illusion. She may be unhappy if she thinks you have forgotten."

Leonidas waved him off. "I'll not tell her," he said. "But back to the subject of her kissing someone. *Who* is worthy of her kisses, Zander?"

"You did not hear this from me."

"I understand, but answer the question."

"Talan."

Leonidas' eyebrows lifted. "I see," he said. "So there *is* something between them. I suspected as much."

Zander nodded slowly, confidently. "The youngest son of

the hereditary king of Anglesey and our Aunt Penelope," he said. "He is barely ten years older than she is and has a good head on his shoulders, Leo. You know that. He's a good match."

Leonidas was pondering the thought of Juliette's young daughter and his young cousin when the door opened and servants came through bearing food and drink. He could smell the warmed-over beef and the fresh bread and, ravenous, he tore into it and forgot all about Catherine and Talan.

At least, for the moment.

Even though he'd known Talan since birth, he found himself looking at his cousin through new eyes. He loved the man dearly and had served with him for years, but at this moment, all he could see was a suitor for Catherine's affections. He was starting to feel like a fool, and possibly even like a real father and that had him snorting ironically as he turned his head away.

Life went on, indeed.

"I am happy to report that Lady Maria is in the vault and in chains," Dayne said as he entered the chamber like a conquering hero. "The old hag is where she belongs, finally."

He noticed the food and wine on the table where Leonidas was standing and sopping up gravy with the fresh bread, and he went straight for the drink. Leonidas let him pour himself a full cup of wine because his attention wasn't on his greedy brother as much as it was still on Talan, who had plopped down in the chair that Leonidas had been sitting in.

Chewing, Leonidas kept his eyes on his food.

"Make sure she at least has food and warmth for the night," he said. "I'll decide what's to be done with her tomorrow, but for now, she is neutralized and I am satisfied. There are more important things to discuss."

Dayne took a big gulp of the good French wine. "I assume you are going to tell us why you've brought Edward's queen here?" he said. "Where's Ken, by the way?"

"Guarding her door upstairs," Leonidas said as he swallowed the bite in his mouth and reached out to take the cup in his brother's hand. He downed it in one swallow before answering. "There is a good deal afoot, so listen closely. Simply put, Phillipa is carrying the heir to the throne, but at the same time, there are rumors that Isabella is pregnant with Mortimer's child and that he plans to do away with Edward, and his bloodlines, to put his own child on the throne."

That was a shocking bit of information and the three knights were in various stages of disbelief. "God's Bones," Dayne said, clearly stunned. "But we do not know, for certain, if Isabella is pregnant?"

Leonidas shook his head. "Nay," he said. "But trust me when I say that the Executioner Knights are trying to get us a definitive answer."

Dayne cocked an eyebrow. "The spies are involved, I see?"

"Of course they are," Leonidas said. "Gideon of Loxbeare is in the thick of it and is the one who told us of Isabella's rumored pregnancy. Meanwhile, Tate decided that Edward and Phillipa should be separated and hidden from Mortimer. If he does happen to locate one of them, at least the other will be out of his reach. That means we, my dear family members, are in charge of Phillipa's safety. It is up to us to protect the next King of England."

He'd delivered the news succinctly. At least they knew what they were up against, or potentially up against. With the exception of Leonidas, these were all young knights, all under thirty years, so their experience as warriors had mostly been on the field of battle. The intrigue of politics was something left to their fathers and uncles and grandfathers, but not to them.

That was all about to change.

They were about to grow up.

"We are at your service, Leo," Dayne said quietly. "Tell us what you need done and we shall do it."

Leonidas nodded. "Good," he said. "I realize this is a good deal to ask of men who came to Ashendon thinking it would be a less hazardous situation, but I'm afraid we are now in the middle of something crucial. Dayne, I want you to have a messenger ready to send north to Castle Questing. Uncle Scott must know of this situation. I also must send word to Papa, but I am unsure where he is at this time. He is normally in London this time of year, and we just came through that city, but I did not have time to stop at Isleworth House. We'll need to send a messenger there also."

Dayne nodded smartly. "It will be done," he said. "Anything else?"

"Aye." Leonidas looked at Zander. "I want scouts all over my lands for any sign of Mortimer or his supporters. That means I also want men in the town, keeping an ear out for anything to do with Isabella or Mortimer. You will tend to this personally and report to me daily."

Zander nodded. "Of course, Leo."

That left Talan. Leonidas found himself looking at the young knight and struggling not to view him as the enemy now. While he hadn't committed any crime, of course, the fact remained that if what Zander said was true, Talan had Catherine's affections engaged, and that was the enemy of any father.

Even a stepfather.

"Talan," he said after a moment, "you and I are going to

ensure that this castle can withstand any siege. We are going to go over every inch of the wall and make any necessary repairs. The moat will be trenched if it seems that it will be too simple for an army to walk on it, because I know that in some spots, the water has receded and ground is left. I realize the walls are twenty feet in some places, but for an army the size of the one Mortimer would bring, we need the barrier of the moat. Am I clear?"

Talan stood up from the chair he'd be sitting on. "I will see to it myself," he said firmly. "Preparations will be made, Leo."

"More than preparations. Impenetrable obstacles."

"It will be done."

"Good," Leonidas said, his gaze lingering on Talan for a moment longer before he looked at the rest of the knights. "You have your orders. Go forth and make it so."

The knights were moving for the door, each one of them on a mission. Truthfully, Leonidas wasn't entirely sure that Mortimer would bother coming all the way to East Yorkshire, but it couldn't be discounted. Prudence was the order of the day.

Better safe than sorry.

A long day was about to get longer.

CHAPTER FIVE

Chateau de Chambrey
France

T HE CHAMBER, FOR all of its vast space and shadowy darkness, had a close feeling about it as the fire snapped in the enormous hearth and sparks jumped out onto the stone floor. The closeness had nothing to do with the size of the room, but more the mood that was within it.

The castle belonged to the powerful Lorraine family and had for centuries. It was a confusing complex of rooms and passages and towers, a mishmash of building that had been done during different times by different owners. That made it feel less like a home and more like a labyrinth, but at this moment, the head of the House of Lorrain was seated in an old chair in front of that spitting fireplace. He'd positioned the chair far enough away that he wasn't being hit by the sparks, but that meant the heat wasn't warming his old bones, and he very much needed them warm tonight.

News from England had arrived.

It had been at least four months since he'd last heard from

his daughter, a highly trained spy who had been placed close to the royal couple of England. That had been a plan he concocted many years ago and, fortunately, it had come to fruition through careful planning and political connections. It was a scheme that would hopefully see the French emerge in a more stable situation because, at the moment, their situation seemed to be somewhat *un*stable.

But that was going to change.

There were several situations afoot when it came to the English and French royal families, but that was something that Bernard de Lorrain hoped to change. Careful plans had been in the works that would see his very own daughter, Christelle, become a close advisor to Queen Phillipa. Christelle's position was twofold in that she was supposed to encourage Phillipa to acquire more French advisors. The French wanted a foothold in the English royal court, but Edward was very much against it because of experience with his father's favorites, and Phillipa also seemed to be against it because she was fully assimilating into the English people. Word was that the English adored her because she was kind and fair and very much wanted the input of the English advisers.

That was not what the French had anticipated.

Therefore, Christelle had been positioned to hopefully combat Phillipa's anglophile attitude, and the time was quickly coming that it was going to be imperative because Phillipa was no longer a child but a grown woman who was expecting a child of her own. The reality was that Phillipa wasn't even truly French, but from Hainault. Still, the House of Lorrain had enough connections to the French that great rewards had been promised to them should they help position French advisers within the English court.

That was most imperative because there was the small matter of King Edward and his claim to the French crown. When King Charles of France passed away, Edward was the nearest male relative by birth eligible to inherit the French throne, but the French preferred Phillip, who had indeed inherited the throne because Edward had his hands full with his troubles in England, including his mother and her lover, Roger Mortimer. That had thrown Edward off the scent of the French throne, and the French wanted to keep it that way.

That was where Christelle came in.

Bernard knew there was a great deal at stake and the pressure was growing by the day. He hadn't heard from his daughter in quite some time and the French were getting restless, so her missive today had been of great relief.

Until Bernard opened it.

Then he wasn't so relieved.

There was trouble afoot.

"What does it say, Bernard?" A man with white hair, slender and fine, had been standing back in the shadows as Bernard read his daughter's missive. "What does she say?"

Bernard sighed faintly. "I fear we may have waited too long, Gautier."

"Why?"

"Because it sounds as if Edward has become a man and is preparing to take control."

Gautier de Leon was part of the French royal court, a cousin to the king, though distantly. He had a grand chateau outside of Paris and another one near Amiens, was a man who craved power and took it when he could, so Bernard's words struck a chord of concern within him.

He couldn't tell if the man was being dramatic or truthful.

"What has happened?" he asked.

Bernard held the missive up to him. "Isabella may be with child," he said. "If she is, that could change the dynamics of Edward's embattlement with Mortimer because Mortimer would want to put a child of his upon the throne. According to Christelle, the decision has been made to separate Edward and Phillipa to keep them safe from Mortimer for the time being."

Gautier was trying to read the opening of the missive, but his mind was on the conversation. "Where are they taking Phillipa?" he asked.

"Ashendon Castle," Bernard said. "It is at the bottom of the message. They are taking her to Hull."

Gautier looked up from the vellum. "Hull," he repeated. "That is to the north."

Bernard nodded. "North of Lincoln," he said. "There is a large port, one of the largest on the eastern side of England. I've never been there, but I imagine the castle is not too far from the port if it is in Hull itself."

Gautier didn't say anything until he finished reading the missive. Then he set it down and began to rub his hands together, thinking.

"Hull," he muttered. "If the queen is in Hull, away from the king and away from his army, then this may be perfect for our cause."

Bernard nodded slowly. "I was thinking the same thing," he said. "Originally, Christelle was placed close to Phillipa simply to keep watch on the young royals. To exert control over the queen if we could."

Gautier was still rubbing his hands together because that was how he did his best thinking, looking like a madman wringing his fingers.

"Listen to me," he said as if a great idea had just come to him. "Isabella is French. Edward is an increasing threat to the French throne because he is, quite honestly, the legal heir. I have always believed that."

"And?"

"And if we were to help Mortimer and Isabella gain the throne, that would put them in our debt," Gautier said. "Isabella is pregnant with a child we can control if we do away with Mortimer after we have helped him gain the throne. We will have a French queen and a French heir to the English throne."

"And how are we to do that?"

Gautier looked at him as if he'd gone daft. "By using Phillipa as leverage against Edward, of course," he said. "Christelle will deliver Phillipa to us, we will bring her to France and lock her in one of my properties, and tell Edward that we will kill her and the child she carries unless he abdicates in favor of Isabella and Mortimer."

Bernard could see his point and he, too, thought it was a sound plan. "My daughter could deliver Phillipa to us quite easily," he said. "And it would not take an army to get the queen. Only Christelle."

"Exactly."

"We will travel to Hull and meet her in secret," Bernard continued. "We can have Phillipa on a cog heading for France before anyone even realizes she is missing."

Gautier was smiling broadly. "Now you understand, my friend," he said. "We can end this situation quite quickly and painlessly, all in favor of France, in a very short time. No bloodshed, no armies. Simply one small woman delivered to us by your daughter. Brilliant."

Bernard looked at him. "And we shall be well paid, of

course."

"Anything you want, my friend."

"One hundred thousand marks of gold should do."

The smile vanished from Gautier's face. "Are you serious?"

"A queen's ransom, my friend," Bernard said, knowing he held the answer to France's problems. "You want a queen? Then you shall have to pay for her."

Gautier wasn't happy about being swindled, the way he saw it. "You are a wolf, Bernard," he said. "A wolf with teeth."

"A wolf who can give France what it wants," Bernard said. Then he leaned in Gautier's direction. "What is it worth to you to control the throne of England?"

Gautier didn't even need to answer that because they both knew what it was worth. Before the night was out, Gautier had sent missives to several French allies informing them of the very real possibility of seizing the English throne and what it was going to cost them.

A ransom all of them, and most especially the French king, would be willing to pay.

And Bernard knew it.

CHAPTER SIX

"**I** DID NOT think you were coming!"

The whispered words had come from Catherine just after she had reached out to grab Talan, pulling him into one of the several towers that lined Ashendon's walls. Most of the towers functioned as stairwells and storage areas, but this one in particular held hay and feed for the stables.

This was Talan and Catherine's secret haven.

They had been meeting here several times a week for the past year, ever since Catherine had managed to flirt her way into Talan's heart. It hadn't been difficult, in truth, because she was a beautiful girl and quite charming, and Talan had succumbed without a fight. He was seven years older than she was, however, and she wasn't yet of age. Almost, but not quite.

But he loved her anyway.

"I had to wait until Leonidas went to bed," he said quietly, bolting the heavy wooden door of the tower. "At least, I assume he has because I haven't seen him. But now that he has returned, we have a problem."

Catherine, with an oil lamp held high so she could see his face, was looking at him with some apprehension.

"Unless you intend to tell him about us, we will simply have to meet in secret," she said. "We have already been doing it for a year. We can continue."

Talan sighed faintly, taking the oil lamp from her and then leading her up the narrow wooden stairs to the loft above. It was mostly empty, with just a few piles of hay and an old stool. He set the lamp on the stool and pulled Catherine down to sit beside him.

"I hate to deceive him," he said quietly. "But his return was unexpected. You and I… We are still coming to know one another, Catie. We are still young. You are young. We do not have to rush into anything."

Catherine knew that Talan wasn't keen on jumping into marriage. They'd already had that discussion. He knew he loved her, knew he wanted to marry her, but at twenty years and four, he wasn't sure he wanted to do it *now*. He was a knight of the de Wolfe empire and would go where he was told to go and fight whomever he was told to fight, and it wasn't fair to a wife.

So he'd said.

She sighed heavily and looked away.

"Then what do you want to do?" she asked. "Continue hiding from him? It is not as if the entire castle does not know about us, Talan. Someone will tell him."

Talan shook his head. "Not necessarily," he said. "Catie, I do not mean to be difficult about this. You know I love you. But I would like my own command or, at the very least, a stable position before I marry. I do not want to leave you at Ashendon while I go wherever I'm told to go. I could end up in Scotland next month and be there for a very long time. How fair is it to you to leave you here, waiting for me?"

She frowned and looked at him. "Who says I will wait for

you?" she said. "I will tell Leonidas to find me a husband and I'll marry a man who wants to be married. You can fight the Scots all you wish and I will not care."

Another old argument between them. Talan shook his head in exasperation. "I do not understand what the rush is," he said. "We have our whole lives ahead of us and I do not think we should be pushed into anything."

"You pushed me into this when you first seduced me."

He averted his gaze. "That is not fair," he said softly. "That is not kind, either. I did not seduce you. You were quite willing."

She had been. That wasn't a lie. "I was willing to give my innocence to you," she said. "I was willing because I loved you and I thought you loved me enough to marry me."

"I do," he insisted quietly. "But I just do not feel as if my position is stable enough for a wife at this time. I have hardly any fortune, hardly anything to offer you. I am the youngest son of the hereditary King of Anglesey and I will not inherit anything. I must make my own fortune. Why is it wrong for me to want a stable position, and some money, before I take a wife? I *cannot* offer you anything right now, Catie."

She gave him a side-eye. "I would think you would appreciate a woman who wanted you for who you are, not the fortune you bring," she said. "I do not care if you have a fortune. I only care that you are mine and I am yours."

"As wonderful as that sentiment is, we cannot survive on love alone," he said. "The reality is that I must be able to provide for you."

It made sense, but it wasn't to Catherine's liking. She couldn't let the subject go without a fight. "But why is this an issue?" she said. "You serve your cousin, the Earl of Hull, who happens to be my stepfather and who will provide a sizable dowry for me, which we can then live off."

Talan grunted unhappily. "I will not live off my wife as the vast majority of my income," he said flatly. "A man with no respect for himself would do that."

"A man who is in love would do that."

He shook his head firmly. "I will not," he said. "If you do not understand my sense of honor, then we have nothing more to discuss."

"But—"

"*Nay*, Catie."

She stared at him a moment. "Then you will not ask Leonidas for my hand?"

"Not at this time."

Catherine felt as if she'd been hit in the gut. She and Talan has spent a year dancing around the subject, but Leonidas' unexpected return had pushed the situation to a new level. She wasn't conniving by nature, but she was young. And reckless at times. In her world, she only knew what she wanted, and after having suffered through a hellish year with Lady Maria, with Talan riding to her rescue and keeping her safe from the odious woman, a marriage with the man who'd saved her from that terrible fate was the only thing that mattered. He was reluctant, but she wasn't.

Perhaps there was a way to force him into it.

"Then I suppose I shall have to rely on your good sense to know when the time is right," she said, though she didn't mean it. "Not to say I'm happy about it."

"I know," he said. "But I must do what I feel is best for us both."

"Does that mean no more meetings between us until you

are certain?"

He looked at her. "Nay," he said. "Just because I do not want to marry at this moment does not mean I do not want to see you, Catie. Of course I do. Why? Do you not want to see me?"

Her answer was to lean over and kiss him, as she'd done so many times. Talan responded to her immediately, like he always did, his mouth fixed to hers. Passion ignited between them so easily, and it was something he'd learned not to fight. He just accepted it. Therefore, he pulled her against his body and began to loosen the lacings on her garment because that was always the next step when their desire took flight. His hands were big and strong, loosening the ties on the dress and sliding it down her torso as she went to work on his tunic.

Everything was coming off.

Talan lost his big hands in the silken mass of her hair, holding her head against his as his lips continued to feast. Catherine gasped and groaned in response to his tender onslaught, willingly lying on her back as he pulled her down atop the scratchy hay. Trapped beneath his big body, she spread her legs wide for him as his big body slipped between them, and she moaned with desire as his tongue invaded the honeyed recesses of her mouth.

But Talan wasn't satisfied with only kisses. His mouth eventually left her lips, moving to the pert nipples he took such delight in. She was round in the bust and in the hips like her mother had been, which he found utterly pleasing. Talan lost himself in her breasts as Catherine cradled his head, encouraging him to suckle harder. She even rubbed her nipples to harden them, and he suckled her fingers when they came near his mouth. He suckled and kissed until the warmth between her legs became a raging fire and she grasped his manhood in an attempt to direct him into her wet heat. Talan didn't keep her waiting. Stretching out over her body, he let her position him so that he could thrust into her, driving his full, hard length until he was fully sheathed within her.

In the grip of passion, Catherine cried out softly, biting off her screams as his heated shaft began to thrust into her. She began to work with him, her pelvis to his, gasping with pleasure each time their bodies collided. Already, she could feel her muscles tightening as her climax approached and she grabbed Talan's hips, wrapping her legs around him so that he was pulled as deep as he could possibly go. He couldn't move very well from the way she was holding him, but he could move enough.

His arms went around her.

"Speak of your love for me, my dearest," he whispered into her ear. "Tell me how much you want me."

Catherine was breathless. "More than life itself," she breathed, digging her fingers into his buttocks as she rubbed herself against him. "More than the moon wants the night, do I want you. You are the size of a bull, my darling boy. Big and thick and…"

All of the grinding she was doing against him produced the desired results as she abruptly exploded with a climax as she tried to finish her sentence. Describing the size of his male member always did that to her. She cried out, and Talan brought his mouth down on hers, trying to drown out her shrieks of passion so no one would hear, but he had enough passion of his own. His release came as hers was dying away.

Usually, he pulled from her body before he released, but this time, her legs were around him and he couldn't pull out in time. He managed to unwind her ankles enough to remove himself, but he'd already spilled mostly inside her at that point. The rest of it ended up on the straw beneath them as he lay upon her, breathing heavily and the least bit perturbed that she'd locked him up with her legs so he couldn't pull out in time.

"You did that on purpose," he said, winded. "Do it once more and I will never bed you again."

She didn't say anything. She just lay there, unmoving, as Talan waited for her to reply. Suddenly, she was pulling herself out from underneath him and, without a word, started grabbing her clothing, pulling it over her head in haste, yanking on her surcoat and slapping his hand away when he reached out to grasp her. He tried to do it again, to stop whatever she was doing, but she kicked at him the second time and stumbled away, cinching up the ties on the side of her garment.

"Catie," he said quietly, "please do not leave. But you know you should not have done that."

Catherine wouldn't answer him. He'd caught her in a plan of her own making and knew exactly what she'd done, but she wasn't going to admit to it. In her mind, she shouldn't have to resort to such things, hoping to get pregnant simply to force him into marriage. Whatever she did was his fault.

At least, she kept telling herself that.

Going to the door, she unbolted it, yanked it open, and charged off into the night, leaving Talan still in the straw, wondering if he'd gotten the whole thing wrong. He didn't think so, but perhaps he had. Perhaps she'd only wrapped herself around him in the heat of passion and nothing more.

Feeling rather bad with the way things ended, he went to find his clothing.

CHAPTER SEVEN

Ashendon Castle

S HE FELT AS if she'd been here for years.

In truth, it had only been several days since their arrival at Ashendon Castle, but it seemed as if so much had happened since they set foot on the grounds that time seemed to lose all meaning. Since the day after they had arrived, Christelle and Phillipa had found a purpose at the enormous castle with its soaring walls and a veritable army of servants, servants who had been living in fear of Lady Maria and the stick she evidently liked to carry around to threaten people with.

They'd learned a lot of things about Lady Maria in the few days that they'd been there.

None of them good.

The woman was, in fact, still in the vault. No one had said much about what was to be done with her, so she hadn't been a topic of conversation. But what *had* been a topic of conversation was the fact that now Ashendon had a young chatelaine in Catherine who hadn't necessarily had a lot of experience in the role, and before Christelle could say a word about it, Phillipa volunteered the both of them to help the young woman with the job.

And with that, they became part of Ashendon's functions.

Phillipa may have been a queen, and she may have had more servants than some countries had population, but that didn't mean she didn't know how to run a household. She knew exactly how to do it and put that skill to work, starting from the bottom—literally. The first thing she and Christelle did was inventory the stores in the great vaults down below the keep. There seemed to be a good deal of dried foodstuffs, like beans and peas, but not anything remotely fresh. The cold locker that usually held meat was empty. Discussions with the cook revealed that Lady Maria would purchase good pieces of meat from a butcher in the town, but then she would divide it up and sell off pieces of it, leaving usually just the bones and scraps for the cook to work with.

There was more monkey business going on with the stores as well.

According to the cook, an old woman who had served generations of the de Cottingham family, the supplies at Ashendon had always been extensive. Lady Juliette, and her predecessors, had been frugal with money but also quite astute when it came to making sure there was enough food for an entire castle. Juliette had ensured the stores of Ashendon were well supplied, but when Lady Maria assumed the mantle of chatelaine, the good stores seemed to disappear. According to the cook, Lady Maria would take the good stores down to the river where the ships were docking and sell them for quite a bit of money. The cog crews were always glad to get a hold of decent supplies, and Lady Maria had readily supplied them.

More tales of Lady Maria unfolded as the days went by,

stories of her not only selling the stores and the books in Leonidas' solar, but also trying to sell a couple of Leonidas' fine horses until Dayne stopped her. It seemed that the woman tried to sell anything that wasn't nailed down, pocketing the money, which was found after a thorough search of her bedchamber. She'd managed to remove a stone in the wall and stuff her ill-gotten gains behind it, so Leonidas was able to get back all of the money she'd stolen from him. But he turned that money back over to Christelle and Phillipa, who summoned merchants from the town to place orders for things that they needed.

The stores began to fill up again.

With a big meal every evening that contained good meat and vegetables and bread, the men were happier. So were the children, who were allowed to sit with Leonidas and his men at the dais as long as they behaved. Catherine had taken over governess duties in the wake of Lady Maria's absence, and given that she loved her brother and sister, she'd done an excellent job so far. The children seemed happy and were definitely well fed, but three nights in a row, Georgiana had shown up to supper with her pet chicken that she insisted eat with her. Given the guilt Leonidas had felt for the Lady Maria debacle, he had allowed it.

Tonight, Christelle found herself staring across the table at a chicken.

It was a small white chicken with black spots and black eyes, and Georgiana treated it like a living baby. She put it on the bench next to her and put bread down for it to peck at, which the chicken did contentedly. It never tried to run. But tonight, it got up on the table, twice, and when it tried to eat Christelle's bread, she waved a hand at it and it flapped its wings, scattering back to Georgiana.

All the while, Phillipa thought it was the sweetest thing in the world.

Christelle thought it was just a chicken.

Even now, she tried not to feel disgusted as the chicken jumped back onto the table and started eating from Georgiana's plate. *Peck, peck, peck.* Christelle finally had to look away, looking to Phillipa, who was beaming as she watched the delighted little girl and her pet fowl. Elsewhere in the hall, men were drinking and singing, and the enormous hearth with the carved stone mantel was burping smoke into the chamber that collected near the ceiling in a blue haze. There was chatter, and laughter, and the smell of the boiled beef that they had procured from a local farmer. After the harrowing journey to Ashendon, even Christelle had to admit that it all seemed rather… normal.

Calm.

Just another evening at the Earl of Hull's castle.

Thoughts of Leonidas had her looking down the table to where he was sitting with his brother and his cousins and Kenneth, who had just come in from securing the gatehouse for the night. The knights had divided up the duties to include Kenneth and even Leonidas now that Phillipa was in residence, so they were all involved in the security of the castle. Also included in that security were two senior sergeants, men who had served de Cottingham for years faithfully. They were also clued in to Phillipa's presence, though the army, as a whole, wasn't. Leonidas thought it better that way. There would be less chance of Phillipa's location getting out, possibly to people who had connections to Mortimer.

The less people who knew, the better.

With the sergeants outside on the walls as the feast went on, the knights were inside the hall, huddled in a group, undoubtedly speaking of things that affected the country. Christelle would have liked to have been included in such a conversation, given her role in Phillipa's protection, but she didn't want to ask and wouldn't insert herself. Her true purpose at Phillipa's side was information gathering for the French, so anything she could get from Leonidas and the knights would make its way back to her father.

Already, she was certain he'd received the missive she'd sent him when they passed through London. Soon, she'd send him another missive to let him know that she and Phillipa had arrived safely. Given that they were in a port town, there would be no shortage of men willing to take a message across the sea to France for the right price. She considered herself fortunate for that.

But something else was eating at her these days, too.

The very reason why she'd come.

That was something she hadn't counted on—liking the people she had been sent to spy on. She'd been with Phillipa for three years, and in spite of her role at the woman's side, she loved the queen like a little sister. Phillipa was kind and compassionate, without a nasty bone in her body, and Christelle loved the childlike innocence about her. An innocence that was threatened by the very world she ruled over, and most especially by the woman who was her protector. Christelle would protect Phillipa to the death, but on the other hand, she'd been feeding her father and the French information about Phillipa and Edward since she'd assumed the position. Phillipa knew that Christelle wrote to her father often and thought it was sweet that she was so fond of her father, but she'd never once questioned the contents of the missives, luckily for Christelle. But her feelings on the situation were creating a dilemma, now more than ever.

Deep down, she wasn't so sure she wanted to be part of something that might potentially hurt Phillipa.

"Christy?" Phillipa addressed her, snapping her out of her train of thought. "What would you say about going to the fish market tomorrow morning and selecting some fine fish for the evening meal? Mayhap even eels if we can find them. I do so love jellied eels."

Christelle looked at her, a smile on her lips. "You love anything," she said, teasing her. "Or, I should clarify, the child you carry loves anything. He is making great demands of you, your grace."

Phillipa laughed as Georgiana, bored with her meal and her chicken, climbed under the table and emerged on Phillipa's lap. The queen pulled the child onto her thighs and hugged her tightly.

"Children are a joy," she said, her head against Georgiana's. "Where is Catherine, by the way? She has not joined us."

Christelle sipped the last of her wine. "She said that her head was aching and she would take her meal in her chamber," she said. "I do like her. She's a fine young lady."

Phillipa nodded firmly. "She is," she said. Then she looked at Georgiana as the child yawned. "And I think another fine young lady must go to bed. It is getting late."

Georgiana whined. "Not yet," she said. "I'm not tired!"

One of the great joys Phillipa had experienced over the past few days was the privilege of putting Georgiana and Gabriel to bed. Catherine had afforded her the honor and Phillipa had taken to it eagerly. Now, with Catherine presumably down for the evening, Phillipa was delighted to be able to put the twins to bed herself.

"I think that you are *very* tired," Phillipa said, standing up with the little girl in her arms. "I think we should all go to bed. Don't you?"

Christelle stood up next to her, moving to grab Gabriel as the boy tried to put the end of a spoon up his nose. Phillipa was carrying Georgiana away, but the child was demanding her pet chicken, so Christelle was forced to snag the fowl. With the chicken in one hand and Gabriel in the other, she followed Phillipa from the great hall and into the keep beyond.

Truthfully, Christelle didn't have the same maternal instinct that Phillipa did, so she left the queen to put the children to bed, standing outside the door as Phillipa told them an old story about two children who were lost in the woods and saved by a woodsman before the wolf could eat them. Christelle leaned against the wall, listening to Phillipa's soft voice and the occasional voice of Georgiana or Gabriel. It seemed like they had endless questions, these children who had been so emotionally abused over the past year. They were coming to realize that they were safe and cherished again, in large part due to Phillipa and Leonidas. Christelle wished she were so adept with children, but she simply wasn't. She'd never had the opportunity.

And she probably never would.

Once the little ones were asleep, Phillipa decided to follow their example. Christelle made sure Phillipa got to bed, and once the fire was banked and the tapers blown out, she was contemplating seeking her own bed but found that she simply wasn't tired enough. Phillipa was safe and secure, but Christelle didn't want to spend the evening standing guard outside her door, so she made her way out of the keep and into the bailey. She could watch the entry door from almost any point in the ward, as there was only one way in and one way out.

With one eye on that door, she made her way up to the wall.

The sea was off to the east and she could see it from where she stood, the moonlight rippling on the water. She could smell the salt and the mildew, as grass sometimes smelled when it was constantly wet. Even so, it was a lovely evening, if a bit cold, and she breathed the air in deeply.

"I thought I saw you come up here," came a voice from the nearby stair tower. "Where is the queen?"

Christelle knew that voice and it was an effort not to feel joy at it. Leonidas emerged from the stairwell as she casually glanced in his direction.

But it was a struggle.

"Sleeping," she said, turning back to the sea view. "The woman is wearing herself out managing her chatelaine duties and the children. She is exhausted."

Leonidas came to stand next to her, leaning on the parapet and looking down the wall to check for danger. "I have told her not to exert herself," he said. "Edward will not be pleased if she works herself into illness."

"She will not do that," Christelle said. "She is more con-cerned for the child she carries than anything, but she *is* exhausting herself."

"She seems happy."

"She is loving it."

Leonidas looked at her. "And you disapprove?"

Christelle hesitated. "I suppose not," she said after a mo-ment. "She really is very happy when she is being useful. Has your daughter always had that stupid chicken?"

He looked at her, sharply. "*Stupid* chicken?"

She broke down into soft laughter. "Forgive me," she said.

"It's simply that where I come from, we do not consider chickens dinner guests. *Dinner*, aye. But not dinner guests."

He grinned, flashing those big teeth. "To tell you the truth, the chicken is new," he said. "She did not have it when I left here a year ago."

"She is sleeping with it now."

"So I have been told."

"I can remove it if you wish."

Leonidas shook his head. "Let her have the chicken if it pleases her," he said. "She's had so little joy in her life, at least over the past couple of years. A chicken is a small price to pay for her happiness."

"You are very understanding," Christelle said. "I am not entirely sure my own father would have let me take a chicken to bed."

Leonidas glanced at her. "Did you have to endure your mother's death and then an abusive nurse afterward?" he said. "Because that is what she has had to endure. If a chicken brings her comfort, so be it."

Christelle shrugged. "I did not endure anything so terrible at her age, but I did endure the death of my mother."

"How old were you?"

"I had seen eight years of age. She died giving birth to a brother, who did not survive."

Leonidas grunted as his gaze moved to the darkened landscape beyond. "I am sorry for you and your father," he said. "God gives and He takes sometimes. I do not understand why, but that is the nature of things. Women sometimes… die."

Christelle looked at him. "You mean your wife?"

He nodded faintly. "Aye."

"Would it be impertinent to ask what she was like?"

He shook his head but didn't seem too eager to answer, at least not right away. When he finally spoke, his voice was quiet. Almost intimate.

"She was short and red haired, and she was the most joyful person I'd ever met," he said. "To be in her presence was to feel light of heart."

Christelle smiled. "That's very sweet," she said. "In a world where few men think so highly of the women they've married, it's lovely that you remember her so warmly."

He shrugged. "I loved her," he said simply, glancing at her. "You find that surprising?"

"I find it delightful."

He nodded, as if pleased by her reply. "Catie has grown to look a good deal like her," he said. "In fact, when I saw her coming out of the gatehouse on the day we arrived, I thought I was seeing a ghost."

"Catie is a lovely young woman," Christelle said. "In fact, all three of the children are lovely. I do not know much about children, but I can only imagine that a good woman with kindness and understanding raised such children. You can tell that they are loved."

He was looking at her as she spoke, as something in his eyes suggested that his guard might be going down a little. As if he were willing to discuss what he considered a forbidden subject because it did his heart good to do so.

Perhaps that meant he was healing, just a bit.

"They *are* loved," he said. "And that is why I will not take Georgiana's pet chicken away. She needs something to love, and to love her in return. It brings her comfort in a world where she's had little over the past couple of years."

"That is understandable," Christelle said. "Does Georgiana

look like her mother, also?"

He snorted softly. "She acts like her more than she looks like her," he said. "She is vivacious and eccentric, which was everything Juliette was. She had her little quirks, too."

"Like pet chickens?"

"Worse," he said. "Pet ferrets. When we were first married, those things would slither into the bed around my feet, and more than once I found myself leaping out of bed because it felt as if serpents had invaded my linens."

Christelle started to laugh. "I cannot imagine anything chasing you out of bed."

"It's true," he said, chuckling. "Not to be indelicate, but they were already in the bed on our wedding night and she refused to remove them. How I didn't kick one of them in the head and kill it is still a mystery."

Christelle was enjoying his tale of ferret woe because as he told the story, he was slightly exaggerating the discomfort of it all.

The man had a sense of humor.

"It is a good thing you did not kill them," she said. "I am certain your new bride would not have taken that very well."

He shook his head in agreement. "Nay, she would not have," he said. "I got used to those damn things after a while. There was not much I could do to discourage them. I would wake up and one would be lying across my neck or on my head. Truthfully, they were warm, so I suppose they served a purpose."

"What happened to them?"

The warmth in his eyes faded. "About two months after Juliette passed away, they caught an illness of some kind," he said. "It killed them both. So, I washed them, wrapped them tightly in one of Juliette's silk scarves, and had the lid to her crypt removed so I could put them inside with her. I buried them with her and the child."

"What child?"

"Juliette died giving birth to our daughter."

Christelle's humor was completely gone. "Oh… Leo, I did not know," she said, sounding deeply remorseful. "You told me she had died, but I did not know it was in childbirth. My deepest apologies for asking about her. I did not mean to dredge up terrible memories. It was very insensitive of me."

He shook his head, putting an enormous hand on her arm because the man, as she had discovered, wasn't afraid to touch her. He was a man who touched others, too, because she'd seen him do it with his men—a hand on the shoulder, even an embrace. Leonidas was a man who valued touch as a form of expression or emotion, and as uncomfortable as she had been with it, she found she wasn't so much anymore.

She rather liked it.

"You did not know," he said, giving her arm a squeeze. "And you did not dredge up terrible memories. My memories of Juliette are all good ones. Until the end, anyway. To be truthful, I was not entirely sure how I would feel upon returning to Ashendon. If the memories would be too strong for me. But that was not the case. I am glad to be back and glad to be with the children again. Juliette is still here, if only in spirit. And I think she would have liked you."

That seemed to perk Christelle up. "Do you think so?"

"I do."

"She would approve Phillipa and me handling the household duties?"

He nodded firmly. "She would be very grateful," he said. "In fact, *I* am very grateful. Christelle, I realize that you and I have not always gotten on well, but I want you to know how grateful I am that you have taken on so much here. The children are happy; the castle is running smoothly. All things that I am deeply appreciative for, and I have you to thank for that."

They were looking at each other beneath the moonlight and Christelle could feel... something. There was something in his eyes that was pulling her to him, like a moth to flame, and she had no idea what to think of it. All she knew was that her heart was beating like a sledgehammer and her breathing was starting to quicken. Her palms were sweating. She'd been attracted to Leonidas for quite some time, and those were feelings that had only increased since they'd left Woodstock. Now, here they were, alone on the battlements, and she was experiencing something she'd never experienced before.

Could it be... romance?

Lust?

Madness?

Smack!

Christelle wasn't sure how her lips suddenly slanted over his, but they did. Her hands were on his face. The *smack* was her mouth as it suckled his, in perhaps the loudest way possible. But, God, it had been delicious. *He* was delicious.

But the glee was momentary.

Realizing what she'd done, Christelle fled the wall in panic, down the stairwell, running for her life across the darkened bailey. She couldn't even look back to see if he was wiping his mouth furiously, trying to rid himself of the taste of her. She could only imagine that was what he was doing.

She'd never been more mortified in her entire life.

But she also wasn't sorry.

Like a fool, she ran all the way back to the keep, throwing the bolt on the entry door and locking everyone inside for the night. Locking Leonidas out should he be following her so he could punish her. But her terror didn't end until she entered Phillipa's chamber, bolted that door, and then rushed into the smaller, attached chamber where her bed was.

Quivering, she undressed, donned her sleeping shift, and climbed onto her mattress, pulling the linens up around her neck.

What have I done?

CHAPTER EIGHT

S HE COULD ADMIT it.

She'd been avoiding him.

Not that it was difficult, especially during the morning hours when the knights were off accomplishing their duties. Every time Christelle thought about what she'd done, she grew red in the face. Trouble was, she knew everyone could tell because her skin was fair by nature, so any hint of color and she looked like a berry. A red, shiny, foolish berry.

God, she was so embarrassed.

Unable to sleep because of what she'd done, she finally gave up and unlocked the entry door just before sunrise. The servants needed access in order to bring food and hot water to Phillipa, so she unbolted the door and stepped out into the ward, inhaling deeply, smelling the dampness of the early morning air. Servants were already coming out of the kitchen yard, and she noticed them as they began to move for the keep. She also noticed Catherine, who was among them, and trying not to be seen.

Christelle's brow furrowed at the sight. She thought Catherine had been in her chamber all night, having given the excuse of an aching head, but clearly that wasn't the case. The young woman had been out of the keep and hadn't made it back in time before being locked out, which made Christelle think that perhaps she'd been busy with clandestine things. Perhaps even a lover. There was no other explanation that would keep a girl out all night. Given that Leonidas had been gone for a year, that was plenty of time for a young woman to gain a suitor and want to keep it from her stepfather.

Pondering that very possibility, Christelle headed back into the keep.

The morning went quickly. Phillipa was late to rise, and the children were already up, being tended to by Catherine, who was bright and cheery and pretending she'd been in the keep all night. By the time Christelle saw her, she had changed clothing and wore a lightweight frock because the weather, even at this time of the morning, was faintly warm. There was heat on the breeze, which wasn't entirely unusual for the time of year.

As Phillipa wearily assisted Catherine with the twins, who were clamoring about wanting to play in the river, Christelle supervised the servants and spoke to one of them briefly about the evening meal. Evidently, Phillipa had expressed her desire to go to the fish market to the cook, also, and already the woman was in town to catch the fishermen as they came in from the sea. The thought of fish pie with onions didn't sit well with Christelle for obvious reasons, but she didn't argue about it. She resigned herself to having bread and cheese for supper.

Once the twins were dressed and fed a meal of warm bread, stewed fruit, cheese, and some of what remained from the previous evening's meal, the cries to play down by the river increased to the point where Phillipa had to quiet them. The children were quite determined. In exasperation, she turned to

Christelle.

"Will you please ask Leo if we can have an escort down to the river?" she said. Then she turned toward a lancet window, feeling the breeze on her face. "It does seem to be warm today. I should think dipping our toes in the water would be quite lovely."

Christelle wasn't thrilled about having to seek out Leonidas, but she nodded. "If that is your wish, your grace," she said. "Are you certain you feel well enough?"

Phillipa brushed hair out of her face with the back of her hand. "Of course," she said, looking to the children. "Moreover, I do not believe they will be stopped. They want to dip their toes in the water, too."

The twins cheered loudly and began to jump up and down as Phillipa and Catherine shushed them. Meanwhile, Christelle was heading out of the chamber, mentally preparing herself for seeing Leonidas. Her stomach was in knots as she quit the keep, out into the day that was growing warm and mild.

The first knight she came across was Zander as he came from the stables. He was blond and bright, and far prettier than a man had a right to be, and Christelle had come to know him a little over the past few days. Just swift interactions, but he was quite amiable. She thought she might take the coward's way out and ask Zander about a visit to the river instead of Leonidas.

"Good morn, Sir Zander," she said, holding up her hand in greeting. "'Tis a fine day already."

Zander grinned, looking faintly like his cousin when he did so. "It is, my lady," he said, squinting into the bright sky overhead. "I think it will be a warm one. Growing up in a land where some men would consider our warm days cool, a day like this is sent from God. I should lie down on the ground, spread my arms out, and bask like a turtle on a log."

Christelle giggled. "I should like to see that."

"You do not believe me? I will prove it right now."

A twinkle came to her eye. "Would you prove it down by the river?"

He cocked his head curiously. "My lady?"

Christelle threw her thumb back in the direction of the keep. "There are two little rabbits in that keep that are jumping like mad, wanting to go down to the river and put their feet in the water," she said. "Would you be so kind as to ask Leonidas for permission and an escort? Just for a couple of hours, until they exhaust themselves and want to go back to the keep."

Zander nodded. "Certainly, I will ask," he said. "But he is in the great hall if you wish to ask him yourself."

Christelle shook her head. "I do not wish to bother him," she said. "I will go and help prepare the children if you will ask him for me. You may fetch us from the keep when the escort is ready."

"As you wish," Zander said.

Christelle turned and headed for the keep before he could ask her any further questions. She didn't want to explain why she didn't want to ask Leonidas personally and, in fact, was very glad that Zander was so willing to do as she asked. She'd managed to avoid Leonidas this time.

But it didn't last.

Georgiana and Gabriel were dressed in linen, something light for their adventure on the river's edge, while Catherine was clad in a simple linen gown. She'd loaned Phillipa a beautiful muslin shift and a lightweight robe that went over it, and Christelle was in another dress belonging to Catherine because they had come to Ashendon with very little, so they had depended on Catherine to provide them with some clothing, which she had done happily. Properly dressed, everyone was ready for the jaunt to the river's edge when there was a knock on the door. Thinking it was the escort, Christelle opened the panel.

Leonidas stood there.

Christelle's heart leapt into her throat, so much so that she started to cough. It was a startled reaction to his abrupt appearance, and she struggled to speak as he stood there, his gaze never leaving her face.

"Your escort to the river is waiting, my lady," he said rather formally. "Are you ready?"

Christelle nodded, still coughing, and turned to gesture to Catherine and Phillipa, who got the children on their feet. But the pair didn't need much prompting, and Leonidas was bum-rushed by eager children. He had to grab them both before they could throw themselves down the stairs in their glee.

"Slowly, please," he told them, handing them back to Catherine and Phillipa. "You will walk slowly and with restraint. Only wild animals run as you did. Are you wild animals?"

Georgiana and Gabriel shook their heads vehemently. "Nay!" they shouted in unison.

Leonidas rested his fists on his hips. "Then you must not behave like one," he said. "If you do that again, I will put a collar on your neck and walk you on a lead. I will even feed you raw fish and animal guts, like a wild animal would eat."

He was trying not to smile as he said it, and the children burst out laughing, declaring that he was not serious. But Leonidas nodded as if quite serious, even though he was no longer able to keep the smile off his face.

Out of the castle they went.

While Leonidas and Zander led the pack, Christelle, Talan, and a dozen soldiers brought up the rear. Dayne, unhappily, had been left in charge of the castle, but it could not be helped. Georgiana and Gabriel were so excited that they could hardly contain it, and seeing this, Zander got the children worked up and began to run, encouraging them to run with him. Catherine and Phillipa finally gave up trying to keep them calm and let them go, watching them bolt after the knight who was leading them on a merry chase. Zander ran up and he ran down, and the children ran after him, squealing. By the time they reached the river's edge, Zander fell down on the bank, exhausted, and the twins gleefully jumped on him. But that horseplay was short lived with the reality of the river right in front of them.

Water began to splash.

Catherine and Leonidas stood right on the riverbank with them, carefully watching the pair. The bank was slippery, and although the River Hull was a wide and seemingly slow-moving river, it had an undercurrent that was swift. Leonidas wouldn't let the twins get any deeper than their knees, and when Georgiana indeed tried to go deeper, he pulled her onto the bank and made her sit down and wait a few minutes before going back in again as punishment.

Unhappy, Georgiana sat there and wept.

But the tears were temporary. Georgiana went back in again, this time with Zander at her side. Catherine was at Gabriel's side as he splashed the water, mostly on her, until she scolded him. But still, he splashed and kicked until she was forced to move away. Delighted she wasn't hovering over him any longer, Gabriel began to roll around in the mud.

As the antics were going on, Christelle stood downriver, alternately watching the water and the frolicking children. She was far enough away from Leonidas that she didn't have to look at him or talk to him, but her stomach was in knots. She still didn't know why she had kissed him, but this morning, she had the added trouble of wondering why she didn't kiss him harder. Or longer. One moment she was attracted to him, and in the next, it was something that had grown deeper. Deep enough to want to kiss him. That big, handsome knight with the scar on his forehead that she had put there had managed to get under her skin, and it had happened so quickly that she was struggling to come to terms with it.

But one thing was for certain.

She had no idea what to tell him when he asked her why.

Why did you kiss me?

As Christelle was looking out over the river and trying to come up with an answer, she made the mistake of losing track of Leonidas. He'd been standing by the children, but suddenly, he was standing beside her. Christelle saw his shadow and her heart began hammering again as she looked up to see that he was fairly close to her. Their gazes locked and, sensing the unspoken question in his eyes, the very question she'd been wrestling with, she blurted the first thing that came to mind.

"I do not know why I did it so do not ask me," she said quickly. "I am ashamed of myself, so nothing you can say can possibly make me feel worse. I would be grateful if you would forget my complete and utter failing so we can simply move past it."

Christelle lowered her head, unable to look at him. If she had been, she would have seen the mirth and, quite possibly, warmth in his eyes. As Georgiana and Gabriel screamed in the background because Zander was splashing them, Leonidas folded his arms across his chest and took another step in

Christelle's direction.

"That is difficult to hear," he said, his voice low. "Clearly, it was a terrible kiss. You did something on impulse and it was the worst thing you had ever done. I understand."

She looked at him then. "What do you mean by that?" she said. "And I did not say it was a terrible kiss."

"You said you were ashamed."

"Of *me*."

He shrugged. "You are simply being kind," he said. "You do not have the heart to tell me that I did not meet your expectations."

She sighed, exasperated. "I did *not* have expectations," she said, waving her hands around for emphasis. "I put my hands on your face and I kissed you and I do not know why. I have never done anything like that before."

"Oh? Why not?"

"Because I've never met anyone I wanted to kiss, I suppose."

Christelle realized he'd cornered her into a confession too late. Her eyes widened when she became aware of what she'd said, and she clapped a hand on her forehead, turning away from him in horror. By now, Leonidas was fighting off a grin because he could see how mortified she was. The truth was that he'd wondered how she felt about her impulsive act.

He'd been wondering most of the night.

He hadn't been at all certain what to say to her when he saw her today. In fact, he'd been in the great hall trying to figure it out when Zander entered with requests for a visit to the river. He mentioned that it had come from Christelle, and even though Leonidas hadn't wanted to frolic by the river's edge today, the fact that the request had come from her had him willing to agree to it. Mostly because it gave him an excuse to see her again.

Odd how he wasn't upset about it in the least.

It was true that he was attracted to her. More as the days went by. It was also true that he was still grieving the loss of Juliette. At least, he thought he was. He thought his return to Ashendon would only exacerbate the grief he was trying to put aside, but the truth was that returning home had given him comfort. He'd been able to face what he left behind—three children and the life he'd once known. What he realized was that his life hadn't changed much. The children still loved him, but more than that, they needed him. Juliette's ghost was here, but he could live with it. He knew she would want him to be happy and perhaps even love again.

The kiss last night… It had given him hope.

Hope that life, for him, would go on.

"Thank you," he said after a moment.

Christelle was wallowing in embarrassment, so much so that she couldn't even look at him. "For what?" she asked.

"For being so brave," he said. "For doing something first that I should have done but did not have the courage to. When one gazes into the sun, the fear of blindness is real."

That statement forced her to pause. Then her head came up and she looked at him. "What does that mean?" she asked.

He smiled. "It means you are a remarkable woman, Lady Christelle," he said. "I am awed every time I look at you because you are, indeed, brighter than the sun. Mayhap I am even a little intimidated by you. Now, if you are truly ashamed of your bold kiss and wish me to forget it, I will. But if you do not want me to forget it, and I hope that you do not, I shan't. I shall treasure it."

She looked at him in wonder. Realizing that her kiss had

not offended him changed the entire mood between them. Instead of shame, Christelle was starting to feel the least bit giddy.

"Truly?" she said.

"Truly," he said. "If you wanted to do it again, I would not put up a fight."

Christelle couldn't help the smile that spread across her lips. A silly, flattered smile. The man was being just the least bit flirtatious with her, but she'd had so little practice with the games that men and women played that she was at a loss for words. Opening her mouth to say something, anything, that might sound witty or pleasing or just plain coherent, she was cut off by a horrifying scream.

"She fell in! She fell in!"

Catherine was screaming from the bank about fifteen feet away as Zander and Talan both jumped in, grabbing for something that was just out of their reach. Gabriel was on the river's edge with Phillipa, but Georgiana was nowhere to be seen. Frantically, Christelle and Leonidas went to the river's edge, as it was flowing in their direction, only to see a scrap of fabric and a foot on top of the water.

Christelle immediately dived in.

The water was freezing and murky, but she swam in the direction of the foot. Unfortunately, the icy water caused her ears to nearly explode with pain and her head came up as she gasped in agony. A few feet away, Georgiana's head came up and the child cried out, struggling for air, but she just as quickly went under again and Christelle began to swim frantically in her direction.

Unfortunately, the undercurrent was strong, and even though Christelle was a good swimmer thanks to a grandfather who had lived by a lake, she couldn't seem to get to Georgiana. The child hadn't come up again and Christelle continued swimming down the river, along with the current, as Leonidas and Talan, and the majority of the soldiers, ran along the banks, trying to catch a glimpse of the little girl. Zander had jumped in and was working the other side of the river, opposite Christelle. At one point, there was a sandbank in the middle of the river and Christelle ended up swimming around it, grabbing for Georgiana in the muddy, cold water.

Time passed.

Too much time, Christelle thought, but she refused to acknowledge it. She couldn't. But deep down, she knew that with every second that passed, Georgiana's chances of coming out of this alive were growing slimmer. Georgiana was somewhere in this freezing water and Christelle was determined to find her. Further downriver, soldiers were jumping in, trying to form a human net that would prevent Georgiana from going any further, and Christelle began to dive again, feeling for anything she could under the water, but the river merged into a bunch of underwater grass and she found herself tangled up in it. She could get her head above water, but her forward progression was nearly stopped. In a last-ditch effort, she tried to dive again, grabbing around for anything that didn't feel like grass, when her fingertips touched something rough.

It was fabric.

Grabbing hold, she yanked as hard as she could.

"I have her!" she cried as her head came out of the water. "Help me! I have her!"

Using the sandbank that was about twenty feet behind her, Leonidas and the others crossed the river to the opposite bank, where Christelle was just lifting Georgiana's limp body out of the water. Zander came frantically swimming in her direction, helping her lift the little girl. The child's face was ghostly pale, her lips blue, and Christelle was so cold and so exhausted that she could barely bring her to the bank. Suddenly, Leonidas was in the water along with Talan, and he grabbed the little girl as Talan grabbed hold of Christelle. As Leonidas rushed the child onto the grass and put her down, beating her on the back and trying to pound the water out of her lungs, Talan managed to drag Christelle onto the bank. Once she was lying on the grass, he helped Zander out as well.

"Lady Christelle?" Talan said as he returned to her. "Are you well?"

Christelle was coughing up river water, but she waved him off. "Aye," she said. "Help Leo. Help him with Georgiana!"

Talan reluctantly left her as she lay there, coughing and trembling. After a few moments of deep breaths, Christelle managed to push herself into a sitting position only to see Leonidas and Talan as they tried to save Georgiana's life. The soldiers were huddled around them, watching, and Christelle staggered to her feet, wandering over to the men as they worked hard on the little girl. At one point, Leonidas even picked her up by her ankles and hung her upside down in an attempt to drain the water from her lungs.

"Is she breathing?" Christelle asked anxiously.

Leonidas laid the child back on the ground. "Nay," he said grimly. He patted her back a few more times and then laid his head against her chest, listening for a heartbeat. Several seconds passed before he lifted his head and stared at the little girl. "Oh, God. This cannot be. This cannot… *be*."

Christelle's eyes welled with tears. Pushing through the soldiers, she fell to her knees beside Georgiana and began to shake her.

"Georgiana!" she wept. "Wake up! You must breathe and wake up!"

Talan, who was standing at the child's head, tried to put himself between the little girl and Christelle. "Stop," he muttered softly but firmly. "She cannot wake up, my lady. She is gone."

"Nay!" Christelle roared. "You did not try hard enough! She is not gone!"

She did the same thing that Leonidas had done, flipping the child onto her belly and pounding the water out of her. She pushed on the child's torso, throwing her weight into it, trying to push the water out of her lungs. She'd seen Leonidas do the same thing, but he hadn't done it hard enough. Or long enough, in her opinion. Christelle even rolled the child onto her back again and blew into her mouth, trying to blow air into her lungs.

But it did nothing.

Georgiana remained still.

Christelle still had her hands on the child but then she realized that Talan had been right. The little girl really *was* gone. Horrified, she looked at Leonidas, who had an expression of horror in his eyes that she would never forget. He'd given up. With that awareness, sobs burst forth as Christelle pulled the little girl against her, holding her tightly.

"I tried," she sobbed. "I tried so hard, but I could not find you. Please forgive me, Georgiana. Please… forgive me."

Every man standing there, Leonidas included, watched Christelle weep her heart out. It was a gut-wrenching scene, made worse when Catherine managed to get to the opposite bank. Seeing her limp little sister in Christelle's arms had her in hysterics, so much so that she fell down, twice, before she even reached her sister. She practically yanked Georgiana from Christelle's arms and wept over her little sister with such pain that even the hardest man was swallowing back tears.

The entire scene was a nightmare.

Christelle was on her arse, weeping heavily as she watched Catherine's grief. The young woman was beyond shattered as she called to Georgiana repeatedly, begging her to awaken. Leonidas, struggling to keep his composure, turned to Talan and Zander, standing behind him.

"Zander," he said hoarsely, "go back and escort Phillipa and Gabriel to the castle. Make sure they are secure."

Zander nodded, wiping the tears from his face. "What do I tell the queen?" he asked. "She will want to know what happened."

Leonidas sighed heavily. "Tell her the truth," he said. "But be gentle. I will seek her when I return."

Zander acknowledged the command, wiping his face one last time before heading upriver, where Phillipa and Gabriel were still waiting with a half-dozen soldiers guarding them. Leonidas watched him go before returning his attention to the sobbing women and the dead little girl.

"We must return to the castle," he said to Talan. "Christelle will catch her death if we do not get her into warm clothing, and we must… take Georgiana back. Send one of the men for blankets immediately, anything to keep Christelle from freezing and something to cover Georgiana with. I do not want her to be a spectacle for curious men when we bring her back."

Talan nodded, leaving Leonidas long enough to send a soldier running for the castle. But he quickly returned, his gaze hardly leaving Catherine as she wept over her sister.

"Now what?" he asked. "Shall we force the women back?"

Leonidas watched as Christelle, no longer sobbing uncontrollably, crept over to Catherine and put her arms around her and Georgiana. She held the young woman, trying to give her what comfort she could. Leonidas knew that it should be him giving her comfort, but the truth was that he was in shock. Absolutely in shock. A bright, warm day had turned deadly, and he simply couldn't believe it. Not only had he lost Juliette and their daughter, but now he'd lost yet another daughter.

Little Georgiana.

It was all he could do not to get sick.

But the knight in him, the man who had been trained to function logically when everything around him was chaos, had to take control. Not the stunned stepfather. He had to dig deep to find that emotionless commander because, at the moment, he was anything but emotionless.

There would be time enough later for him to grieve.

"I WILL TAKE Catherine and Georgiana," he finally said. "You take Christelle. I am certain they do not wish to move, but I am equally certain that we cannot leave them here, in the open, for all to see. Let us return to Ashendon and do what needs to be done."

Talan nodded, following Leonidas over to the huddle of women. Carefully, Leonidas bent over Christelle, putting his big hands on her shoulders.

"My lady," he said softly, steadily, "we must return to the castle. May I help you stand?"

Christelle lifted her head from Catherine's shoulder, looking up at him with pain in her eyes. "For pity's sake, give her a few moments," she said hoarsely. "Let her grieve."

Leonidas squatted down next to her. "Georgiana is wet and cold," he said. "Does she not deserve the dignity of dry clothing and a little peace? And does Catherine not deserve the opportunity to grieve in private? Please, Christy. Help me get Catherine back to the castle."

Christy. He'd never called her that before. That made her take a second look at him, and she could see his reasoning. After a few moments of deliberation, she nodded reluctantly and returned her attention to Catherine, giving the young woman a squeeze.

"Georgiana needs dry clothing," she muttered. "And we must take her somewhere so that men are not gawking at her. We must protect her, Catherine. Let us return to the castle."

Catherine was still weeping, her face buried in the top of Georgiana's head. She lifted her face, looking at Christelle with complete devastation in her expression.

"She was standing next to me," she wept. "I was holding on to her dress. *I* was holding her. But she slipped away."

Christelle nodded sympathetically. "I know," she said. "She wanted to play in the river. She loved the water. What happened was an accident, Catie. Just an accident. No one is to blame."

Those gently uttered words only caused Catherine to cry harder into Georgiana's hair. Christelle put her hand on the little girl's face in a comforting gesture.

"She is cold, Catie," she said. "We must take her to the keep and dry her off. Then you may hold her as long as you wish. Please?"

Catherine was still weeping, still struggling, but at least she wasn't openly fighting her. After a few more moments, tense moments because Christelle wasn't sure the girl was actually going to take her advice, Catherine finally turned to Christelle.

"Will you please help me?" she whispered.

Christelle nodded and immediately reached out to take the little girl. Catherine relinquished her without a struggle, and Christelle quickly turned the child over to Leonidas, who held the little girl tightly against his chest as he stood up. Christel helped Catherine to her feet and they began to walk with Leonidas, slowly heading upriver to the sandbank so they could cross to the other side. The entire time, Leonidas kept Georgiana clutched against him, her face pressed into his chest and a big hand over her head, protecting her from prying eyes and the elements. Protecting her in death as he'd tried to protect her in life. He still half expected her to suddenly cough and start crying, but she never did.

She remained still.

It was a sad procession that headed back to the castle.

They were just nearing the gatehouse when a couple of soldiers emerged bearing the blankets that Leonidas had requested. Talan took one and immediately tossed it over the little girl. The second blanket went around Christelle, who was still wet and cold, but she shared it with Catherine because it seemed to her that the young woman needed some kind of protection and comfort at the moment.

The blanket shielded them both.

By the time they hit the bailey, it was clear that everyone knew what had happened. The soldier that ran back for the blankets had told the men at the gatehouse, and the rumors had spread like wildfire. All of the activity at the castle seemed to come to a halt as Leonidas led the party with a dead child in his arms, covered in a dusty blanket. But Leonidas didn't acknowledge anyone. He continued to the keep, where he would leave Georgiana with her sister and the queen and

Christelle. The three women would ensure that the little girl was properly taken care of.

That was the best Leonidas could hope for.

God help him, it had been an extremely costly day.

CHAPTER NINE

Carlisle Castle

S HE RECEIVED THE note last night.

Now, she was on a mission.

It wasn't usual for Elizabetha de Lara, Countess of Carlisle, to be on a mission of any kind. As the wife to the man who should have been king, Toby, as she was known, was content to raise her children, run her house and hold, and also manage the entire city of Carlisle as the local magistrate. The truth was that Tate technically oversaw the city government, but Toby stood in for him and he considered her a better justice, anyway. She had a no-nonsense but fair way about her that was much appreciated by all.

And that's why she was going to handle this situation.

No-nonsense and to the point.

In reality, the message that had come last night had been addressed to her husband. Tate and Toby had such a symbiotic relationship that whenever a missive arrived for Tate, Toby simply opened it, and if she could deal with the situation, she would. There weren't any secrets between them and they both preferred it that way, so the missive that had come for him last night was something Toby was going to handle on behalf of her husband.

Truthfully, he didn't even know about it.

How she managed to keep it from him with a castle full of soldiers who had big mouths and an extreme loyalty to the Earl of Carlisle, she didn't know. The man was wrapped up in the politics of the country and Toby was happy to take whatever load she could off him, but in this case, she was more than determined to take care of this situation because she didn't want her husband alone with the person who had sent the missive.

In fact, Toby wasn't so sure that the missive to Tate hadn't been a ruse of some kind.

Not a ruse that would put him in danger, but more a ruse aimed at seduction. Toby knew the sender of the missive all too well, as she had years of experience with the woman. The message sender had always possessed a soft spot for Tate, and Toby wasn't going to give her a chance to get the man alone.

Not even in a game of political high stakes.

Therefore, she traveled alone into the town of Carlisle, having slipped from the postern gate, and lost herself in the many avenues and alleys that constituted the city of Carlisle. She'd left her trusted maid at the small, fortified gate, waiting for her. If she returned within the hour, all well and good. But if she didn't, the maid was instructed to tell Tate, who had been shut up with Stephen and a couple of other men in his solar all day long. Things were changing quickly at Wigmore Castle, where Roger Mortimer was located, and Tate was trying to stay ahead of the man. But the very woman Mortimer was using to cling to power was here, in Carlisle.

In a tavern called, ironically enough, The King's Head.

Toby had been there before with her husband, many times, so she knew how to slip in unnoticed. She went in through the kitchens and spoke briefly to the tavernkeep, who knew her. He directed her to a chamber accessed under the stairs, a small entrance that led to a larger chamber that faced the street. Thanking him, Toby made her way to the chamber.

Carefully, she opened the door, her gaze moving swiftly over the chamber. It was dark and cold inside but for a small bank of lit tapers against the wall. A weak fire burned in the hearth, hardly enough to give any heat. A lone woman sat at a table meant for several people and looked small sitting there, small and vulnerable, but there was nothing vulnerable about this woman. When the chamber door opened, she turned to it swiftly, but when she saw who it was, she pulled the hood from her head.

Isabella of France made herself known.

"I should have known it would be you," she said in a heavy French accent. "Somehow, I knew you would not let your husband come alone."

Toby removed her hood, revealing a carefully coiffed crown of dark blonde hair and piercing green eyes. She didn't come away from the door.

"And you were correct," she said evenly. "We know each other well, your grace."

"We do," Isabella said. "You are looking well, Toby."

"As are you," Toby said. "You are ageless. I am envious."

That wasn't exactly true, but Isabella was susceptible to flattery. Her smile grew. "You are kind," she said. "I feel as if I've lived a hundred years and a hundred different lives at times. I feel… tired."

Toby finally decided to come away from the door, removing her cloak, and sat down at the table. Not across from Isabella, but next to her. Though they'd never been friends—far from it—there was respect there. Toby respected her even if she didn't trust her.

But this was a highly unusual circumstance.

Out of the blue, the former queen had appeared.

"I can understand that," Toby said after a moment. "You have endured much."

Isabella nodded. "Not as much as some, but more than others," she said. Then her hazel eyes fixed on Toby. "How is my son?"

Toby knew she was prying. This was what she wanted to do to Tate, only she could use her feminine wiles on him. Or at least try to.

Toby would be more difficult.

"Well, so I am told," Toby said. "And how are you? I hear there is a child coming."

She went right to the point, essentially firing a warning shot across Isabella's bow. Whatever information Isabella was going to try to get out of her, Toby would not be willing to divulge, but Toby wanted it made clear that she knew a few things about Isabella, also. If they were going to dance, then it was time to get started. Isabella seemed initially surprised at the statement, but a cool smile flickered on her lips.

"I do not know where you heard such a thing," she said steadily. "Other than those I already have, there are no more children to speak of."

Toby nodded faintly, but her gaze was appraising, as if she didn't quite believe the woman. "I hope your other children are well, then," she said.

"They are, thank you."

"Good," Toby said. "Now that we have the pleasantries out of the way, you will tell me why you sent my husband a summons."

Isabella waggled her eyebrows, softly clearing her throat as she averted her gaze. "Am I to understand he is too occupied to see me?"

"He is."

"Then, mayhap, I should wait until he is less occupied."

Toby wasn't going to tolerate foolery. "That time will never come where it pertains to you," she said. "He spends all of his time trying to keep this country from falling into your lover's hands, so *you* are the reason he is so occupied. Now, tell me what you want or I will leave and your journey to Carlisle will be at an end."

Isabella's smile faded as the conversation took a decidedly unfriendly turn. As Toby had once fired a warning shot, she was about to do the same.

"I know my son is at Carlisle," she said, watching Toby's face for any hint that such a thing was true. "I wish to speak with him."

Toby was very good at keeping a neutral expression. "What makes you think he is at Carlisle?" she said. "Woodstock is his home."

"Aye, it is," Isabella said. "Do you truly think I do not have spies at Woodstock? Of course I do. They tell me that Tate took Edward north, and if Tate is in residence at Carlisle Castle, then I am certain Edward is with him. He would not have left my son off somewhere."

A glimmer came to Toby's eyes. "That is a logical assumption."

"I am also told his wife is with child."

There was no possibility that Toby was going to give anything away with her expression, which she maintained quite well. "That is not what you've come to discuss," she said, avoiding the statement. "I want to know why you are here. What do you want of my husband?"

Isabella sat back in her chair, pondering the question, knowing she would get nothing out of Toby where it pertained to a future grandchild or her son. Tate wouldn't have told her either, but she would have enjoyed the chase with him. She'd always had a soft spot for him and Toby knew it, which was why she was here.

Smart woman.

"You and I have been through a few difficult situations, have we not?" she said after a moment.

Toby nodded. "A few."

"I hope that I was always courteous to you."

"You were."

"I also hope you understand that it is not in my nature to lie."

"What have you lied about?"

Isabella shook her head. "Nothing," she said. "I refer to what I am about to say. I would not lie to you, Lady Carlisle. I have no reason to."

Toby eyed her for a moment. "Very well," she said. "I am listening."

Isabella paused, which made Toby both curious and suspicious. When Isabella did continue, her voice was barely above a whisper.

"I believe that Roger and I are at an end," she said.

Toby's brow rippled in confusion. "End?" she repeated.

"Why does that mean?"

"Precisely what I have said," Isabella said. "*Fin de notre chemin*. The end of our path."

"*What* path?"

Isabella sighed sharply. "All he speaks of is of his rule," she said. "All he craves is power. It is not easy for me to say this, Toby. It was different when Roger's enemy was the husband I hated. But now… now, he speaks of my offspring. He knows of Edward and Phillipa's child and he speaks of controlling the child, being a regent to his rule."

Toby was careful in her reply. "The throne is Edward's, not any future child's," she said. "Not yet, anyway."

Isabella's gaze flicked up to her. "If Edward was not here, the throne would belong to the child."

Now, Toby was getting a sense of what she meant. "You mean that Mortimer means to do away with Edward as he did with his father?"

"Aye," Isabella said, clearly distressed. "I was hoping it would not come to this, but I fear that it has. He cannot control my son because he has good men to advise him, your husband included. That is a lost cause. But the child Phillipa carries… He intends to get his hands on Phillipa so that when the child is born, it will be forever under Roger's control."

Toby digested what she was being told for a moment. "Did you come here to warn Tate about a plot against Edward?" she said. "Is that why you are here?"

"I have come to tell you where Roger will be in the autumn so that your husband, and my son, can rid themselves of him once and for all."

Toby frowned. "You would orchestrate an ambush?" she said. "An assassination?"

Isabella sighed again. She sat back in her chair, her gaze moving to the hearth that was barely glowing with warmth. Toby watched the woman closely, noting that she seemed to have aged a decade in just the past few moments. The stress of living with Mortimer and the stress of English politics had taken their toll on the once-beautiful woman.

It was happening right before Toby's eyes.

"It was different when Roger's focus was on my husband," Isabella said quietly. "Edward and I… There should have never been a marriage. He did not want to marry. His father forced it on him and on me. Edward could have made the best of it, but instead, he chose to humiliate me and degrade me with his actions. That is why I was glad for Roger. In a sense, he helped me regain some dignity. He saved me from a man who only wanted to shame and torture me. When he captured Edward and ordered his death, I was glad. I was relieved. But now, he is focusing on my son and I cannot stand by and do nothing. You are a mother, Toby. You understand what it means to protect your children. You will do it to the death. Even from a man you trusted and loved, once."

Toby was genuinely astounded by what she was hearing. Isabella of France was many things, but as she'd stated, she was not a liar. That was never her reputation, nor had it ever been Toby's experience with her, so she took her words at face value.

Very serious words, indeed.

Pondering what she'd been told, she sat back in her chair and thought about what she should do at this point. This was beyond what she had expected and, if absolutely genuine on the part of Isabella, beyond what she had a right to mediate.

She needed her husband.

But first, she needed assurance.

"If what you are saying is true, then it changes everything," she said. "But I want you to look me in the eye and swear before God, upon the lives of your children, that this is true. That it is not some sort of tactic to gain my trust or Tate's trust."

Isabella fixed her in the eye. "It is not a tactic, I swear."

"Prove it," Toby pushed. "Tell me who your spy is at Woodstock."

"The privy chamber servant who tends Phillipa," she said without hesitation. "An older woman named Alba. She used to be my servant, but when Phillipa became queen, I sent her to serve the new queen. She tells me everything."

Frankly, Toby was shocked the woman had told her who it was. She didn't know the servant, but Edward probably would. And he would remove her. Isabella knew that, so for her to confess who her spy was told Toby that Isabella was serious, indeed. Of course, the woman could be lying, and there could be more than one spy, but that went back to the beginning of the conversation when Toby knew that Isabella wasn't known by reputation as a liar.

The seriousness of the situation, for Toby, became more critical.

But so did her confusion.

"And you expect me to simply believe you?" she said incredulously. "Isabella, we have been at war with one another for years. Men have died because of your loyalty to Mortimer, and now you simply expect us to believe that you want him dead? That you're tired of him, like an old coat? Did you truly think it would be so easy?"

Isabella lifted her shoulders, weakly. "I have come all the way to Carlisle with only two men as my escort," she said. Then she lifted her hand. "Look around, Toby. Do you see Mortimer's army? Do you see anything to suggest I am traveling like the queen that I am? Nay, I am not. In order to come here, I had to convince Roger to allow me to travel to Leeds, where a former lady-in-waiting is in the midst of a health crisis. The lady is a longtime friend and although she is dying from a cancer, she is willing to be my alibi for my journey to Carlisle. In fact, the men I traveled with are her men so that my own escort cannot tell Roger that I traveled to Carlisle. It has taken me four long days to get here. Is that not proof enough that I am serious?"

In truth, it was. Toby didn't disbelieve her for a moment. No wonder the woman looked so exhausted. Clearly, she had gone to great lengths to get to Carlisle, and in that moment, Toby decided that Tate needed to hear everything.

This was a burden she couldn't bear alone.

She stood up.

"I will order a meal for you," she said. "You will eat it and rest and I will return."

Isabella looked at her, concerned. "Where are you going?"

Toby was already turning for the door, but she paused to answer the question. "To bring back the man you originally sent the missive to," she said. "But know this—he will be accompanied by knights, who will enter this room before him. If, by any chance, all of this is a ruse to assassinate my husband, know that he will not be alone. If you have assassins hiding in these walls, they will be killed by my husband's men. And then I will kill you personally. Do you understand?"

Isabella's gaze lingered on her for a moment. "Still the lioness, Toby."

"Always," Toby whispered.

Isabella had no doubt whatsoever.

CHAPTER TEN

Ashendon Castle

"THIS IS A terrible situation for all of us, Leo," Phillipa said softly. "But I agree with you. We must bury Georgiana sooner rather than later. I freely admit that I shall miss her."

Standing in the entry of the keep, cool and dark and quiet, Leonidas and Phillipa faced one another. Phillipa had just come in from a walk outside with Gabriel, who wasn't faring well these days. He missed his sister deeply. The child had run back outside, leaving Leonidas and Phillipa in a sad little group.

But, then again, everything at Ashendon was sad these days.

"I will miss her also," Leonidas said, his heart heavy. "But I wanted to thank you for taking charge of her, for ensuring she was washed and prepared. You should not have to be this brave, your grace, but I am grateful. I am not sure how much help Catie has been to you."

Even as he said those last few words, they both knew the answer. Catherine had been a mess since the moment she realized her sister had drowned, nearly useless in every way. Being young and emotional, and having just suffered the loss of her mother two years earlier, she was overwrought with anguish.

"She is devastated," Phillipa said gently. "She feels personally responsible. She was holding Georgiana's skirt when the child slipped in."

Leonidas shook his head. "She is not responsible," he said. "No one is. It was simply an accident."

Phillipa couldn't disagree. "I know," she said. "But it is not only Catherine who feels that way. Christelle does, too. She tried so hard to save her."

Leonidas nodded with sorrow. "She did, indeed," he said. "I thought she was going to drown, too. But there was nothing more she could do."

Phillipa was genuinely concerned. "For someone who strives for perfection as Christelle does, I do not think she knows how to accept defeat," she said. "She has the mindset of a knight, you know. She is taking this very hard."

"I am aware."

"What can we do to help her?"

Leonidas wasn't sure. It had been two days since the death of Georgiana, and everyone was taking it hard. Even the soldiers seemed to be saddened by the little girl who had been great entertainment at the evening meals with her pet chicken. In fact, Gabriel had taken over carrying the chicken around, talking to it as if he were speaking to his sister. On the night of Georgiana's death, he'd spent hours sitting next to her as she lay upon her bed, telling her how angry he was that she wouldn't awaken for him.

That day, and night, had been something of out of a bad dream. Leonidas had delivered Georgiana to Phillipa, who had stoically taken the child and proceeded to remove her wet clothing, wash her, and then put on a clean frock. Phillipa had even washed and braided Georgiana's hair, and between her and Christelle, they managed to properly prepare the little girl as Catherine stood by and sobbed. She'd tried to help, but she was so distraught that Phillipa had simply encouraged her to sit down and rest while she and Christelle did all of the work.

Two days later, Catherine was still distraught.

So was Leonidas, but he was better at controlling himself. Once the shock had worn off, he'd made the decision to bury the little girl with her mother. He didn't see any reason to have a coffin built for such a little child and he knew that Juliette would have preferred to have her daughter buried with her. When he told Catherine of his decision, she seemed to agree with it, although he really couldn't tell with all of the crying going on. As the days went on, she didn't seem to be able to control her emotions any better and had spent both nights sleeping next to her sister's corpse. That concerned Leonidas, but Phillipa begged him to be patient. Everyone grieved differently, she had said.

Catherine was simply grieving in her own way.

Therefore, he had gone about his duties, and that included speaking with the priests at Hull Minster, the enormous cathedral down by the waterfront where Juliette was buried. Generations of de Cottinghams were buried there, in fact, so Georgiana would be in good company. Leonidas had made arrangements to bury the child after mass on market day, which was two days away. He hoped that Catherine would be better able to reconcile her grief in that time.

Or, at the very least, stop weeping hysterically every day.

"To be honest, I am not certain what we can do to help Catherine," he said belatedly to Phillipa's question. "This situation is as shocking for me as it is for her, and as terrible for me as it is for her. I lost my wife and daughter in childbirth. Now, one of Juliette's remaining daughters is gone. I feel like a failure for not having protected these women—*my* women—so I am still struggling with this, too."

Phillipa was immediately sympathetic. "I know," she said. "I am very sorry. I did not mean to sound unfeeling. You have endured something terrible, Leo. Please tell me if there is something more I can do to help."

He smiled weakly. "You have done more than enough, your grace," he said. "If such a thing had to happen, then I am glad you are here to help. You have helped me shoulder a great burden."

Phillipa smiled in return, but quickly, her eyes filled with tears and she lowered her head. "Forgive me," she said. "I was fond of Georgiana and I have moments when I cannot help the sadness. I do not mean to trouble you with it."

Reaching out, he took her small hand and squeezed it. "To know that she made a mark upon you means that she will never be forgotten," he said quietly. "Mayhap you will tell your children of the little girl you once knew who slept with her pet chicken."

Phillipa broke down into soft laughter, wiping the tears from her eyes. "I will not tell them about the chicken for fear they will want one, too," she said, putting her hand on her gently swollen belly. "But the short time I have spent with Georgiana and Gabriel helps me understand what it means to raise children. They have helped me a great deal."

"Good," Leonidas said, a glimmer in his eye. "Now you can focus your attention on Gabriel. He's been carrying around the chicken, just like his sister did."

Phillipa shrugged. "He feels closer to her when he does," she said. "It helps him deal with the loss."

Leonidas nodded as he looked up to the keep. "I should spend more time with him," he said. "Catherine needs time to recover. The least I can do is shoulder the responsibility for Gabriel. And… and he is my son. My wife's son, but mine nonetheless. He has lost his mother and father and sister all in a short amount of time. I am sure he is feeling rather lost."

"I think it would be good for him to spend time with you," Phillipa said. Then she cocked her head as she gazed at him. "You are a good man, Leo. Most men would not show concern for another man's son."

"He was entrusted to me by marriage. I would not neglect him."

Phillipa smiled at him. "As I said," she murmured, "you are a good man."

He lowered his head humbly. "You are kind, your grace," he said. Then his gaze trailed over to the staircase that led to the upper floors, a spiral flight built into the wall. "I came to the keep to see how Catie is faring, in fact. I saw you walking out with Gabriel but not with her. Or with Christelle."

Phillipa gestured toward the floors above. "Catie is in her chamber, I believe," she said. "But Christelle went outside earlier. You did not see her?"

He shook his head. "I did not."

"She likes the garden in the kitchen yard, you know," Phillipa said. "She likes flowers. Did you know that?"

He frowned. "Her?" he said. "I should think she would be the last person to like something most considered feminine and useless."

Phillipa eyed him. "She is a woman, Leo," she scolded him

softly. "I realize she is different from most, but at heart, she is a woman of flesh and blood and feeling, like any other. I get the impression that her father was disappointed that she was born female, so he treated her like a man. Truthfully, I think she is very confused."

"About what?"

"About what she is supposed to be."

It was his turn to eye her. "She is a Blackchurch-trained warrior," he said. "That is an astonishing accomplishment. *That* is who she is."

Phillipa shook her head. "That is what she was trained to be," she said. "It is not who she is."

"Who do *you* think she is, then?"

Phillipa fought off a smile. "I think she is someone who is quite fond of you," she said. "I think it would help her were you to spare her a kind word about what has happened. Mayhap you should speak to the woman, not the warrior."

He scoffed, but perhaps with a little too much bluster. "I do not intend to speak to the woman *or* the warrior," he said, trying to convince her that he had no interest. "What she likes or feels is inconsequential to me."

Phillipa wasn't stupid. She'd seen the way Christelle looked at Leonidas when he wasn't looking, and she'd seen Leonidas look at Christelle when she wasn't looking. Neither one of them seemed to be willing to engage the other in anything other than a completely proper, completely professional relationship, which she found both amusing and sad. In her opinion, however, Christelle needed some comfort after her heroic efforts to save Georgiana had gone awry—and Leonidas was just the person to do it.

If he would stop being so stubborn.

"Of course, Leo," Phillipa said as if she believed him. "I did not mean to imply otherwise. But if you could say a kind word to her, as the father of the lost child, I am sure she would appreciate it."

He simply nodded. With a lingering smile, Phillipa headed up the spiral stairs, leaving Leonidas standing in the entry, pondering the queen's comments. He'd protested a little too much when he said he didn't care what Christelle liked or what she felt. That was far from the truth, only he didn't want Phillipa to know that. But something told him that she hadn't believed him.

He didn't blame her.

He was an idiot.

Turning for the keep entry to seek out Christelle, wherever she had gone, he slowly came to a halt. A thought suddenly occurred to him and he turned back for the stairs, heading to his chamber on the top level. It was the chamber he'd shared with Juliette, a vast thing that covered the entire floor. It still had all of Juliette's things in it, things he hadn't the heart to move or give away, so one entire wall where the wardrobe was had trunks and barrels full of items. Even Juliette's dressing table hadn't been touched. He hadn't been able to bring himself to do it prior to departing for Woodstock, but now that he was back and facing all of his wife's possessions on a daily basis, he was thinking of having Catherine help him go through everything. Perhaps it was time.

Someday, anyway.

Reaching the chamber, he stepped into the enormous room, feeling the cross-breeze coming from the windows. It was a messy chamber, and a little dusty, although Dayne had told him that Lady Maria had tried to claim it for herself while Leonidas was away and the knights had taken a hard line against her. It was bad enough that she had commandeered the solar, but they drew the line at the master's bower.

It was difficult to stand in the chamber and not see Juliette everywhere. In front of the wardrobe as she lamented that she needed new clothing, or in front of her dressing table lamenting that her hair was not pretty enough or tame enough. He smiled when he remembered that because he would stroke her hair and it would fly away sometimes, sticking to his hand, and she would swat him.

That made him laugh.

Her dressing table.

There was something in that table he wanted to find.

CHAPTER ELEVEN

T HERE WAS A frog.

Christelle had been gazing at it, and the little pond it sat in, for the better part of two hours. The garden in the corner of the kitchen yard used to be much more of a flower garden decades ago when a de Cottingham ancestor filled it with flowers from a trip to Rome and beyond. Nowadays, there were still flowers, and an enormous, thorned vine that grew over one wall, but it was mostly a home to a small pond where things like frogs and fish thrived.

The frog had already hopped in her direction before heading back again, toward the pond. He reminded Christelle of the story of the frog and the monk, and the frog was so loud that the monk prayed that God would silence it. A silly tale from her childhood that she recalled. She also recalled Georgiana proudly showing her the frogs on her second day at Ashendon.

That recollection further depressed her.

Her turmoil, these days, was great.

Logically, she knew she'd done all she could to save the little girl. But in her heart, she was certain she hadn't done enough. Even now, the child was in the chamber next to Phillipa's, lying upon her bed, tightly swaddled in a fine linen shroud that Leonidas had produced from Juliette's possessions. It was really a shawl, not meant to be a shroud, but it served the purpose.

A very sad purpose.

Talk was that the child was being buried in a couple of days. At least, that was what Christelle had heard Phillipa say to Catherine. Truthfully, Christelle couldn't bear to be in the keep any longer and couldn't bear to look at Catherine, seeing the anguish on the young woman's face and knowing she could have prevented it if she'd only swum faster and harder. If she'd only *tried* harder. But she didn't want to keep running in that circular logic, over and over again, so she found herself down in the garden.

Looking at frogs.

Wondering what in the hell she was doing here.

Perhaps she should forget about everything and just go home.

Ah, but that was the problem. She *couldn't* go home. Her father had sent her to England on a specific mission, and she couldn't simply leave. Even now, he was probably waiting for more news from her even though she'd only just sent him word about her movements with Phillipa recently. But her father was greedy. He wanted constant communication, which was difficult considering what she was doing. Over the past few days, she'd realized that she didn't want to do it any longer.

She just wanted some peace.

"I was hoping to find you here."

The voice came from behind, and she knew who it was even before she turned to look. Leonidas had entered the garden area, heading in her direction. She was glad to see him, as much as she could be, but it also occurred to her that things like stolen kisses and foolish, giddy feelings really didn't matter anymore. A young girl had died and she was starting to question her very existence. But she did the polite thing and acknowledged Leonidas.

"I like this place," she said, returning her focus to the pond. "It is peaceful here."

He nodded as he looked at the pond, too. She was sitting on the only large bench in the garden, one made out of wood, so he lowered himself onto one end of it.

"I've not spent much time here," he admitted. "Juliette used to bring the children here quite a lot. They liked to watch the fish and play with the frogs."

"Georgiana showed me the frogs when I first arrived."

"She considered them her friends."

The subject of Georgiana came up quickly, and Christelle didn't reply right away. If she was feeling bad, she could only imagine what Leonidas was going through, as her stepfather. Christelle knew she'd been very selfish about her own feelings on the matter when she should have been thinking about his. When she finally replied, her voice was hardly above a whisper.

"I am so very sorry, Leo," she said sincerely, closing her eyes and hanging her head. "For Georgiana, I cannot begin to convey how sorry I am that I did not grab her when I could. I close my eyes and I can still see her foot drifting past me. I can still hear her cries when she was just out of my reach. That you have to go through this yet again with another member of your family… I am so deeply sorry."

He looked over at her, hearing the tears in her voice. Her head was lowered so he couldn't see her face, but he could imagine her expression. Reaching out, he put an enormous hand on her head in a gesture of comfort.

"I know you are," he said softly. "And I will say again that you are not to blame. Christy, your actions were heroic. I have never seen a woman so heroic. You have made your family proud, you have made Blackchurch proud, you have—"

She cut him off with a snort. "Blackchurch," she muttered. "Do you want to know the truth? I am not heroic. I was not even good enough to complete Blackchurch. That is the truth. I failed at an assignment a year before I was to finish and they tossed me out, so I remained in England for that year before going home and telling my father that I had completed the Blackchurch training. But I didn't. I failed at it like I failed at saving Georgiana. Do not call me heroic, Leo. Please. Don't ever say that again. There is nothing heroic about me."

Knowing Christelle like he did, Leonidas knew that must have been an incredibly difficult admission to make. She'd seemed so proud of her Blackchurch training. Truthfully, it didn't surprise him because he knew men who had failed out of Blackchurch, too. Excellent men. Blackchurch was one of the most difficult training guilds in the world, so hearing her confession didn't change his opinion of her one bit.

In a sense, perhaps he respected her even more for admitting her failing.

"Heroism takes many forms," he said after a moment, his hand still on her head. "It can be in jumping into a river to save a young lass. It can be in admitting failure. It can be in showing loyalty and selflessness when it comes to a young queen. I know many warriors who are heroic and they never even made it into Blackchurch, though they tried. Regardless of what you think of your failure, you were heroic in trying to save Georgiana. I was there and I saw the entire event. I will go to my grave telling people how brave you were, how strong you were. I have never known anyone more heroic in my life."

She turned to look at him then. Tears were swimming in her eyes. "But I *failed*."

He smiled at her faintly and moved the hand on her head to her face, stroking her cheek gently with the back. "Is that what you think?" he murmured. "You would have failed had you *not* done anything. Had you not jumped into that river. Failure would have been to stand on the riverbank and scream, all noise and no action. It would have been to watch Georgiana drown and not try to do anything about it. Nay, lady, you did not fail. You succeeded in finding her when no one else could."

Christelle fought off a sob, but the tears rolled down her face. "It was too late," she whispered. "I found her too late."

Leonidas shifted in his seat, sliding so that he was sitting next to her, and his arm went around her shoulders, pulling her against him. "But you found her," he insisted softly. "That is the important thing. You succeeded in bringing her to the bank so she did not die in that river with no one around her. As it was, we were all with her when she passed. The last thing she knew was my hands on her and then you holding her. She heard your voice before she went to be with her mother. Better still, Juliette heard your voice. She saw how you tried to save her daughter. I know without question that Juliette was standing on that bank, waiting to take hold of Georgiana's hand so they could be together once again. I also know she would have appreciated your efforts so very much. In fact, I brought you something that Juliette would want you to have to show her gratitude."

Christelle was wiping at her face, head against his big shoulder, as he pulled something out of his tunic pocket. He held it up and she could see the glint of gold. Closer inspection showed that it was a round golden pendant with a big green stone in the center, surrounded by a ring of smaller green stones and finally a ring of small pearls. It was attached to a golden chain, a perfectly beautiful piece of jewelry.

"It's lovely," she said, sniffling.

He extended it to her. "This was given to Juliette when the twins were born," he said. "She said that Edmund had it specially made by a goldsmith in London. The emeralds represent life and fertility and the pearls represent God's blessings for the children."

Christelle took it reluctantly, examining the truly beautiful pendant and flipping it over to see an inscription scratched on the backside.

"*Iubar*?" she read aloud.

He pointed at the letters. "It means 'my sunshine,'" he said. "Juliette said that Edmund always called her Sunshine because of the color of her hair. It was golden red and glistened. Like sunshine."

Christelle wiped the last of her tears and sat up, smiling at him. "That's very sweet," he said. "The man was a romantic."

"He seemed to be," Leonidas said as he watched her inspect the front of the pendant again. "Juliette would want you to have this, Christy. Let it always remind you of a little lass with a pet chicken. Let it always remind you of the day you did not fail."

Christelle was starting to tear up again. "I do not know if I can keep it," she said. "You should give this to Catie. It belonged to her mother, after all."

He shook his head. "Trust me when I tell you that Catie will have more jewelry than she will know what to do with," he said. "I am giving you this because of the special significance with Georgiana. Please take it."

Christelle probably should have fought him on it a little

more, but she couldn't manage to do it. Leonidas' wisdom and words had helped ease the terrible grief she felt a great deal and, in fact, had her looking at him a little differently. The Leonidas de Wolfe she had known before the journey to Ashendon was a serious man of few words and little kindness, but the man she'd come to know since embarking on this adventure was a man of thought and compassion.

And her feelings for him were growing deeper by the day.

"My thanks," she said. "I will cherish it, always."

"Good," he said, a weak smile on his lips. "Juliette would like that. I do, too."

Christelle smiled weakly in return, gazing into the man's blue eyes before she realized how close they were. He still had his hand on her back because she had sat up when she took the necklace from him. No longer did she have her head against his shoulder, and she was disappointed to realize that. There had been such immense comfort in that gesture, simple as it was.

She could feel her cheeks start to flame.

"I suppose I should go into the keep and see if Phillipa needs me," she said, averting her gaze. "I have been away from her overlong."

"No need," he said. "I left her not long ago. She was going to see to Catherine."

"What about Gabriel?"

Leonidas looked back in the direction of the kitchen yard. "He is around here somewhere," he said. "You know the knights look out for him, so if he is outside, somewhere, he is being watched. Truthfully, I thought I might find him in this yard with the chicken."

They were both looking over in the kitchen yard now, searching for the errant child. "Mayhap I should go look for him," Christelle said. "He must be feeling terribly lonesome without his sister by his side."

She stood up, pausing only to put the necklace on. When it became caught in her hair, Leonidas stood up beside her and pushed her hands away, silently untangling her hair from the gold chain. Even when he was finished untangling it, he still pretended to fuss with it simply for the chance to touch her hair. In spite of the fact that she didn't seem to know what a comb was, it was very pretty and very soft. He fingered it for a few moments longer before dropping his hand.

"Turn around and let me see it," he said as she turned to face him. He admired the pendant as it rested against the green broadcloth surcoat she was wearing. "It looks lovely on you. Speaking of lovely, Phillipa mentioned something to me and I wonder if it is true."

Christelle was looking down at the pendant, straightening it out. "What did she say?"

"That she thinks you are quite fond of me," he said softly. "Is it true?"

That statement caught Christelle off guard. She stopped fingering the pendant, looking at him with an expression between shock and disbelief. There was horror in her eyes, but also something cool. Almost appraising. Clearly, she was trying to figure out how to answer him—but after a moment, she simply gave up and averted her gaze again.

"She said that?" she asked, sounding resigned.

"She did."

"I did not say anything to her if that is what you are asking," she said. "I would never do that."

"I believe you," he said. "But I want to know if her observations are true."

Christelle thought on the question. Was it true? Of course it was true. But she couldn't tell him.

... could she?

The mood unexpectedly began to shift.

"What does it matter?" she said. "You have only just lost your wife and now your daughter. You are in no position to entertain anyone's affections and, quite frankly, I am offended that you would ask me such a thing. It is true that I kissed you, and I have apologized for being an opportunist, but that does not mean I am in love with you. I would not tell you if I was, so do not ask me such a thing."

She was looking at her feet, speaking angrily, and Leonidas had to fight off a grin.

"I lost my wife two years ago," he said. "I have grieved. I will not spend my life mourning a loss I can never regain because I am not a man who engages in futility. I loved Juliette but that does not mean I cannot love again."

"I did not say that you couldn't."

"I know what you said," he said, becoming more aggressive with her because she was almost being belligerent. "Christ, you're a stubborn woman. Would it make it easier for you if I told you that I'm quite fond of you also? That I've always thought you were something lovely and wild, like an untamed horse, someone I have long admired? I already told you that I shall not forget your kiss and that you were brave for delivering it, but if it is not something you wish to repeat, and if you truly have no admiration for me in the romantic sense, then all you need do is tell me and we shall never have this conversation again. Am I clear?"

Her head snapped up, her eyes flashing. "You are clear."

"Well?"

"Of course Phillipa was correct. You'd have to be blind and stupid not to realize that!"

"I thought so."

"Then why did you ask me?"

She was literally yelling. He cocked his head curiously. "Why are we shouting at each other?" he asked. "I am not clear on that."

She opened her mouth to reply, loudly, but she suddenly burst into laughter. Gales of it. Leonidas joined her, those big canines front and center, and laughed until he cried. Reaching out, he grasped the pendant resting against her chest and held it up for her to see.

"Here's something else we can shout at each other for," he said. "Remember the inscription on the back?"

He was holding it right in front of her face and she had to tilt her head back in order to actually see it. "*Iubar*?"

"Exactly," he said, lowering the pendant. "*Iubar*. My sunshine. Edmund never put it there for Juliette. I lied about that. I took a nail and scratched that on myself."

She looked at him, incredulous. "Why did you do that?"

He cocked a dark eyebrow. "Now who's being blind and stupid?" he said, jabbing a finger at her. "Do you not recall when I said that I am in awe when I look at you because you are brighter than the sun?"

She nodded. "Of course I do."

He shook his head as if she were, indeed, too dense to get his meaning. "You are sunshine, Christelle de Lorrain," he said softly. "Mayhap someday, if you'll stop being so stubborn, you will indeed be *my* sunshine."

She bit her lip, looking away coyly in a gesture that was natural and sweet. She may not have had any practice flirting, but there was something innate in her that knew how. Still, he could see that she was blushing to the roots of her hair.

"How will we know when I am?" she asked. "Must I give permission?"

"Probably," he said. "Will you?"

"May I think on it?"

"What is there to think about?"

"Are you going to force me into it, then?"

He rolled his eyes. "Do you not know when a man is trying to court you?"

"Is *that* what you're doing?"

He clapped a hand on his forehead in a gesture of disbelief. "Evidently not well enough if you do not recognize it," he said. Then he grew serious. "Must you truly think about it?"

She could see a flash of vulnerability in that question and it amused her. "Probably not."

"*And?*"

"And I think I shall try to blind you if I can."

"Are you giving me permission?"

"I'm telling you that I may possibly kiss you again."

"Christ, woman, can you give me a straight answer?"

She burst into soft laughter. "I thought I was," she said. "Leo, if you think a relationship between two stubborn people might actually be something we won't regret, then I give you permission."

That was all Leonidas needed to pull her against him, so forcefully that she grunted when their bodies collided. But his lips slanted over hers, firmly and tenderly at the same time, and Christelle succumbed without a fight.

That was the furthest thing from her mind.

Leonidas kissed her fiercely, or at least as fiercely as he

dared, but the truth was that there was a great deal of joy behind his actions. Joy he hadn't felt in years. In fact, when he first met Juliette, it had been at a meeting orchestrated by his father and he already knew that he was going to marry her. There was no courtship to speak of other than the actual marriage. Leonidas married first and courted later. Fortunately, that had worked out for both him and Juliette, so the fact that he was actually courting a woman now before marriage was something of a new event to him.

But he was liking it very much.

He thought he might compare Juliette to Christelle when it came to the physicality of a relationship. It seemed strange to be kissing a woman who wasn't his wife, but on the other hand, Juliette's tender kisses had been nothing like the fire he was feeling from Christelle. Perhaps it was the fact that this was so new, or perhaps it was because he was wildly attracted to this woman. In any case, his lips feasted on hers and she gave him absolutely no resistance.

He wanted more.

His hands ended up in that wild hair of hers, holding her head against his, her lips against his. He suckled her top lip and her bottom lip before finally using his tongue to gently open her mouth. She was sweet, like honey, and he licked her teeth and her lower lip, feeling her shudder against him. He could also feel her stirring the embers of desire within him, desire that he had experienced a few times in his life, but not like this. What he was experiencing with her was something quite different.

Something he very much wanted to explore.

It should have occurred to him that he was standing in the middle of the garden and anyone on the walls or even in the kitchen yard would be able to see them, but it didn't. He was so caught up in the feel and the taste of her that it didn't occur to him until he nearly rubbed her lips raw with his forceful attentions. When he realized what he was doing, he stopped kissing her but didn't let her go. His big hands were still in her hair, but now he found himself staring at her as if trying to figure out why that kiss had nearly consumed him for all to see.

"I cannot promise that I will not do that again," he said huskily. "If I frightened you, I apologize."

Christelle, who was somewhat dazed, shook her head in a quick gesture, trying to shake some sense back into herself. "Nothing frightens me," she said. "Have you not realized that by now?"

"Then you liked it?"

"Did you?"

"I asked you first."

She started to chuckle, shaking her head again at the ridiculous conversation. "If this relationship thrives, it will be a miracle," she said. "Aye, I liked it. I let you do it, did I not?"

"I had my hands in your hair. You could not go anywhere."

"If I wanted to go anywhere, you would not have stopped me."

He conceded the point. "True," he said, stroking his chin. "I will admit that I've never seriously courted a woman before. Mayhap I need your father's permission in addition to yours?"

Her smile faded as she thought of Bernard de Lorrain. The man who had, only and always, used his daughter like a pawn. Now, the reality of her feelings for Leonidas was coming to bear because he had feelings for her also. That was something she had never anticipated. Had he not returned them, it would have been a simple thing for her to stick to her mission, the one she no longer wished to be part of, but telling her father would be a complex and possibly dangerous thing. And having Leonidas ask the man for permission to court her might throw everything into jeopardy.

She wondered what Leonidas would do if he found out she was a spy.

"I would not worry about my father," she said quietly. "He would not at all be pleased with an Englishman courting me, so it is best that he does not know."

Leonidas looked at her. "Not even if he knew you would be a countess if we married?"

She shook her head. "It is the fact that you are English," she said. "The weight of a title would not outweigh his disdain for your country."

"Then you do not wish to tell him at all?"

"Should we decide to marry, and I am assuming that is what you mean by courting me, we will tell him after the fact," she said. "That way, he can do nothing about it."

Leonidas grew serious. "What would he do?"

She shrugged. "If he knew before, he could have his men remove me from my post," she said. "My father has an army, Leo. He is a powerful warlord."

Leonidas grunted. "He has not met the de Wolfe empire," he said. "My family has more than two dozen castles and other properties all over England and a combined army of twenty thousand men. I do not think your father can match that."

"Hopefully he will not try," she said. "But let us not speak of him now. We will speak of him later, if we decide that the two of us can establish a relationship that is amiable to us both."

A smile played on his lips. "I am willing to try if you are."

Christelle could feel herself blushing again. "I let you kiss me, did I not?"

"That you did."

She averted her gaze, but not before casting him a brief, if somewhat flirtatious, glance. "I'm certain it will not be the last time," she said. "But not out in the garden where everyone can see us. Rumors are probably already spreading like wildfire."

He chuckled. "Then mayhap you had better tell Phillipa before she hears it from someone else."

She nodded. "I will," she said. "But for now, I think I would like to find Gabriel. He may need a friend. Would you like to come with me?"

Leonidas shook his head. "I have a few duties to attend to," he said. "But I will see you tonight, at supper."

"We are having roast pork."

"I look forward to it. And to you."

Christelle's cheeks were on fire as she headed out of the kitchen yard, trying not to look at him because every time she did, she was certain her red cheeks grew redder. Once they quit the yard, he headed toward the gatehouse and Christelle headed toward the stable, thinking Gabriel might have gone in there. The twins had been known to go into the stable and play, so she hoped to find him there.

An hour later, with no sign of Gabriel to be found, the entire garrison began to hunt for the child.

CHAPTER TWELVE

"IS THAT ALL there is? Where is the meat?"

Wrapped up in a dirty blanket, the only real comfort she had, Lady Maria turned her nose up at the food the servant had brought her. The servant, having served under Lady Maria and having no real love for the woman, slammed the tray against the bars and the food went flying into her tiny cell.

It splattered everywhere.

With a gasp at the flying food, Lady Maria was enraged. She rushed the bars of her cell and tried to grab the servant, who stood just out of arm's length and laughed. Lady Maria clawed at her for a few seconds before realizing that it wasn't going to work.

Nothing was working as she'd intended.

Her life included.

She was going on five days in this hellhole. Because of the high-water table, water seeped in through the floor, through the walls, and through the ceiling. The ceiling seemed to be more condensation than actual water leakage, but the end result was the same. Lady Maria had spent days in this wet and molding environment, a far cry from the fine chamber she had created for herself in the keep and her days of ruling the roost from the elegant solar.

This was a far cry from *anything* she had ever envisioned for herself.

The prostitute's daughter who had forged documents so she could obtain legitimate positions was finally at the end of her lies. She had been trying to reconcile that very fact for the past several days, and the only conclusion she could come to was that she refused to let it end. She had grown accustomed to power and to fine things, and she wasn't going to let this little setback deter her from what she wanted out of life. Somehow, someway, she was going to get out of this predicament and go find another family that would let her take charge of the children and possibly even the entire castle. Ashendon wasn't unique. She still had the letter from the Earl of Carnforth that she'd paid a clerk to forge. There were hundreds of other places in England where her services would be appreciated.

But first, she had to get out of here.

The knights hadn't come to check on her once since they had incarcerated her, and the only people she saw were the servants as they brought her meager meals. Even the blanket on her back had come from a servant, and she was positive they'd gone into the stable to get the dirtiest horse blanket they could find. It was rough and dirty and smelled like animals. Given the fact that knights hadn't checked on her since depositing her in this hole, it would be easier for her to plan her escape.

That was where the servants came in.

And it was going to start now.

Even as she turned away from the iron bars of her cell, it was all part of a ploy that she had been planning since nearly the moment she was jailed. As soon as she stopped grabbing for the servant who threw the food, she groaned as if in great pain and fell to the floor. Her hope was that the servant would show enough interest to open up the cell to check on her, and if that was the case, she had a sharp piece of stone that she had been carrying around on her body, something she had found in this very cell because it had fallen from the ceiling.

Sharp enough to use as a weapon.

As Lady Maria fell on the floor, she made sure to grasp the stone, which had been wedged into her skirt by way of a hidden pocket. Many women had such things sewn into their garments, and the dress she was wearing was one of the finest money could buy. She'd used some of the money from the books she sold to have a local seamstress make it. There were secret pockets everywhere to store things like money and keys and valuables, and anything else she happened to steal.

Now, she'd put one of those pockets to good use.

And she waited.

The servant laughed at her. Cursed her. Even spat on her as she lay there. She wasn't so sure the woman would come inside the cell and, eventually, the servant left. That had Lady Maria picking herself up from the floor, irritated that the servant didn't fall for her deception, but that didn't really matter. There would be another meal at some point and she would pretend she was ill again, anything to get the servant into her cell.

Rising from the floor amidst the splatter of some kind of stew, she waited.

Oddly, she didn't have to wait until suppertime. Not a half-hour after the spilled stew and her fall to the floor, the door to the vault opened and light from above hit the stairwell and floor, illuminating the truly dismal conditions. Quickly, Lady Maria moved herself back to the floor and into the same position she was before. She lay there, still as stone, as two servants came down the stairwell.

She could hear them whispering.

"What happened tae her?" one servant with a heavy Scottish accent asked.

"I don't know," the other servant, the one who had thrown the stew, said. "But she fell down and she hasn't moved. Should we tell Lord Hull?"

Lady Maria could only hear shuffling going on behind her, as her back was to the cell door. She didn't dare move for fear she'd be seen and they would know she was feigning unconsciousness, so she remained perfectly still, even when one of them threw something at her through the bars. Once it struck her in the hip, it clattered to the floor a few feet away—from the sound, she assumed it was a spoon or some other utensil.

More hissing, more whispering. She heard something about *let's see*, but what they wanted to see, she didn't know. She suspected they might want to test her because they made no attempt to be quiet when they walked away, speaking of what they were having for supper and making sure they spoke loudly enough. People didn't normally do that sort of thing when someone was lying unconscious. If Lady Maria was one thing, it was clever. She was cleverer than they were. Because she thought they were trying to trap her, she simply lay there and didn't move.

She lay there for over an hour.

Then they were back. She wasn't sure if it was the same women, but it sounded like it. She could hear a heavy Scottish accent in the mix and they were deciding what to do with her. Someone suggested they go in to see if she was dead.

And that was exactly what Lady Maria wanted.

She hadn't counted on two servants, however. She was going to have to think fast in order to kill both of them without one of them at least having a chance to run away or sound the alarm. She could hear the cell door opening as the tumblers and the old lock clicked. There was a screeching sound as the door swung open on the rusty hinges.

Footsteps entered the cell.

The first thing they did was roll her onto her back. Lady Maria knew that she wouldn't have a second chance at doing what she needed to do, so she had to take this opportunity and take it quickly. When the Scottish woman knelt over her and lifted an eyelid to see if her pupils would react to the light, Lady Maria suddenly brought up the broken stone and stabbed the Scottish woman in the neck.

The fight was on.

As the Scottish woman fell away, mortally wounded, the servant who threw the stew shrieked and tried to escape, but Lady Maria was fast. She was able to throw out a foot and trip the woman before she could get out of the cell. The servant stumbled over Lady Maria's kicking feet and fell, face first, into the cell door. She hit herself in the nose and in the mouth, and as she stumbled back with her hand over her bleeding mouth, Lady Maria landed the razor-sharp stone into her foot. The servant cried out and staggered, falling onto her side, as Lady Maria pounced.

Jamming the stone dagger into the woman's eye ensured quick death. Mostly, anyway. She took some pleasure in watching the woman suffer for the last few seconds of her life. Winded, and terrified that the battle had been heard up above in the gatehouse, Lady Maria rushed to the bottom of the steps, listening for any hint that the soldiers had been alerted. But everything seemed calm up above and she gradually returned to the cell where two dead women lay on the wet floor.

Now was time for her to act.

Heart pounding, Lady Maria stripped the clothes off the servant who had thrown the stew because her clothing was the least bloodied. She then proceeded to strip off her own clothing and dress in the servant's clothes, including wrapping her head up in a woolen wimple. Then she put her clothing on the dead servant and lugged the woman over to her bed, tossing the old blanket over her so it looked as if she were sleeping. The Scottish woman who had bled out on the dirty floor she crammed underneath the cot and made sure the horse blanket covered up any sign of her.

And with that, she was ready to run.

Terrified she would be seen, Lady Maria made her way out to the stairwell again, looking to the floor above to see if there was anyone. There didn't seem to be, so to complete her disguise as a servant, she picked up the tray that had held her meager meal. It had been left leaning against the wall. Head down, tray against her chest, she mounted the stairs to the gatehouse only to see that absolutely no one was paying any attention to the door that led down to the vault. There were only a few soldiers at the front of the gatehouse, talking to each other, and there were a few of them in the bailey near the gatehouse.

It was strangely vacant.

But Lady Maria didn't question it. Keeping the tray clutched to her chest and her head down, she left through the gatehouse and no one stopped her. No one even looked at her. She walked quickly, glancing over her shoulder to make sure she wasn't being followed, all the way down the road and into the outskirts of the village. Once the various small cottages and little farms appeared, she began to run.

All the way to the river's wharf.

All the way to freedom.

CHAPTER THIRTEEN

"**I** DO NOT know what I shall do if Gabriel is gone," Catherine said, her voice trembling. "He is all I have left. We must find him."

Christelle was listening to Catherine chatter about her brother in between crying jags. The poor woman was overwrought and Christelle didn't blame her for being so despondent. They'd been searching for Gabriel for several hours, using the soldiers to leave no stone unturned. They even went to the river, which was where Leonidas was with the knights at this very moment. He made Christelle and Phillipa remain with Catherine, who was on the verge of crumbling into a thousand pieces. He didn't think she could take seeing her little brother's body in the water.

Christelle didn't think she could take it, either.

None of them could. She cast a concerned glance at Phillipa, who wasn't feeling particularly well this day. Her belly had been upset and she was generally tired, but that hadn't stopped her from actively comforting Catherine since the search for Gabriel began in earnest. The two of them had huddled together and Phillipa had done most of the talking as Catherine sadly listened. Christelle had simply stood back and monitored the situation, still feeling guilt over Georgiana, now horrified at the prospect of Gabriel's demise. She was trying not to think the worst, but with the history of this family and death, she simply couldn't help it.

It was a dark day, indeed.

A knock at the chamber door roused her from her thoughts. Before she could even turn for the door, Catherine was running for it, throwing it open only to find Kenneth standing there.

The big knight was dirty from having been an active part of the search for Gabriel. His tightly curled, short blond hair even had leaves and chaff in it from his adventures down near the river. Before he could say a word, Catherine was practically throwing herself at the man in her eagerness to know about her brother.

"Well?" she demanded. "Did you find Gabriel?"

Kenneth shook his head. "Nay, my lady."

Catherine immediately broke down into tears. "Why not?" she cried. "He is only a small boy. He did not simply disappear!"

"I know, my lady."

"Then where is he?"

"Leonidas has sent me to ask you a few questions, if you feel strong enough," he said. "It might help us in our search. May I?"

Catherine began to sob. "I just want him to be found," she wept. "Why can't anyone find him?"

Christelle's sympathetic gaze moved from Catherine to Kenneth. "What do you wish to ask her?" she asked quietly. "As you can see, she is terribly distressed by all of this."

Kenneth nodded patiently. He was the most stoic, perhaps

most frightening knight of any Christelle had ever encountered because the man never had his guard down. It was as if there wasn't an ounce of humanity in him. But those ice-blue eyes had a flicker of sympathy at the moment, which was surprising.

Even Kenneth understood the tragedy that was unfolding this day.

"I know she is," he said. "But I shall be painless, I promise."

Christelle sighed faintly. "Be gentle," she said. "But if you truly want an answer, you will have to be firm with her. Her coherency has not been the best today."

He gave her a nod and stepped into the chamber where Catherine was currently weeping on Phillipa's shoulder. Phillipa eyed the big blond knight as he came near. When he silently gestured toward Catherine, Phillipa reluctantly nodded. That had Kenneth crouching down before reaching out to take Catherine's hands with surprising gentleness.

"My lady," he said, forcing her to look at him. "I must have your attention, please. I know this is very difficult for you, but I must ask you to be brave. Information you give me may help locate your brother. Do you understand?"

Catherine sniffled and nodded. "Where do you think—"

He interrupted her, though not cruelly. "We haven't much time," he said. "I need to know if your brother has a favorite pony, one he might ride away on. Talan and Dayne and Zander do not seem to think so, but you might know differently. Can you tell me?"

Catherine didn't want to answer questions. She tried to pull her hands away from Kenneth, but Phillipa stepped in.

"Please, darling," she said gently, as only Phillipa could do. "You want us to find Gabriel, don't you? Try to think of something that we've not discovered yet. Did Gabriel have a favorite pony? Or a favorite place where he would play?"

Catherine was shaking her head quickly, back and forth. "Nay," she insisted, sniffling. "You are wasting time asking me these questions. There was no place!"

"Did he have any little friends he would play with?"

She managed to yank a hand away from Kenneth. "Gabriel only had Georgiana," she insisted. "There is nowhere else he would... *Wait*... Mayhap there is because... *The chicken!*"

The last two words were blurted and her entire countenance changed. Kenneth, Phillipa, and Christelle looked at her with surprise.

"What about the chicken?" Kenneth asked.

Catherine immediately stopped weeping. She began to wave her hands, quickly, as if the motion would help her bring forth the idea that had occurred to her. In fact, she stuttered a bit before her words were able to gain traction.

"The chicken," she said, her eyes wide as she looked at Kenneth. "There is a grove of trees to the north where there are some wild chickens. They must have escaped from a farmer somewhere, or somehow, but that is where Georgiana found her pet chicken. Sometimes she would take it back to the grove of trees because she said the chicken wanted to visit her family."

"And Lady Maria allowed this?" Christelle asked.

She hadn't really meant to say what she was thinking, because it seemed odd that a young girl would run around outside of the castle, alone, but Catherine shook her head firmly to the question.

"She did not know," she said. "Lady Maria left the children on their own a great deal of the time. I minded them during those times, but they liked to wander. Sometimes they evaded me. One time, I found them at the edge of the forest with those wild chickens. That must be where he has gone!"

Kenneth was already heading for the chamber door. "North, you say?"

Catherine bolted past him, heading for the stairs. "I will show you!"

Kenneth had no choice but to follow her. As he darted after Catherine, Phillipa moved to follow, but Christelle stopped her.

"Nay, your grace," she said. "This is sure to be a mad flight and you must not exert yourself in your condition."

Phillipa was clearly anxious about it. "If I cannot go, then you must go," she said, waving her hands at the door where Catherine and Kenneth had been. "If she grows distraught, you will need to calm her. Hurry!"

That was probably true. Catherine was an excitable girl, and if Gabriel wasn't where she thought he was, then she would surely be distressed. But Christelle was indecisive about leaving Phillipa for a split second because she didn't want to leave the young queen alone.

"Very well," she finally said. "But bolt this door when I am gone. Do not open it for anyone but me or Leonidas."

Phillipa nodded firmly as Christelle dashed out, following the path of Kenneth and Catherine out of the keep. She had no idea where she was going, but she caught sight of them departing the bailey astride Kenneth's big, dappled warhorse just as she came out of the entry. That caused Christelle to rush into the stable yard and confiscate a mare that a groom was brushing. The horse had a bridle on but nothing else, and she swung herself onto the horse's back and took off after Kenneth.

The mare was excitable, so it was a bit of a wild ride following Kenneth down the road and to the north. It was clear that he wasn't going to stop to tell Leonidas and the others about

Catherine's hunch, possibly so as not to cause false hope, so he flew down the road and finally crossed a field that was quite muddy in places. Christelle knew this because the mare plunged into the field, throwing up dirty water, which splashed on her. But she didn't lose sight of Kenneth, not even when he drew near a grove of ash trees that was within distant sight of the castle. He slowed his animal, but Christelle didn't. She caught up to him, kicking up water and clods of earth, about the time they reached the edge of the trees.

Chickens began to scatter everywhere.

"Gabriel!" Catherine cried, sliding off Kenneth's horse. "Gabriel, answer me!"

Kenneth and Christelle were dismounting their respective animals as Catherine ran into the grove, calling for her brother.

"*Gabriel!*"

"Oy!"

Gabriel emerged almost immediately from behind some trees, carrying chicks in his hands. Catherine shrieked when she saw him, running to him and throwing her arms around him. Since Gabriel didn't particularly like hugs, he made a face as his sister wept all over him.

"Where have you been?" Catherine said. "We have been searching for you all day!"

Gabriel managed to pull free of his sister. "I'm here," he said, simply turning back the way he'd come. "There are lots of chicks. I've been building them a house."

Catherine was beside herself. Gabriel wasn't the least bit concerned that she was weeping or that three adults were clearly concerned for him. Instead, he was speaking of houses for chicks.

"Gabriel, *stop*," Catherine said, no longer sobbing. Frankly, she was growing perturbed. "You left and did not tell anyone where you went. Why did you do that?"

He didn't answer her, still holding the chicks, until she reached out and grabbed his arm. He tried to pull free, but she held him fast.

"Let me go," he demanded. "I have to finish."

"Not until you tell me why you did not tell anyone where you were going," Catherine said. "We have been searching for you all day. Did you not hear men calling your name?"

Gabriel was looking at the chicks. "I am not going back," he said. "Not while she's still there."

Catherine looked at him, greatly puzzled. "*Who* is still there?"

Gabriel wouldn't look at her. He managed to pull away and back from her again so she couldn't grab him.

"I cannot go," he said. "You are keeping her there, but it is not her. She is cold and she smells but you keep her there. I won't go back. She... she whispers to me when I am sleeping, and I can't sleep anymore."

Catherine had no idea what he was talking about. "Who are you speaking of?" she said. "If you mean Lady Maria, she is gone. Who whispers to you?"

Gabriel was looking at the chicks in his hands. "Not Lady Maria," he mumbled. "*Her*. My sister."

Christelle and Kenneth were both listening closely. "Do you mean Georgiana, Gabriel?" Christelle said. "Is that who you are speaking of?"

He nodded. "Catie won't let her go," he said. "She makes her stay."

Catherine looked at him in shock. "Why do you say such a thing?" she said, hurt. "She is our sister. Why would you want

effort," she said. Then she held up her hand, flexing her fingers. "She was almost in my grasp, Kenneth. While she was still alive, I mean. But she went under again and floated past me, and that river is so muddy. I simply could not see her in the water."

Kenneth had grown serious again. "Nothing heroic is ever a wasted effort," he said. "Even if you did not succeed. The bravery is in the trying."

"It does not feel that way," she said glumly. "Zander jumped in, too, I believe. I do not know where everyone else was, but I do know that Leo remained on the bank."

Kenneth's pale eyes glimmered. "Do you know why?"

"To direct the efforts, of course," she said. "Why else?"

"Because he cannot swim," Kenneth said quietly. "He probably would have died himself had he jumped in to save the girl. But you prevented that from happening. In a sense, you saved Leo's life, too. And you saved his dignity."

She looked at him in surprise. "I did not know he could not swim."

Kenneth nodded. "Not a stroke," he said. "But do not tell him I told you. It will be our secret. I think if he was aware that you knew, he might feel ashamed. But I wanted you to know so you did not think him a coward."

Christelle shook her head. "I never thought he was," she said. "Truthfully, there was so much chaos going on that I did not even think on it."

Kenneth simply nodded, hoping that Leonidas would never find out that he'd told Christelle about possibly the one thing in his life he never mastered—swimming. The man was fearless on a ship and Kenneth had seen him plunge into moats in an attempt to get to a castle, but the horse swam so he didn't have to. Leonidas had never said anything about his failure to jump into the river to save Georgiana, but knowing Leonidas like he did, Kenneth suspected the man had some deep-seated guilt about it.

He simply wanted Christelle to know.

"I should probably find where Catie and Gabriel have gone to," he said, heading off into the trees. "It will be a joyous meal tonight, knowing the lad is safe."

Christelle had to agree. It was a joyous day, indeed.

But that was about to change.

CHAPTER FOURTEEN

"**H**E SEEMS WELL enough," Phillipa said. "He ate his supper and went right to sleep."

It was late on the evening of the day of the enormous search for Gabriel. Arrangements had been made to put Georgiana in the vault where it was cold, until she could be buried, and Gabriel seemed to be in better spirits because of it. In truth, everyone felt guilty that the boy's feelings had been neglected. No one had even thought to ask him if his sister's unburied body disturbed him, but it clearly had. Enough for him to run off to live with the chickens, as he put it. But now, all was still and quiet and the keep was once again a place of warmth and comfort.

"I think the same will be said for everyone in the search party," Christelle said. "They are so exhausted that they will eat supper and go right to sleep."

They were standing on the landing, in the open chamber door, and Phillipa smiled faintly as she looked at the little boy who was dead asleep on his bed. There were two beds in the chamber and one had been occupied by Georgiana until about two hours ago, when Leonidas himself carried her down to the vault. All that remained behind was the chicken, roosting on the bed as Gabriel snored away on the other.

"We were so concerned for Catie's feelings over Georgiana that we never bothered to think about Gabriel's," Phillipa said. "I feel terrible that we did not ask him."

Christelle shrugged. "Everything is as it should be now," she said. "We will not neglect him again."

"Nay, we will not."

"Neglect who?"

The women turned to see Catherine approaching from the stairwell. Phillipa immediately smiled and held her hand out to the young woman.

"You," she said simply. "We will never again neglect you or Gabriel. You are the most important people to us."

Catherine smiled weakly. "I have behaved foolishly," she said. "Poor Gabriel has suffered because of my selfishness."

Phillipa squeezed her hand. "You were not selfish," she said. "You were grieving. Gabriel is, too, but in a different way. We must be mindful of both ways."

Catherine's gaze lingered on Gabriel sleeping with an arm flung off the mattress. "It is difficult to know what boys are thinking," she said. "I find it... confusing. If I'd only known how he felt, we could have done something about it, but instead, he ran off and frightened us all to death. Why are men like that?"

She said it with such passion that Christelle and Phillipa passed curious glances. Something told them that the question wasn't necessarily limited to Gabriel because of the way she'd said it.

"Like what, darling?" Phillipa said. "Mysterious and lacking communication? Because that is what makes them exciting.

Men keep us guessing."

She meant it as somewhat of a jest, but Catherine didn't find it funny. She frowned. "I do not like to guess," she said. "I am angry with Gabriel, but I am also very glad that he did not come to harm. I suppose my confusion makes me mad."

Phillipa squeezed her hand again. "It makes you a woman who loves her brother," she said. "Do not feel bad."

Catherine sighed faintly. "I suppose I shall overcome my anger," she said. "But men… Are they ever any less confusing?"

That confirmed it. Christelle and Phillipa realized she was no longer speaking of Gabriel. There had been rumors since they'd arrived at Ashendon, rumors about Catherine and a certain young knight, but no one gave them any credence. Castles were rumor mills, churning them out by the dozen, so Christelle had brushed off the servants' whispers even though she'd told Phillipa. That had only been their second day at Ashendon, and the servants had the good sense not to gossip around them anymore because Christelle frowned upon such things.

But perhaps those rumors had some validity.

It was just a hunch they had.

"As I said, men are mysterious creatures," Phillipa said. "I do not suppose you are referring to any man in particular? Mayhap if I knew him, I could tell you. Has someone been toying with you?"

Catherine looked at her with some surprise. "No one has toyed with me," she said indignantly. "I would not allow it."

"Good girl."

"But that does not mean I find men simple of thought."

"No one does."

"Especially not a de Wolfe."

That had Christelle's attention. "Who?" she said. "Leonidas?"

Catherine shook her head. "Not him."

"Dayne?"

"Talan."

The light of realization went on and Christelle and Phillipa passed yet another glance between them, this one rather knowing. Phillipa fought off a grin as Christelle addressed it.

"I do not know much about Talan," Christelle said. "But if he is part of the de Wolfe family, then he is undoubtedly a man of his word. Do you have your eye on him?"

Catherine blushed furiously, which told Christelle and Phillipa all they needed to know. She looked between the women as fear rippled across her expression. "Please do not tell anyone," she said softly. "Least of all Leo. Swear it."

Christelle nodded. "Of course we swear it," she said. "It is none of his affair. Unless you think it should be. Why? Has Talan declared his interest for you?"

Catherine was still fearful to admit that which she did not want to admit, but she'd gone through a year of not having anyone to talk to about this. No women she could share her feelings with. Truth be told, she desperately needed some advice.

"Aye," she said softly. "Remember… you promised not to tell Leo."

"I will not," Christelle assured her. "Does he wish to marry you?"

"He *must* marry me."

"Why?"

"Because he has bedded me."

Christelle's eyes widened and she looked to Phillipa, who

realized the seriousness of the situation. If Catherine and Talan were intimate, then this went beyond a mere infatuation.

Lila took both of Catherine's hands in her own.

"Did he force himself upon you?" she asked with genuine concern. "You may tell me. I promise that I only wish to help."

Catherine shook her head firmly. "Nay," she said. "He is not that kind of man. But he feels that he has nothing to offer me by way of marriage and he wants to earn his fortune and mayhap gain property or possessions, things of value, before he asks for my hand."

Phillipa didn't think that was a bad idea, but she didn't come out with it. She fidgeted a bit, trying to decide what to say that wouldn't make Catherine feel like she was in the wrong.

"But you want to marry him now?" she said hesitantly.

Catherine lifted her shoulders. "Why not?" she said. "Talan and I love one another. I am already his wife in body if not by law. I do not understand why he feels it necessary to earn his fortune before he takes a wife. What does it matter?"

"Because you cannot live on dreams and youthful hope," Christelle said. She was a little more direct than Phillipa. "You must let Talan feel as if he can support you. You must let the man have his pride, Catie. There is no rush, after all. You are very young. If he loves you now, he'll love you when you come of age. Is the man not worth waiting for?"

Catherine shrugged. Then she nodded. It wasn't the answer she wanted, but it was perhaps the one she needed to hear. Talan had tried to tell her essentially the same thing, but she thought he was being cagey, purposely delaying their marriage.

But perhaps he'd been telling the truth.

"I suppose," she said, feeling dejected. "But I do not understand what difference it makes if he has money or doesn't."

"Who is going to pay for your clothing?" Christelle said. "Your food? Your needs? And do not tell me you can use your dowry. Although I imagine you have a substantial one, nothing would kill the man's pride more than having to live off his wife."

"You think so?" Catherine said hesitantly.

Both Christelle and Phillipa nodded. "I do," Christelle said. "I would think that part of being a good wife is to understand your husband's needs and fears. You cannot always think of yourself and what you want. Think about what he wants, too."

That was as much beat-down as Catherine wanted to hear, true though it might be. "Very well," she said sadly. "Thank you for speaking with me about it. And for keeping my secret."

"Of course, Catie."

"I think I'll retire now. After today's search, I'm feeling weary also."

"Go," Phillipa encouraged her. "Sleep well, Catie. We'll speak more on the morrow about this if you wish."

Catherine simply nodded and turned for her chamber. When she was inside with the door safely shut, Christelle turned to Phillipa and gave her an expression that suggested she was shocked by the entire situation.

"He has *bedded* her?" she said. "My God, if Leo finds out, he'll kill Talan."

They were still out on the landing. Phillipa shushed her, pulling her toward the connecting chambers they shared. "He'll not know by our tongues," she whispered, entering their chamber with Christelle behind her and quietly closing the door. "We will not say a word. Swear this to me."

Christelle nodded. "Of course I will not tell him," she said. "I would not be the one to divulge that kind of information. It is not my right."

Phillipa nodded. "Nor mine," she said. "But Catherine should know that she is playing with fire. Talan, at the very least, should know. He is a good deal older than Catie is."

Christelle shrugged. "She is a lovely girl," she said. "Talan is handsome and strong. Being attracted to one another is not a crime, but bedding her… It is a very risky thing to do."

"Especially with Leo," Phillipa said. "I shudder to think what that man would do if he were truly angry because Talan has bedded Catherine. He is already feeling sad and despondent about Georgiana, so I fear he would take it out on Talan if he knew Catherine had been compromised."

Christelle didn't reply immediately. She let that fact settle between them, a weighty bit of knowledge that seemed to fill the very air around them. Phillipa wandered over to the wardrobe where her collection of borrowed garments were hanging on pegs or neatly folded. She began to prepare for bed, and Christelle went to the stairwell and called down to the servants who were sweeping down in the entry, summoning a maid to help Phillipa. Once that was in motion, she went back into the chamber and shut the door.

"I would be remiss if I did not mention something else to you, your grace," she said softly.

Phillipa looked up from removing a necklace she had been wearing. "What is it?"

Christelle was hesitant. "Before the maid arrives," she said. "This has been a most eventful day and I do not want to throw one more log on the fire, but something has come up that you should be aware of."

Phillipa looked at her curiously. "What is it?"

"Leo has asked to court me."

Phillipa's mouth popped open in surprise. But a grin spread over her lips and she stood up, putting both hands on Christelle's face, cupping it.

"Is this true?" she said excitedly. "He wants to marry you?"

Christelle couldn't keep the smile off her face. "So he says."

Phillipa laughed happily. "Oh, Christy!" she said. "That is wonderful news! What did you say?"

"That I would let him."

"Good!" Phillipa said with glee. "What about your father? Will you write and tell him?"

Christelle tried not to let the mention of her father dampen her joy. "Eventually," she said. "For now, Leo and I are simply going to enjoy the opportunity to know one another better. Truthfully, stitching that red cross on his forehead was mayhap the best thing I ever did. He must have thought I was flirting with him."

Phillipa continued to chuckle. "Were you?"

"Not at the time."

Phillipa dropped her hands from Christelle's face. "I am certain that has changed by now," she said, eyes twinkling. "Truly, this is the very best news. Thank you for sharing it with me."

"You are welcome," Christelle said. "I do not have any sisters or mother to share the news with, so thank you for allowing me the privilege."

Phillipa sat back down. "I have three sisters," she said. "I love them all, but I've not seen them in some time. You are the closest thing I have to a sister here in England, and I cherish that. I cherish *you*, Christelle. I hope we are always as close as we are at this moment."

You wouldn't if you knew why I was really here.

The thought ran through Christelle's head. She'd been questioning her purpose for some time now, but hearing that Phillipa viewed her as a sister caused a landslide of doubt. She'd come to spy, but the truth was that she'd bonded with those she was supposed to spy on. She wasn't hard pressed to admit that she loved Phillipa. She even loved Catherine and Gabriel, and she had nothing but affection for the knights she was surrounded with.

Leonidas most of all.

Phillipa asked her if she was going to send word to her father about Leonidas. She was, but that missive would also contain the news that she no longer wished to be part of his plans. She would marry Leonidas and be a good wife to him because here, at Ashendon, was the life she wanted. Married to a man who adored and respected her. A countess to rule benevolently over her vassals.

Children.

Perhaps even love.

Aye, this was the life she wanted for herself.

She couldn't think of anything better.

"I am honored, your grace," she said softly. "It means more than you know. I have never truly belonged anywhere, with anyone. You have given me a home."

Phillipa reached out to grasp her hand. "Leo will serve Edward always," she said. "After you are married, you can—"

She was cut off when someone knocked at the door, and Christelle went to open it. A maid scurried in, the same one who had tended the children and Catherine and even Lady Maria. She was an older woman with red hair, bald patches in places, but she was clean and efficient. She rushed straight to Phillipa, but her movements were sharp and hasty.

"Forgive me, your grace," she said. "All of Ashendon is in an uproar!"

"Why?" Phillipa asked. "What has happened?"

The old servant threw up her hands. "Something terrible!" she gasped. "Lady Maria has escaped!"

A dark evening was about to get darker.

CHAPTER FIFTEEN

ALL OF ASHENDON seemed to be in an uproar, just like the
servant had said.

After rousing Catherine and Gabriel, Christelle carried the
sleeping little boy into Phillipa's chamber and put him to bed
with the queen. Catherine took Christelle's bed in the small
alcove. With Lady Maria on the loose, her whereabouts
unknown, Christelle had made the decision to put the children
to bed with Phillipa for their own safety.

Phillipa was more than happy to have them.

With the children secure behind a bolted door, Christelle
proceeded to clear the keep of any servants, searching every
crevice and every chamber, before putting a soldier inside and
having him bolt the entry door and protect it with his life. She
then went outside to see if she could help in the search, but it
seemed to be systematically organized. Torches were lit and
men were moving everywhere she looked. A group had even
gone into Hull to search for the woman there, but with no
results. Christelle was told that Lady Maria had killed the two
women who had bought her a meal and stolen the clothing off
one of them, which was why she had been able to slip out

unnoticed.

All of the knights were wrapped up leading search parties, so Christelle made her way to the wall to watch the activity and help if she could. So far, everything seemed to be under control, so she simply watched and waited.

The night deepened.

At one point, Talan returned leading a search party. After what Catherine had told her and Phillipa, Christelle found herself looking at Talan through new eyes. He had the dark de Wolfe good looks and was certainly a sharp and accomplished knight, but the truth was that he was young as far as knights went. Because he was a de Wolfe, however, he had skill and breeding, so it was easy to overlook his age—but the reality was that he was still quite young.

Catherine, of course, didn't realize that because she was even younger than he was. To her, he was a man, and men and women married when they loved one another. And he loved her. She could hardly see beyond her own wants, and that was evident. The truth was that Talan was older than Christelle was, but she had the maturity of somebody twice her age. There were times when she even *felt* twice her age. That was what a difficult life and a demanding father had done to her. But she was a young woman in her prime and now, with Leonidas' interest, she felt as if his declaration had somehow given her existence more value. More importance.

A future to look forward to.

Oh, she knew exactly how her father was going to take the news that she no longer wished to spy on the queen. The more she thought about it, the more she knew there was going to be trouble. Bernard would not take the news lying down, and she was starting to regret telling him that the queen had been moved to Ashendon Castle. He knew where she was, so even if she told him she no longer wished to spy, he could very well come to Hull looking for her.

That meant she was going to have to throw the man off her scent.

The solution, of course, was to send her father another missive saying that they had been moved elsewhere. She'd pick a castle in Wales or even Scotland, somewhere far away that would send her father on a wild goose chase should he decide to pursue her. But the truth remained that, at some point, she was going to have to tell Leonidas her true purpose in coming to England. She didn't want to tell him now because their interest in each other was so fresh and new that she didn't want to damage it. If the truth of her purpose had come out at some point earlier in their association, all she risked was exile. But if it happened now, she risked something worse.

Heartache.

Perhaps when she and Leonidas built more trust between one another and their feelings deepened, the information wouldn't be so bad. But for now, she wasn't going to tell him.

She wasn't going to tell anybody.

As the search for Lady Maria continued into the night, Christelle remained on the wall. She saw clearly when Dayne and his search party returned, and then when Zander and his party returned. Leonidas and Kenneth returned toward midnight, having taken an enormous contingent into the town of Hull to search every inch for the murderous nurse. But it was clear that they'd had no luck and the search was called off for the night.

Christelle went down to the bailey to greet him.

"I heard what happened," she said as she approached.

"From what we knew, Lady Mary was a power-hungry thief, but murder didn't seem to be in her purview. No luck finding her?"

Leonidas had just dismounted, sending his horse off with a stable servant as Christelle came near. "Nay," he said, removing his helm and scratching his dark head. "We searched businesses and homes, but no one has seen her. And they know her in town, so they would recognize her on sight. My suspicion is that she managed to buy or barter passage on one of the many ships coming in and out of the mouth of the river. She is probably halfway to London by now."

Christelle listened intently. "And the entire castle was searched?"

"From top to bottom," he said. "We did that first. There is no place she could have been hiding that we would not have found, so I am confident she is not here."

Christelle trusted his word. "I put Catie and Gabriel to bed with Phillipa just to be safe," she said. "I searched the keep myself and have a soldier stationed inside behind the locked entry door."

"Good," Leonidas said. Then he eyed her a moment, with appreciation. "Walk with me. I want to get out of my mail."

Christelle did. As Zander and Dayne and Talan disbanded the search parties and Kenneth went to the gatehouse, Leonidas and Christelle headed toward the eastern side of the bailey where the troop house was. There were also a series of small, one-room cottages built, hardly big enough for a bed and some gear, but they were intended for the knights. Leonidas, even though he was the Earl of Hull and Ashendon was his castle, chose not to stay in the keep because the queen was in residence, instead residing in the largest cottage next to the troop house, and that was where they were heading.

"It seems that you've had two big searches today," Christelle said to make conversation. "First Gabriel, then Lady Maria. You must be exhausted."

He grunted. "That would be a fair assessment," he said. "How is Gabriel faring, by the way?"

"Quite well," Christelle said. "Once you moved Georgiana out of the chamber, he settled right in."

"And Catie?"

"She feels guilty that we were all focused on her grief and not Gabriel's."

He glanced at her. "She will come to terms with it," he said. "I hope. Though I've never had any luck deciphering females. You will have to help me."

"I will if I can."

He flashed her a grin and she responded in kind. It was a new day between them, a new moment, and the newness of it wasn't lost on either of them. How many times had they walked together or served together, with nothing more than professional intentions? But this was different.

Very different.

With smiles on their faces, mostly looking giddy and foolish, Christelle and Leonidas ended up over at Leonidas' cottage. Opening the door, he slung his weapons onto the bed and turned to Christelle, holding his arms up.

"Help me out of this, please."

It was a surprising request, but she didn't hesitate. The belts and scabbard came off, as did the tunic. He bent over and she deftly pulled off his mail coat, which weighed quite a bit. It also clung to him because he was sweaty, so she had to give it a few good pulls to get it off, grunting all the way, until it slipped off into her grip.

"Who usually helps you undress?" she asked, handing him the mail so he could put it on a frame. "Surely you do not do this all alone."

He was down to his padded tunic and boots. "Not usually," he said. "I've never had a squire, but there are plenty of soldiers to help. Will you do something for me?"

"Surely."

"Send for hot water, please."

Christelle did. She stepped outside the cottage, which had the door open the entire time, and summoned a nearby servant. As the man went running, Leonidas managed to strip off his padded tunic and the thin linen tunic underneath. Those went on the frame along with the mail, so by the time Christelle stepped back into the cottage, she was faced with a half-naked man who was pulling off his boots.

She froze in the doorway.

"Wh-what are you doing?" she stammered.

He had no idea what she meant. He paused and looked around, confused, before answering. "Removing my boots," he said. "Why? What do you think I am doing?"

She pointed at him. "I turn my back for a moment and you are nearly nude."

He looked down at himself and shrieked. "My God," he gasped, pulling the nearest blanket over his bare chest. "I am! I'll not be your feast for the eyes, you brazen woman."

Christelle's moment of shock was replaced by laughter. She laughed until she wept, until the servant returned with the hot water and Leonidas had his boots off. Unfortunately for him, his feet smelled horrible, and that made Christelle laugh harder. Leonidas stripped down to a pair of linen breeches and that was all, but she hardly noticed. She stayed in the open doorway as he washed his face and hands and feet and chest, everything that wasn't covered with cloth. He had soap that smelled heavily of pine and even had bits of pine in it, so when he scrubbed, that scent filled the entire cottage.

But Christelle still stood back by the open door.

"Feeling better?" she asked.

He was washing his right foot. "Much," he said. "Contrary to what you might think, I do not enjoy my own smell when I've been sweating. I confess that I do bathe when I'm able."

She dared to come away from the door, wandering inside. "That's a woman's privilege."

"Then I'm a woman."

"You are definitely *not* a woman."

He looked up from his foot, grinning. "You noticed, did you?" he said. "Good. If I want to court you, then there should be something about me you find attractive."

"I do," she assured him. "Why do you find that surprising?"

He lifted an eyebrow at her before returning to his foot. "*Le Morsure.*"

She'd heard that before, long ago. "The Bite," she said, smiling. "I heard that about you when you first came to Woodstock. Then I saw you with your helm on, and how it frames your mouth, and I understood. Most helms are not designed like that."

He shrugged. "Most men do not have teeth like I do," he said. "When I realized I could make myself look like a wolf, which suits the name, I had the helm designed. *Le Morsure* was a moniker my trainers gave me as a squire. Even as a lad, they said a strike from my sword was as sharp as a bite. That was something that made my father very proud."

"Edward?"

He nodded, finished with his foot and rinsing it off. "My father is the son of the greatest knight in the north," he said. "He could fight well enough, but he had five brothers who lived and breathed battle. He was the diplomat of the group and I think he always felt different because of it. I am his fifth child, but firstborn son, so when I was born, you can imagine how thrilled he was. And when I became a knight to take my place among the best de Wolfe knights in the family, I think he felt somewhat vindicated. That he could father so great a knight."

"So your teeth had nothing to do with *Le Morsure?*"

He grinned. "Of course they did," he said. "My maternal grandfather had a smile similar to mine, only my canine teeth are a bit more prominent."

"Like fangs."

"Exactly."

"I think you have a lovely smile."

He laughed softly. "It has never been called that before, but I thank you."

"You are welcome."

"Close the door."

"Why?"

"Because I want to kiss you and I don't want it to be a spectacle."

Christelle fought off a grin, looking at the open door as if debating his request. "You do realize that people will talk if they realize I am in here with you and the door is shut."

"Am I allowed to tell men that we are courting?"

"Why should you want to?"

He frowned. "So no one else will try to court you, foolish woman. Why else?"

She was terribly flattered. "No one has ever said that to me."

He huffed. "Well and good," he said. "I hope they never do. I hope I am the only one who ever says it."

"I am certain you will be," she said. "You are rare in my world, Leo."

"Why is that?"

"Because you look beyond the warrior," she said. "Every man I've ever met has only looked at my skill and training. I'm not sure anyone has ever looked at me."

"As a woman."

"Aye."

Leonidas put both feet on the floor and stood up. He was more than a head taller than her, a very big man who now smelled of pine. He approached her, drawing close, and came to a halt when he was just a few inches from her. For a moment, they simply stared at one another in a deeply intimate moment. His bare chest was right in front of her face and Christelle's cheeks were so hot that she was certain she was about to burst into flame. No man in her life had ever provoked such a reaction, and it was both wonderful and intimidating. She knew she wanted something from him but wasn't sure what. That kiss he asked for? A simple touch? A kind word? Her body was yearning for something she couldn't put her finger on.

All she knew was that she needed it.

"I see you," he whispered, sending chills up her spine. "I see the woman and she is exquisite. Mayhap she could brush her hair once in a while or bathe with my pine soap. If she did that, she would be the most magnificent woman in all of England, but the truth is that it does not matter to me. I will take you as you are, Christelle de Lorrain, with your wild hair and dirty face. I will take you with your breeches and tunics, or borrowed dresses. I will take you with your stubborn nature and red crosses stitched into my forehead. Even if you do not want to take me right now, I will wait for you because I've been married once. I know what it is to feel for the woman you have married. You make me feel as I did for Juliette, only stronger somehow. There is a pull from you to me that I cannot deny. So, aye… If you do not want me now, I will still wait for you. I will always wait for you, as long as it takes and for as much as it is worth. Because you are worth everything."

The last words out of his mouth were like an aphrodisiac to Christelle. She'd never felt anything like it. His words made her want to embrace his naked flesh and kiss it, and embrace and kiss it she did. She wrapped her arms around his waist and kissed him right on the chest, on the flesh that was directly in front of her, and she heard Leonidas groan low in his throat. So she kissed him again and again, kissing his chest and the soft matting of hair across it, kissing it as her fingers dug into his back. She kissed his powerful breast, even kissing his left nipple, and suddenly, his hands were in her hair and he was pulling her head back. His mouth descended on hers and she was trapped.

Their kiss was powerful and passionate. His tongue licked at her lips, inviting them to open for him, and she did. It was her turn to gasp as his tongue licked her teeth and his lips suckled her own tongue. He kissed her so hard that he nearly drained the life right out of her, and probably would have had she not pulled away so she could take a breath. But he didn't stop his onslaught.

He simply moved to other parts of her body.

Christelle was aware of his lips on her shoulder, his arms tightening around her, but she didn't care. She was lightheaded, feeling each new sensation as if they were bolts of lightning. Every move caused her to tremble. When his big hands moved down her back and gently grasped her buttocks, both of them, she flinched.

Leonidas held her fast, his mouth coming up from her shoulder. "I am sorry," he murmured. "Did I hurt you?"

She shook her head quickly. "You did not," she said, meeting his lusty gaze. "But this… this is all new to me."

"If you do not want me to touch you further, I will not."

Her eyes glimmered. "I think you should," she said. "No one else has. I think I'd like to know what I have been missing."

He chuckled softly. "You are ever-fearless," he said. "But I do not want to make you uncomfortable."

"I will not know until you do it."

"Then let me show you," he said softly. "If you decide you do not like it, then I will never do it again."

Christelle nodded. It sounded fair enough. On this night, she was wearing one of the garments loaned to her by Catherine, the simple broadcloth she'd been wearing since her arrival. The garment was laced between her breasts, which she filled out better than Catherine did, so there was some strain to the material. Leonidas began to carefully unlace the bindings. One by one, the holes were unlaced until the string was cast aside. The shift was now nearly open to her navel. As the noise from the bailey infiltrated the closed door and small, coverless windows high in the chamber for ventilation, Leonidas very gently pulled her shift off her shoulders, exposing her tender, pale skin. He watched the top of her breasts become more exposed until the edge of the fabric was just above her nipples. But he would go no further.

"May I?" he whispered.

Christelle was breathing so unsteadily that she was certain she was going to faint. It was an overwhelming experience but an extremely intimate one. She probably should have stopped him but it didn't occur to her to do it. She was as curious as he was, and her body was on fire for reasons she did not understand. All she knew was that Leonidas had sparked the blaze. When he asked the question, she swallowed hard.

"May you… what?" she managed to ask.

He smiled. "I am asking permission to show you."

"Show me what?"

Her naïve question had him laughing softly. "Must I tell you?" he said. "Can it be a surprise? I promise it will not hurt. If you do not like it, I will stop."

She considered his proposal. "You are aware that we should not be doing this at all," she said. "The only time I have ever been kissed by a man was by you. And now, here we are, alone in your cottage as you unlace my bodice."

"Do you not like what we are doing?"

She nodded, her cheeks growing hot as she lowered her head. "I do," she said. "Leo, I have spent my entire life alone. Because of my father's insistence that I train like the son he never had, I have always been misplaced wherever I've been. Phillipa was the first person who accepted me for who I am. She has never made me feel odd."

"Have I?"

Christelle shrugged. "Not really," she said. "But you have never treated me like a colleague, either."

"You are not."

Her brow furrowed. "I am a warrior, like you."

He shook his head. "But you are not a knight," he said. "You may have trained as much as a woman could train, but you are not a knight."

"That does not make me inferior."

"Have you ever fought in a battle?"

She sighed sharply. "Nay, I have not."

"And you still think you are my equal?"

"Why on earth would you want to court a woman you consider inferior to you?"

"That was your word, not mine."

Frustrated, she began pulling up her bodice. "My whole point in telling you all of this was to say that I have always felt misplaced," she said with some anger. "I was going to tell you that you have made me feel accepted, and wanted, but now the truth comes out. I am not a comrade. I am not a knight. I am nothing."

He watched her jerky movements. "You are not a colleague and you are not my equal," he said. "I can out-fight you and outthink you. I am stronger than you are. I can easily overwhelm you. But you are, without a doubt, the bravest, strongest, and loveliest woman I have ever had the good fortune to meet. We are not equals, Christelle. But we are quite alike, you and I. I do not think there is another soul in all the world that I respect and admire more than you."

That brought her pause. One side of her bodice was up, but the other was still hanging down around her arm.

"You have a strange way of complimenting me," she said.

He shrugged. "It is not a compliment," he said. "It is truth. I will never lie to you and I suspect you will never lie to me, either. I've always thought you to be a woman of honor. Am I wrong?"

Christelle felt as if she'd been kicked in the gut. Was he wrong? Of course he was wrong. She'd been lying to him since the day she met him. She'd been lying to all of them. But gazing into his blue eyes, she just couldn't tell him that. She knew that if she admitted it, he'd never speak to her again. To a man like Leonidas, honor was everything.

And she had none of it.

Withholding her true self hadn't been an issue before he declared his desire to court her. Certainly, she'd thought about it, but more in the context of keeping it from those around her and doing what she'd been sent to do. But that all changed the moment Leonidas declared his interests. Now, it was front and center. Perhaps she should throw caution to the wind and simply experience this moment with him. She hadn't planned on letting it go any further than the kiss he requested, but here she was with her bodice down around her shoulders. He wanted more of her and she was letting him take it without a fight.

Truth be told, she wanted to experience the magic she never thought she'd know.

"Very well," she said quietly, peeling down the side of her bodice that she'd just put back in place. "You wanted to show me something?"

He smiled faintly, realizing they were past whatever conflict might have popped up. He hadn't really meant it to, so he was glad to see that she didn't want it to either. Now, the tops of those lovely breasts were calling to him and he took her in his arms, lowering his head and tenderly kissing the swell of her bosoms.

They tasted as good as they looked.

But he could only take so much. Chaste kisses and tantalizing visions were going to be the death of him. He gave a little pull and the right side of the shift pulled away, exposing her right breast.

Christelle gasped and weakly tried to cover up again, but he put his hand up to stop her. She didn't fight him on it in the least. He gently suckled the flesh surrounding the nipple but made no move to do more. At least, not at the moment. He continued to kiss, very tenderly, and brought a hand up to very gently cup her breast. Then Christelle felt something warm, wet, and firm against her nipple.

He suckled hard.

Christelle couldn't help the moan that escaped her lips. Leonidas pulled her against him once more, tightly, suckling her furiously. Christelle cried out at the pleasure of it, her arms going around his head as he feasted. The tighter she held his head, the harder he suckled. They were engulfing each other.

It was like a firestorm.

For as gentle as he had initially been, Leonidas quickly deteriorated into lusty oblivion. He'd never had anything so sweet. He pulled the shift off her and laid her upon his bed, his big hands and searing mouth doing things to her that made Christelle feel faint. She was gasping for every breath as his mouth moved between her breasts, licking and suckling furiously. His hands were on her thighs, moving to cup her silky-skinned bottom with both hands as his passion overwhelmed him. She was soft and warm, and he was out of control.

Leonidas forgot himself as his mouth moved down her torso. He kissed and suckled every inch of it, listening to her gasp with pleasure. He vaguely remembered removing his breeches, and suddenly, they were naked together on his bed. Christelle grunted when his weight came down on her, instinctively parting her legs so that his weight slipped onto the mattress below them. Leonidas felt her legs part for him and the world seemed to stop for a brief and powerful moment. He knew what he was about to do. Perhaps he should stop himself, but he couldn't. All he could think of was Christelle and her beautiful body. But it was more than her body—it was her mind, her spirit, and that damned stubbornness. There wasn't anything about her that he didn't find perfect, and the strength of his feelings was never more evident than it was at this moment.

He was in love with her.

He'd known that for a while, but he'd been denying it. Somehow, it seemed disloyal to Juliette's memory even though he knew that was foolish. He'd loved his wife. Now, he had the opportunity to love again, but in a different, more powerful way. Juliette had been all soft and tender moments, pleasing and kind.

Christelle was like the fire of lightning.

He wanted to get burned.

Pulling her against him, he fused his lips to hers, thrusting into her hot and yielding body gently, swallowing her gasps of surprise with his delicious kisses. He withdrew and thrust again, pushing further into her and feeling her tense beneath him. He kept his kisses warm and passionate, hoping to relax her as his hands caressed her back and buttocks. Then he withdrew a third time and thrust once more, sliding into her wet folds with a great deal of ease. Seated to the hilt, he savored the moment.

The feel of her fed him like nothing he had ever experienced.

He withdrew fully and thrust again and could hear Christelle gasping, but she was no longer tense. She seemed to be relaxing against him, becoming acquainted with a man's body for the first time and discovering that she liked it. His hands caressed her torso, her breast, as he thrust again and again, carefully at first but increasing in power and passion.

More thrusts, more friction, and Christelle was moving with him, groaning softly with delight. Her legs wrapped around his hips and he held her buttocks tightly, his pelvis against hers, as he powerfully thrust into her.

Leonidas was consumed with the feel and smell of Christelle. He could see her nude outline in the weak light, the flare of her hips and the rise of her breasts. He thrust into her, feeling himself approaching his climax but not wanting to see the moment end. It was an incredibly powerful and important moment for him, coupling with this woman who had quickly come to mean a great deal to him. He thrust one final time, hard and long, acutely aware when her slick walls began to tighten around him. He held her tightly as she experienced her first release, listening to her gasp with surprise and joy, before taking his own.

But their passion did not die completely. There were sparks long after the explosions had settled. Leonidas continued to move within her long after their powerful climax, still wanting to be a part of the woman. She'd been so surprising in so many ways and, truthfully, he still found it difficult to comprehend that they were together. That he had admitted his feelings and she had returned them.

He felt like the most fortunate man in the world.

When the gasping and groaning finally died away, Christelle fell into an exhausted sleep in his embrace and he succumbed shortly thereafter.

They slept like that all night, the best night's sleep either one of them had ever had.

CHAPTER SIXTEEN

"CATHERINE?"

Startled by the sound of her name, and recognizing the voice, Catherine stood up swiftly from where she'd been leaning over the chicken coops in the kitchen yard. But she whacked her head, yelping as she put her hand on what was surely going to be a lump as she turned to Talan, who had come up behind her. He winced at the sound of her skull hitting the wood.

"Did you hurt yourself?" he asked, coming closer.

She shook her head. "I do not think so."

He pulled her hand away. "Let me see."

She flinched as he ran a finger over the top of her head, already feeling a bit of a bump. "You should put a cold compress on it," he said. "But it does not look terribly bad."

Catherine's hand lingered on her head for a moment longer before she tried to shake it off. "I can hardly feel it," she said. "Did you want something? Or did you come here simply to startle me?"

His gaze lingered on her for a moment. He already sensed this was going to be a testy conversation based on her mood. "I wanted to tell you that I am very glad Gabriel was found," he said. "But I am surprised he went off to find those chickens. I completely forgot about them, too, until Leo told me where he'd been found."

Catherine nodded. "I do not know why it didn't occur to me earlier, but I'm thankful to have remembered," she said. "And I am thankful that he did not go back to the river. That was my fear."

"I know," he said softly. "I am so sorry about Georgiana, Catie. I've not had the chance to tell you that yet. I cannot tell you how much my heart aches for you."

Catherine averted her gaze. There were so many raw emotions she was dealing with, not the least of which were what she considered a rejection from Talan and her little sister's death. Still. Those things had been foremost in her mind for days. So much horrendous emotion that she was having difficulty dealing with.

"I came out here because Georgiana's pet chicken seems to have wandered away," she said, avoiding commenting on his sympathies. "I thought it might have ended up in the coop with the other chickens."

Talan looked over her shoulder at the wooden coop. "It's not in there?"

"Nay," Catherine said. "But it must be around here somewhere. It does not stray far."

"I will help you look for it."

"That is not necessary," Catherine said. "I'm sure you have duties to attend to. It is beneath you to hunt for a chicken."

She was being difficult. She'd had a very hard few days, so he knew her mood was brittle. He felt very sorry for her. He wished he could make it better.

"Catie," he murmured.

"What is it?" she asked, not looking at him.

"I love you."

She laughed bitterly. "Not enough to marry me," she said. "I wonder how much you actually do love me if it is not enough to marry me?"

He didn't want to argue with her. "It was not my intention to make things worse for you by extending my sympathies," he said. "I am sorry to have troubled you."

She looked at him then. "Is that so?" she said. "Talan, you cannot pick and choose the moments you wish to be kind to me. You are either kind all of the time or not at all. And it is horrible for you to tell me that you love me. You are trying to manipulate my feelings."

He rolled his eyes. "I am doing nothing of the kind," he said. "I thought it would make you feel not so alone."

"I *am* alone," she said. "The man I love does not love me enough to marry me."

"I am sorry you feel that way," he said.

He didn't say any more, which only seemed to infuriate her. "And that is all you have to say?"

"I do not know what more you want me to say."

"Aye, you do," she said. "I want you to say that you will speak with Leonidas and ask permission to marry me. I know you have reservations, but they are not my reservations. Why can you not see that I am simply a woman who loves you, no matter your financial situation? No matter if you do not have titles or riches? If anyone marries you for your wealth, then they are not worth having."

He was quickly growing weary of the conversation. "You are correct," he said. "I would never marry a woman because she wanted my wealth."

"And I do not."

"But *I* want to be able to support my wife comfortably," he said through clenched teeth. "If you do not understand that, then we are an impasse because I will not ask Leo for your hand. The more you push me on this, the less willing I am to talk to him."

Catherine looked at him as if she'd been struck. Tears were welling, but she fought them. "Then you do not love me as you say you do," she said hoarsely. "You have lied to me."

His head snapped to her, and he fought off the fury that was threatening to erupt. "You will not call me a liar again," he growled. "As for the rest of it, I can only say that I came here to try to give you some comfort, but I can see that you do not need any. If you think that I do not love you, that is your prerogative. If you do not wish to have anything more to do with me, that is also your choice. You will not have to worry over me any longer, and you can find another fool to marry you on command. Best of luck to you."

With that, he turned on his heel and started to march away from her. The next thing he realized, an egg hit him on the arm. He paused, lifting his right arm to see shell and yolk dripping off it. Increasingly irritated, he continued walking away—and another egg hit him on the bottom. Frustrated, he wiped it off the back of his breeches as he turned to Catherine.

"Behave like a child and I will treat you like one," he said. "Children do not get married."

Frowning, Catherine marched up to him. "Then let us be plain," she said. "In your eyes, I am old enough to love, old enough to bed, but not good enough to marry?"

He sighed heavily. "I will not discuss this with you again."

"You *will* speak to Leonidas. Please, Talan."

"I am not going to speak to him."

"Then I will tell him you bedded me and you will be forced to marry me."

He looked at her, incredulous. He took a few steps back in her direction, closing the gap between them so their conversation wouldn't be overheard. "Is that how you want to gain a husband?" he said. "By forcing me into marriage?"

"If that is my only choice, then I will take it. I will do what I must."

He couldn't believe what he was hearing. "If you do that, you will marry a man who will resent you," he said. "Is that what you want? My animosity forever? Because I will not be threatened, Catherine. If you feel that you must tell Leo, then tell him. But I will deny it and it will be your word against mine. More than that, I will return to Wales and you will never see me again."

She was deeply insulted. "You would dare deny our relationship?"

He leaned into her so she could hear him clearly. "By your threats, you are proving to me just how immature you are," he muttered. "How dare you threaten me like that. You do not love me. You only want to be married and you do not care how you obtain a husband, only that you do. Had I known this side of you a year ago, I would have never engaged with you. You are making me regret everything."

With that, he marched away from her, heading out of the yard. Catherine watched him go, infuriated and insulted until those emotions turned into genuine hurt. Not that she didn't deserve everything he said, but it was still difficult to hear.

In tears, she turned back for the chicken coop.

CHAPTER SEVENTEEN

Hull

One week later

H ULL WAS A surprisingly vital sea town.

On a bright day with scattered clouds across the sky, the cog from Calais arrived just as the fishing boats also came in with their morning haul. Fishmongers were down on the riverbanks, calling to the fishermen, and the cog from Calais docked with hardly any notice because of it. That meant Bernard, Gautier, and Gautier's knight, a man who went only by the name of Mort, disembarked the ship and no one cared why they'd come. No one questioned them. They were able to go straight to the wharf where a line of taverns and businesses sat, and they selected a tavern at the end of the row called The Flying Fish.

It was a larger establishment with a second floor, which were rooms for let, and the first thing Bernard did was make an arrangement with the tavernkeep. He would rent two rooms, meals included, and Gautier would allow Mort to guard the common room and keep out the rabble. Mort didn't have much say in the matter, but then again, he was a monster of a man who spoke little and had a broken moral compass. He didn't much care. Gautier kept him around because he would do anything on command, including kill, hence his name—Le Mort.

Death.

The chambers that Bernard had secured were on the street level, overlooking the river and the boats coming in, so it was a prime location. Bernard took one chamber and Gautier took the other, and as Bernard was removing his writing kit from his baggage, Gautier wandered into his chamber.

"Your room is bigger," he said, looking around. "Mine is not so grand."

Bernard could hear the jealousy in the man's voice, something that was prominent when he didn't think he was getting his due. "You can have this one if you wish," he said, carefully unpacking his kit. "Mort can sleep in here with you. It is large enough."

Gautier snorted. "The man does not sleep," he said. "Speaking of sleep, did you see the castle on the rise? A nice, calm castle."

Bernard nodded. "I am preparing to send a message to the castle now," he said. "I am certain we can find a runner here at the tavern. Men to deliver the missive for a coin."

Gautier went over to the window, leaning against the sill and watching the activity below. "Now that we are here, we should make firm our plans," he said. "We brought Mort for a reason, and that reason is to subdue the queen so we can take her with us back to Chambrey. Should we have Christelle bring her here? There would be far less chance of failure."

Bernard shook his head. "I doubt they will let Phillipa out of the castle," he said. "Even if they do permit her to come out, she will be heavily guarded. What we do, we must do with stealth. That is the only way this will work."

"Then what do we do?"

Bernard looked at the writing kit before him, the vellum, the cheap ink. He fingered the yellowed sheets thoughtfully. "I will send my daughter word of our arrival," he said. "I will suggest she come and greet her father and bring a guest with her. Christelle will know who I mean. Our only chance, and we will only have one, is for Christelle to bring Phillipa with her. It must be under a pretext—mayhap shopping or something else. Christelle will have to think of something. Once she has Phillipa free of the castle and free of her guard, she becomes ours."

Gautier pondered that. "Do we even know whom the castle belongs to?" he said. "Mayhap I should go to the common room and see what I can discover. Or ask Mort to keep his ears open. Mayhap he can learn something about the castle and who is guarding the queen, other than your daughter. Christelle does not work alone."

"I know," Bernard said. "I know that both Edward and Phillipa have been shadowed by elite knights, but Christelle never mentioned who. It wasn't pertinent to our conversations but now I am wishing she had. If she—"

A knock on the door interrupted them, and Gautier went to the panel, opening it. A thin woman with badly cut red hair and her short, round counterpart stood in the doorway, a tray of steaming bowls in their hands.

"Your meal, my lord?" the red-head said.

Gautier stood back and ushered her in. The women went straight to the table and set down the heavy trays. They began removing the bowls, the bread, the utensils and the like. They were moving quickly and efficiently and Bernard wasn't much interested in them until a thought occurred to him. He turned his attention to the pair, eyeing them, as Gautier stood back by the door.

"Have both of you lived in this town all of your life?" Bernard asked.

The women didn't respond right away because they were unaware they were being addressed. The rounder one finally figured it out and elbowed the woman with the wild hair, who focused on Bernard when she realized he was speaking to her.

"Nay, my lord," she said in a voice that was strangely refined. "I have only worked in this town, but Aldis was born here."

Aldis nodded fearfully in support of the statement but didn't speak. Bernard fixed on the woman who had answered his question.

"It is a big town," he said. "When is market day?"

"The day after Sunday, my lord," the woman answered. "It is mostly a fish market, but others come to sell their wares."

Bernard nodded to the information. "I see," he said. "And the castle? Who is the lord?"

"The Earl of Hull, my lord," the woman said without hesitation. "Leonidas de Wolfe is his name. An unfair and unscrupulous man, if you were thinking of doing business with him."

"Oh?" Bernard said with interest. "Why do you say that?"

The woman took both of the trays off the table and handed them to Aldis, who fled with them. When the round woman was gone, the red-haired servant focused on Bernard.

"It is best not to say things in front of her, my lord," she said quietly. "It would not do for my words to be repeated."

"Why not?" Bernard asked. "What about Lord Hull?"

The woman grew serious. "He steals from his servants," she said. "He hires people and does not pay them. He has been known to inflict cruel punishment on his children. He has three of them, though he inherited them through marriage. Simple children without much of a mind. The entire castle is… dark. Dark with his wickedness."

Bernard found that very interesting. "That is troublesome news," he said. "It is just him and his children living at the castle, then?"

The woman's gaze lingered on him for a moment. "You are quite curious about the castle, my lord," he said. "I could tell you more. For a price."

So much for the free information. Bernard glanced at Gautier, who nodded shortly. Bernard dug into his purse and tossed the woman a coin.

"There," he said. "What is your name?"

"You may call me Mary, my lord."

"And how do you know so much about Lord Hull?"

"I was one of the servants he stole from," she said. "He exiled me, took all of my money, and I have been forced to work so that I may build my purse and return home. However, I would caution you from telling him you spoke with me. My life would be in danger."

"Then you have a score to settle with the Earl of Hull."

Mary shrugged. "He is a powerful earl and has the ear of the king," she said. "I can do nothing against him. But I would like to get my money back."

"Tell me what I wish to know and I will help you replenish what you lost," Bernard said. "Do we have a bargain?"

Mary nodded. "Gladly, my lord," she said. "What do you

wish to know?"

Bernard looked at Gautier, who came away from the door and stood in front of the woman. "How many ways are there to get into the castle?" he asked.

"Two," Mary said. "The gatehouse and the postern gate near the kitchens. Both are heavily protected."

"Does the castle have an army?"

"It does, my lord. A large one."

"And does it ever open the gates to do business?"

"Every Monday," Mary said. "Farmers and fishmongers, mostly, though priests have been known to wander in and there is the occasional minstrel who stays the night and entertains during supper."

Gautier looked at Bernard, both thinking the same thing. *Minstrels.* But they shook their head at the same time because it would be a very bad idea, as neither one of them could sing or play an instrument. Also, they weren't farmers or fishmongers, so entering the castle on market day was out.

Still, they'd been told what they wanted to know. They knew that the Earl of Hull was in charge and the castle was fortified. That would have to be enough for now.

"You want to get into the castle, my lords?" Mary said, breaking into their train of thought. "Do you want to find a way in? I could possibly help you."

Neither Bernard nor Gautier were going to divulge why they'd asked so many questions, so Bernard dug in his purse for a few more coins and handed them to her.

"Thank you for the information, Mary," Bernard said. "You may go now."

Mary did, heading to the door. She paused by the door as if to say something more, but Gautier opened the panel for her and she was forced to take the hint. He shut the door behind her, holding out a hand to Bernard to keep him silent until they were sure the servant wasn't lingering by the door, listening. Several long seconds passed before Gautier spoke softly.

"We know there are two fortified access points and that the Earl of Hull has a large army," he said. "Bernard… why must we behave so covertly?"

Bernard looked at him curiously. "What do you mean?"

Gautier sat down on a small chair that was hardly large enough for a child, listening to it groan under his adult weight. "What is preventing you, as Christelle's father, from visiting your daughter?" he said. "No one other than Christelle knows of your true allegiance. It would not be considered unusual for a father to visit his own child, would it?"

"I suppose not."

"Then why can we not simply go to the castle and ask for Christelle?" Gautier asked. "Why send a missive if we can go ourselves?"

Bernard considered that. "We could," he said. "But what reason would we have for being in Hull?"

Gautier shrugged. "Is a visit to the daughter you've not seen in years not reason enough?"

As Bernard contemplated that very simple and not entirely outlandish plan, there was a knock at the door. It was so faint that they thought they'd not heard it correctly at first, but the knock came again. Curious, Gautier rose and went to the panel, opening it to find the round servant girl standing outside.

"Please, my lords," she said, her voice trembling. "I came to warn you."

Gautier frowned. "What about?"

The girl looked around nervously. "Not out here, my lord,"

she said. "May I come in?"

Gautier indicated for her to step into the chamber, and she did. The pale and quivering servant looked as if she'd seen a ghost. She focused on Bernard.

"I do not want any money for what I am about to tell you," she said. "But the servant you just spoke to is not who she seems to be. Be cautious."

That had their interest. "What do you mean?" Bernard said.

The girl was clearly terrified. "She has stolen from nearly everyone here, my lord," she said. "She stole from my mother, and when my mother confronted her, she stabbed her in the face. My mother has a big gash on her cheek now."

"She sounds dangerous," Bernard said. "She said her name was Mary and she used to work at the castle."

The girl nodded quickly. "She did," she said. "We all know her. She used to come here to sell meat from the castle to the tavernkeep. She stole from the earl, and when he came home, he discovered her treachery and put her in the vault. I heard her tell Morley that she had to kill in order to escape. When men from the castle came looking for her, she cut her hair off with a knife and used something from the apothecary to color it red. Morley did not tell the men from the castle that she was here because she has been warming his bed since she arrived."

It was intriguing news. "So you think she is giving us incorrect information?" he said. "That she is somehow trying to fool us?"

The girl shook her head. "Even now, she is leaving from the rear of the tavern," she said. "She is fleeing. What she does, she does for the love of money. What did you ask her?"

Bernard was concerned that the woman he'd just spoken to was evidently running off to parts unknown. Something told him that wasn't a good thing. "We asked her about the castle," he said. "Just a few questions."

"Do you intend to travel to the castle, my lord?"

"Possibly."

"And do what?"

"I did not tell her and I will not tell you."

The girl thought on that a moment. "If you were asking about the castle, mayhap she is going to warn them," she said. "If you did not tell her your purpose, then she can make up anything she likes."

Bernard stood up, looking at Gautier. "What better way to ingratiate herself to those she sinned against by telling them that there are men in the village who threaten the castle?" he said with some urgency. "Tell Mort to catch up to her. She must be silenced."

Gautier was already heading out of the chamber. As he left, Bernard turned to the serving girl.

"Ardis is your name?" he said.

"Aldis, my lord."

He nodded. "Aldis," he repeated correctly. "Thank you for telling me this."

Aldis nodded. "What she did to my mother was unforgiveable," she said. "I… I just want to see her punished."

"She will be," he said. "You will not see her again."

Aldis was visibly relieved. "I hope so, my lord," she said. "Thank you."

"But you must not tell anyone about this conversation," Bernard said. "Can you do this?"

"I will take it to my grave, my lord."

"If you do not, the grave will come sooner than you think," Bernard said for good measure. In spite of the woman saying she wanted no money, he dug into his purse and tried to give her a few coins. "Here. For your trouble."

But Aldis shook her head. "I did not do this for money, my lord," she insisted. "I did it to see the woman punished."

"Understood," he said. "What do *you* know about the castle?"

Aldis shrugged. "I know the de Cottingham family used to live there," she said. "The old earl was a kind man. He was well liked. When he died, his widow married a de Wolfe. But I have never been there, my lord, so I could not tell you about it."

Bernard simply absorbed the information and thanked her. He didn't want to press her for fear she might grow suspicious, too. He already knew what he needed to know, anyway. As Aldis left the chamber, Bernard went back to his writing kit. He still thought that sending his daughter a missive was the best course of action. He'd just sat down and picked up his quill when Gautier came back into the chamber and shut the door.

"Mort is following her trail," he said quietly. "He will not let her reach the castle alive."

Those were prophetic words. As Lady Maria ended up on the road leading to the castle, she was set upon just outside of town. For the woman who lived by her own rules, who cheated and lied and stole, who abused children with no repercussions, ended up with her throat slit in a ditch. A fitting end to life poorly lived.

A missive was heading to the castle within the hour.

CHAPTER EIGHTEEN

Ashendon

"YOU WANTED TO see me, your grace?"

Leonidas was standing in the doorway of the queen's chamber on a rather chilly but bright morning. The chamber was warm courtesy of a blazing fire and fragrant because the servants had brought in fresh rushes. Phillipa looked up from the needlepoint she was working on, smiling at Leonidas as she waved him in.

"I did," she said. "Thank you for coming."

"My pleasure, your grace."

"Do you know where Christelle is?"

He nodded. "With Gabriel and Catherine," he said. "They took some soldiers with them to the chicken woods, as Gabriel called them. He wanted to see the chicks again. Thankfully, this time he told us where he was going."

He was referring to the horrific day they'd spent hours searching for the young lad, waggling his eyebrows at the memory. The inference wasn't lost on Phillipa.

"Hopefully he has learned his lesson," she said. "But, more

importantly, we may speak without fear of Christelle hearing us."

Leonidas looked at her curiously. "There is something you do not want her to hear?" he said. "I am intrigued."

Phillipa motioned him to sit down, which he did. She turned her chair so that she was facing him. Her expression went from warm to serious in the blink of an eye.

"I understand that you have asked to court Christelle," she said.

Leonidas fought off a grin and averted his gaze. "Ah," he said. "That's what this is about. I realize that it may seem strange, considering Christelle and I have never really gotten on, but the situation has changed. Trust me when I tell you that my intentions are only honorable."

"Then you did ask to court her?"

"I did, your grace, a few days ago."

"And you are happy about this?"

He let his smile break through. "Delighted," he said. "You must understand that my marriage to Juliette was arranged by my father. I did not pick her. But Christelle… I picked. I am completely delighted with my selection, and she seems to be delighted, too."

Phillipa sighed faintly. Then she turned to the table next to her, upon which sat an open vellum envelope. She picked it up, looking at it as she spoke.

"I grew up in a family that was entrenched in politics," she said, her tone and manner subdued. "One of the things my father instilled in me is to never fully trust those around you. Even people you think are your friends."

"Wise words, your grace."

Phillipa indicated the vellum. "Christelle does not know

this, but I read every missive she sends to her father and every missive that comes for her," she said. "It is only prudent that I know about everything in and out of my household."

"Quite astute."

Phillipa looked up from the vellum. "Leo, there is no easy way to tell you this, but given you have asked to court Christelle, I feel that I must," she said. "Our dear girl is a spy."

The warm expression on his face quickly vanished. "A spy?" he repeated. "But… you cannot be serious."

"I'm afraid so."

"It's not possible."

"Sadly, it *is* possible," Phillipa said. "You know I would not tell you this unless I was absolutely certain."

Leonidas knew that. God help him, he did. But he was quickly falling into the realm of disbelief. "My God," he said. "What makes you think so?"

Phillipa smiled without humor. "Because every missive she sends her father has contained detailed reports on Edward and me," she said. "Our movements, our visitors, our conversations. Everything. She even sent word to her father before we left Woodstock that we would be traveling to Hull. This missive in my hand is from her father, who has arrived in Hull. He asks that she come to visit him and bring a guest, which I can only assume means me."

Leonidas was flabbergasted. "But why should it mean you?"

Phillipa could see the utter shock on his face and tried to be gentle. "You have not read all of the missives I have," she said. "The ones from her and then the ones from her father. I am always the subject. Her father is very interested in me. Therefore, it is my assumption that he means me."

That didn't seem to clear things up for him. "I do not understand any of this," he hissed. "*Why* should she be spying? And why does her father care?"

Phillipa handed him the vellum. "As I said," she said, "my father told me never to fully trust those close to me, so anyone who has been placed close to me or to Edward is fully examined. As much as they can be, in any case. Edward told me that Christelle's father, though his family is ruled by the Holy Roman Emperor, has ties to France. My husband has a claim to the French throne, of which he has been more vocal about as of late. Of course, that threatens the French. Christelle has been placed close to me to watch the royal couple, report on our movements, and now her father is in Hull and asking Christelle to bring me to him. Can you guess why?"

Leonidas was shocked. He stared at the vellum, reading through it and hardly willing to comprehend the implications. "If the French held you hostage, they could force Edward to surrender all rights to the throne."

"Exactly."

Leonidas stood up. He had to. It was rare when he was surprised about those he knew because, like Phillipa, he was careful with those close to him. But it never occurred to him that he should be guarding himself from Christelle. That stubborn, beautiful, tough woman had a secret. A terrible secret.

He could hardly believe it.

"And she has pretended to be fond of me to further inch her way into the royal circle," he finally said. Then he sighed heavily, as if all of the life had just been sucked out of him. "My God. How could I have been so stupid?"

Phillipa watched him wrestle with the news. "Her fondness for you may very well be real," she said. "It may have nothing to do with her position close to me. But I felt you should know the truth before you make a decision that could affect the rest of your life."

Leonidas looked at her a moment before lifting the vellum again and rereading it. There wasn't much to it, but it most definitely asked Christelle to bring a "guest" to meet with her father. Leonidas wasn't stupid. Knowing what he'd been told, he could read between the lines.

It was true.

Oh, God…

"If you knew this about her, why did you not send her away?" he asked in what was bordering on an impassioned plea. "Why did you allow her to remain?"

Phillipa could see how much he was hurting. "Because I thought we could feed the French false information," she said. "Spies can be used to our advantage, Leo. Surely you know that."

He took a deep, ragged breath, trying to steady himself. "I do," he said. "Then why did you not share this with me before?"

"Because there was no reason to," she said. "I was watching the situation. But now that you have asked to court her, I could no longer keep it from you. Believe me, I have wrestled with it. I do not want to destroy your happiness, but I find that I simply cannot remain silent. You must know."

Leonidas rubbed his eyes wearily, trying to reconcile what he'd just been told. It was all so overwhelming. "Then I thank you for telling me," he said quietly. "I suppose… I suppose I have some thinking to do."

Phillipa watched him sadly. "I know this is difficult," she said. "Mayhap you should simply ask her about it. Tell her that you know."

He shook his head firmly. "If her father is sending missives that request she bring you to him, then there is nothing to discuss," he said. "She is a danger to you, your grace. She can no longer serve you. I want her gone."

Phillipa sighed heavily. "I thought you'd say that," she said. "If you would please send her away, I would be grateful. I do not think I can do it. I love her, you know. Even though I knew who she was and what she was, I grew to love her."

Leonidas simply nodded. He loved her, too, but now... now, he was devastated.

There was nothing more to say.

"Is there anything else, you grace?" he asked.

Phillipa shook her head. "Nay," she said. "Again... I am sorry, Leo. I know this must be difficult for you."

Leonidas didn't trust himself to speak. Silently begging his leave, he was heading for the door when there was a knock on the panel. Hoping it wasn't Christelle, because he wasn't exactly sure how he was going to react to her, he pulled the door open to see Kenneth standing there.

"Good," Kenneth said quickly. "I found you."

"What's amiss?" Leonidas asked.

Kenneth's gaze moved between Leonidas and Phillipa. "Tate and Edward are approaching," he said. "They are less than an hour away."

Phillipa stood up quickly. "My husband is here?"

Kenneth nodded. "He is, your grace."

Phillipa led the stampede out of the keep.

⌇

LLAFN Y DDRAIG.

The knight with the dragon blade.

Tate rode in through the gatehouse of Ashendon, hearing the whispers from the soldiers around him about his dragon-headed sword. There wasn't one fighting man in England who didn't know that he should have been king, so the reverence was real.

Even if it was taking place next to the king himself.

But Edward was used to it and he didn't care, especially now. His wife was within his sight and that was all he was concerned with. Phillipa was standing near the gatehouse with Leonidas and Kenneth, and the moment Edward dismounted his steed, Phillipa flew to him and they joyfully embraced.

It was touching to everyone but Leonidas.

He was watching the reunion with a sick feeling in his stomach, knowing that kind of joy had eluded him. He had been close, but it had been cruelly snatched away from him. In fact, he couldn't even watch Edward and Phillipa.

He had to look away.

"Leo," Tate said as he came near, holding out a hand in greeting. "'Tis good to see you."

Leonidas took the man's hand, forcing a smile. "And you."

Tate shook his hand, followed by Stephen, who had also ridden escort. "The queen looks happy and healthy," Tate said.

"She has been no trouble at all."

Tate watched the happy couple for a moment before returning his focus to Leonidas. "I suppose you're wondering why we arc hcrc," he said. "There is much to tell, my friend. Let us go inside. Feed me and I will tell you everything."

Leonidas turned toward the keep with Tate beside him. "I must say your arrival is most unexpected," he said. "Surprising is more like it. And I do not get a good feeling about it."

Tate glanced at him before looking around the vast bailey of

Ashendon. "This is your seat?" he said.

He had deliberately avoided Leonidas' comment, and Leonidas was well aware. He nodded to the man's question.

"It is."

Tate nodded in return. "Well done," he said. "It suits you."

"I think so."

"And how are your children?" Tate asked. "There are three of them, correct?"

Leonidas sighed. "We had a tragedy shortly after our arrival," he said. "My youngest daughter, Georgiana, drowned in the river."

Tate came to a halt and faced him, horrified. "Oh, God," he breathed. "Leo, I'm so very sorry."

Leonidas put his hand on the man's arm. "It was an accident," he said as they began to walk again. "We buried her with her mother, but you can imagine how it has affected everyone around here. Phillipa was quite distraught about it."

They paused again, turning to the royal couple, who were still embracing. Kenneth and Stephen were standing watch, but Tate lifted a hand to Stephen, who took the hint and got the pair moving for the keep.

"She is a woman of deep feeling," Tate finally said as they resumed their walk. "Truly, Leo, I am very sorry for your loss. If there is anything I can do, I hope you'll let me know."

Leonidas shook his head. "There is nothing, but I thank you," he said. "We are still recovering from it, as you can imagine."

"And how are you getting on? I can only imagine the toll it has taken on you."

Leonidas shrugged. "Men like us are trained not to collapse in grief," he said. "But I will admit that, as of late, I feel sorely tested.”

Tate sensed something in those words, so he didn't press. When they made their way inside the keep, the mood shifted as Leonidas proudly showed them his solar. Of course, generations of de Cottinghams had filled it with treasures, but he was proud to show off those treasures. Many of the valuable books were missing thanks to Lady Maria, but there were still plenty of things to admire. Tate walked the length of the walls, inspecting the books and the trinkets, including a valuable bejeweled box that Lady Maria had somehow managed to miss.

"Impressive," Tate said. "This is a fine property, Leo. I'm very happy for you, my friend."

"Thank you," Leonidas said as he sat down at his table. "But you did not come to talk about my property."

"I did not."

They could hear people in the keep entry and eventually, Kenneth, Stephen, Phillipa, and Edward wandered into the solar. Leonidas couldn't help but notice how Phillipa and Edward were clinging to one another, and that only emphasized the grief he was feeling. Like a knife had been rammed into his back and twisted. He couldn't even look at them, felt sickened and embittered.

"Now that we are all here, do you want to tell me why you rode several days to get here?" he said, trying to shift his focus from the loving couple to the business at hand. "It must be something serious."

Tate found the wine, but no cups. He picked up the pitcher and drank from the neck before answering. "It is," he said, smacking his lips. "The time to subdue Mortimer once and for all is at hand. We have formulated a plan."

Leonidas' eyebrows lifted. "Subdue him?" he said, surprised.

He looked between Tate and Edward, who was whispering something in Phillipa's ear. "Who made this decision? You?"

Tate shook his head. "Isabella," he said. He watched the expression on Leonidas' face and put up a hand to ease the man. "I know what you're thinking, but she took a great risk to come to Carlisle and tell me that Mortimer's plan to murder Edward is moving forward, but the stipulations have changed."

"Changed?" Leonidas said. "How?"

Tate took another long drink, finishing off the pitcher. "Isabella is not pregnant," he said. "However, she has spies in the royal household who have told her that Phillipa is, so it is Mortimer's intention to remove Edward and control his child. He can continue as regent for a very long time if he does."

"This is my decision," Edward said. He let go of his wife long enough to face the powerful warlords around him. "Make no mistake, Leo—this is my decision. It is time to end Mortimer's grip on my throne. My mother can no longer tolerate his wickedness and has agreed to help me claim my right once and for all."

Leonidas was listening with a good deal of skepticism. "And you trust her?" he said. "I mean no offense, your grace, but Isabella has proven time and time again that she cannot be trusted. Are we truly going to trust her this time?"

The last question was posed to Tate, not to Edward. Tate could hear the disbelief and even anger in his voice. They'd been dealing with Isabella, evading Isabella, and just plain hiding from Isabella—and Mortimer—for years, so the suggestion of allying with her wasn't sitting well.

Tate could hardly blame him.

"I spoke to her at length, Leo," Tate said quietly. "You are well aware that I've known the woman longer than anyone in this chamber. If anyone should have a reason to doubt her, it is me. But I believe her. She is going to help orchestrate Mortimer's move to Nottingham, which is where we will capture him. I have already sent word to several allies, and we shall make a show of force in Edward's favor. Mortimer's days are numbered, Leo. This I promise."

Leonidas wasn't convinced. It was all over his face. But, to his credit, he didn't say so. "If that is true, then it is a welcome relief," he said. "You have my full support, of course. When are you planning this action?"

"Soon," Tate said. "According to Isabella, we will rendezvous with Mortimer in October at Nottingham, and there are still several allies we must contact before this can take place."

Leonidas nodded. "Then I will have my brother begin preparing my army to move out," he said. "But I should tell you that our trouble is not only aimed at Edward. I have made a few discoveries whilst here at Ashendon."

Tate looked at him curiously. "What about?"

"It seems we have a spy close to us."

"Who?"

"Christelle."

The announcement came from Phillipa, not Leonidas. She was still holding her husband's hand as she stepped forward to address the knights. She looked at Leonidas, but their eyes met for a moment and all he could do was hang his head. He couldn't seem to voice what they both knew. As he averted his gaze, Phillipa took the lead.

"I know it is difficult to believe, but I have only told Leo today," she said to the group. "Ever since Christelle came to serve me, I have been monitoring the missives she sends to her father. My father once told me not to trust anyone completely, so I do not. In Christelle's case, it was wise advice. She has been sending her father information about Edward and me since the beginning, including our movements and any conversations she may have heard. She even sent him a missive about our journey to Hull, and this morning a missive came from her father. He is in Hull and has requested that she bring me to meet him."

Tate's expression was deadly serious. "For what purpose?"

Phillipa shrugged. "Her father has ties to the French," she said, looking to Edward. "My husband has told me that. What better leverage to use me against my husband so he will renounce his claim to the French throne?"

Now, Tate's eyebrows flew up in disbelief. "God's Bones," he muttered. "*La protecteur de la reine* is a spy? I cannot believe it."

"It is true."

Tate moved his stunned gaze to Kenneth and Stephen, to see if they'd had any inclination about Christelle, but they were as stunned as he was. After a moment, he simply shook his head.

"She came highly recommended by allies in the French court," he said. "Not only that, her father's liege is the Holy Roman Emperor."

"He has French ties," Edward said quietly. "I have spies, too, Tate. I thought it best not to tell you about Christelle because it would make you view her differently. She is a smart woman—she would have suspected something. If you are wondering why I allowed her to remain, I thought we could use her to our advantage at some point by feeding her false information to her father."

That was a surprising bit of information for Tate and Stephen and Kenneth—and, quite frankly, it was rather insulting that Edward hadn't chosen to tell them. But Edward was beyond question, so they simply accepted it.

"As you wish, your grace," Tate said. "But it seems that with her father in Hull, we now have a problem. Is Christelle aware of the missive?"

Phillipa shook her head. "Nay," she said, indicating it on the table where she had set it when they'd been on their way to greet Edward. "I have not given it to her yet because she has been with the children all morning. I was going to re-seal the wax and give it to her, so she does not think it has been read, and see how she reacts. From the missives I have read between her and her father, there was never any mention of his coming to England, so I suspect the visit is unexpected."

Tate fell silent as he pondered the situation. Leonidas sat there with his head down, still reeling from the news. Hearing it a second time didn't make it any better. He was still puzzled, still deeply hurt, still feeling foolish that he'd allowed himself to be sucked in by a spy. Phillipa was watching him, sadly, which clued in both Tate and Stephen that there was more going on in this situation. They could see how depressed Leonidas was, and that was greatly puzzling.

Puzzled or not, however, they had decisions to make.

"Although I can appreciate why you let Christelle remain close to you, your grace, I'm afraid that now we know who she is, she cannot remain at your side," Tate said. "She is a danger to you, a very real and close danger, and I cannot permit that."

Phillipa was well aware. "I know," she said. "Leo and I were just discussing dismissing her when you arrived. I believe Leo was going to do it immediately."

That was Leonidas' cue to stand up. He couldn't sit there anymore, not when his life was about to come crashing down around him. He couldn't stand the sympathetic expression on Phillipa's face, and once he left, he knew she would tell the rest of them what had happened with Leonidas and Christelle. How Leonidas had been stupid enough to fall in love with a spy.

How he had been stupid, period.

"I will find her and send her along her way," he said. "But my suggestion would be that we follow her. She will undoubtedly go to her father, and there is a chance we may be able to overhear their conversation. It might help us discover any further dangers to Edward or Phillipa, at least from the French. We will deal with Mortimer once Christelle and her father are neutralized."

"An excellent idea," Tate said. "Will you tell her now?"

"Aye."

"Then we'll be ready to follow," Tate said. "But I will confess that I am disappointed to hear this. I liked Christelle. 'Tis a pity, truly."

Leonidas simply nodded, grasping the missive from Christelle's father before heading from his solar, feeling as if he were about to go to his execution. It was the same theory—the life he hoped for would be over. The woman he wanted to marry would not be his. It was the death of a dream, if nothing else.

The death of *his* dream.

But he had to face it.

As he'd predicted, once he'd cleared the solar, Phillipa told the knights everything.

CHAPTER NINETEEN

I T WAS SUCH a magical world.

That was the only way Christelle could describe it. The past few days, ever since she and Leonidas had consummated their relationship, had been days that she'd never thought she would experience. For a woman who had always lived a rather cold existence, doing what her father told her to do, the introduction of love and affection into her life had changed it completely.

She had spent the morning with Catherine and Gabriel, children who would soon belong to her. The very thought was extraordinary because she never thought she would have children. Never mind that she didn't give birth to them. It didn't matter. She loved them both, so whether they were her flesh and blood it didn't matter.

She and Leo and Catherine and Gabriel were going to be a family.

That was another thing. She was actually going to have a family of her own. That was a new concept. She had her father, and her father had a few relatives, but there was no real family, as families went. Those relatives were simply people who happened to be related to her. She wasn't close to any of them. In the short few weeks that she had been at Ashendon, she had been shown what it meant to be part of a family. This was the world that she wanted to be part of.

A world of her own.

It was late in the morning as they were heading back to the castle after their visit to the wild chickens. The afternoon was full of bright skies and fair breezes, and she could smell the salt blowing off the ocean. Gabriel was being followed by Georgiana's chicken, but he also had another small bird in his hands. It wasn't quite a chick, but it wasn't full grown.

He thought it was the best pet in the world.

As they approached the castle from the north, Christelle could see a figure in the distance, heading in their direction. It didn't take her long to figure out that it was Leonidas, and her heart leapt with joy at the sight of him. This time of year, the grass was about knee-high and she could see him plowing through it, tall and strong and handsome.

And hers.

As he drew nearer, she waved to him and Gabriel took off, running for Leonidas to show him his new chicken. Catherine skipped after him, and as Christelle watched, they proudly showed Leonidas the bird. He patted Gabriel's head and pointed to the castle, clearly telling them to get inside. That meant it would be Christelle and Leonidas in that big field, just the two of them, and she was giddy with anticipation.

"Now that you've gotten rid of the children, whatever do you intend to do with me?" she asked, grinning. "Though keep in mind that we are within range of the walls. Every sentry on duty will see whatever it is you intend."

Strangely, he wasn't smiling at her. He simply extended

what looked like an open vellum envelope to her, and she took it curiously.

"What's this?" she asked.

"Read it," he said without humor.

She did.

Dearest Christelle,

I await you at The Flying Fish in the village of Hull. It is time I come to you and more importantly, that our intentions come to fruition.

Please visit me and bring your guest with you. I wish to see her because it is time to move forward.

Papa

The smile faded from Christelle's face as she read the words again. She had a sick feeling blooming in the pit of her stomach because, clearly, Leonidas had read the missive. He would want to know what it meant. Everything she'd kept from him, everything she'd hidden, was about to come out, and she found that she was wholly unprepared for it.

God help me!

"When did this come?" she said, looking up at him. "I suppose you would like an explanation."

It was all Leonidas could do not to explode at her. "It came today," he said. "Phillipa had it."

"Is she the one who opened it?"

"She is," he said through clenched teeth. "You see, she has read every missive you have ever sent to your father and every missive you have ever received from him. She knows you have been spying on her, Christelle. She has known from the start."

Christelle went pale. He could see it. She looked at the missive one more time before lowering it.

"I see," she said. "Then I am glad. Glad she knows. As the days went on, it became a horrific burden to bear. I am relieved that I may speak of it now."

Leonidas shook his head. "I do not care how relieved you are," he said. "I want you gone."

She snapped her head up to him, stunned. "Gone?" she said. "Will you not even allow me to explain?"

He snorted bitterly. "Do not push me, lady," he snarled. "Congratulations. You have hurt me. But it ends now."

Realizing he didn't want to hear any explanation, Christelle began to tremble. "Leo, please," she said softly. "There is no use in denying that I was sent to spy on the queen, but you must understand something. I had no choice. My mission was dictated by my father. I told you that he had been a hostage of the French king as a child, but what I did not tell you was that it made him loyal to the French. I lied when I said he was opposed to them. They want Phillipa because they can use her as leverage to force Edward to relinquish his claim in the French throne."

Leonidas' jaw was twitching fiercely. "Tell me something I do not already know," he growled. "We have figured out your purpose."

"I was not going to deliver Phillipa to him, if that was your concern."

He snorted rudely. "You say that now because we have discovered you," he said. Then he shook a big finger in her face. "As you know, spies are usually killed, so count yourself fortunate that I am allowing you to leave with your life. But go now before I change my mind."

She stared at him, realizing he had gone to the hard Leonidas she'd first met. It had taken a long time to break that man down, the one who was always on his guard.

Now, he was back.

Like stone.

Christelle was armed. Without another word, she stripped off her scabbard, sword intact, and tossed it to the ground a few feet away from him. Then she fell to her knees, arms at her side, and faced him.

"You are correct," she said, her voice loud but quivering. "I am a spy. That was my purpose. But what I did not count on was becoming emotional about the people I was sent to spy on. Phillipa is like a sister to me, a sister I never had, and you… Everything about you is part of me. Part of my heart, part of my mind, and part of my soul. Without you, I have nothing, so please… show mercy and end my life. It is right of you to do so to protect your queen."

She closed her eyes, bracing herself for what was to come, as he stood there and stared at her. The woman he loved. The woman who had betrayed him. The woman he'd hoped to spend his life with.

The pain was more than he could bear.

Reaching down, Leonidas unsheathed her sword and marched over to her, sword held in both hands and over one shoulder like a club. She had heard him unsheathe the weapon and his approaching footsteps, so she knew he was coming for her.

"Be swift, Leo," she whispered. "That is all I ask."

Grinding his teeth furiously, he came alongside her. He lifted the sword, knowing what his duty was. Knowing what he *should* do.

But then he heard her speak softly.

"Before you end my life, know that my feelings for you are real," she murmured. "That was never part of my mission. I love you with all of my heart, and that is the truth."

He brought the sword down, but instead of plowing it into the back of her neck, it went sailing over her head and landed a dozen feet away.

He began pacing around like a madman.

"Shut your lips," he said, waving a hand at her in a chopping motion. "Everything out of your mouth is a lie, so stop speaking. I will not believe anything you say."

Realizing he hadn't cut her head off had her nearly passing out from sheer relief. Christelle slouched, putting her hand down so she would not fall over completely. "Is there nothing I can say?" she asked. "I will swear on whatever icon you wish. I will swear on my own life. What can I do to make this right?"

"Nothing."

She looked up at the man as he stopped pacing and came to a halt several feet away. "So this is the end?" she said. "Leo, I never lied about my feelings. I am sorry if you do not believe me, but it is true. What is also true is that I was going to write to my father and tell him I would no longer spy for him. I have grown to love Phillipa and you and even Catherine and Gabriel. You have shown me a side of life I never knew to exist. I do not have a family, only my father, and he treated me like a tool. No better than a hammer or an ax. I served a purpose and that was all I meant to him. But you... you have shown me such joy, such warmth and acceptance. Please do not take that away from me."

He was looking at her, grinding his jaw again. "To be clear, I've done nothing," he said. "You have ruined everything with your deceit."

"Do you not love me enough to forgive me?"

He hesitated before answering. "Nay," he said hoarsely. "I must protect Catherine and Gabriel. I will not marry a woman who lies with such ease and lives such deceit. The children have been through enough."

"Forget about the children," she said. "What about *you*? Can you not find it in your heart to forgive?"

He looked at her. Really looked at her. For a brief moment, Christelle thought he might be willing to believe her, but that flash of longing was quickly gone. Averting his gaze, he simply shook his head.

"Nay," he said. "I… I cannot."

He would have done less harm had he slapped her in the face. The result was still the same. Christelle's head snapped back and she looked at him in anguish. But, on the other hand, she could hardly blame him.

She knew he was right.

It was over.

Christelle wanted to throw herself at his mercy. She wanted to beg for his understanding. But anything she did right now only made her look desperate, as if she would say or do anything for his forgiveness.

Congratulations. You hurt me.

Those words would haunt her for the rest of her life.

"What do you want me to do?" she asked, head lowered. "May I at least collect my things?"

"Nay," he said. "You will not collect anything. Your father is in the village. Let him buy you what you need."

It was a harsh command and the tears started to come. Christelle blinked and they rolled down her cheeks, but she held her tongue. She didn't plead with him and embarrass herself.

But her guts were being ripped out and the pain was unbearable. All of it, unbearable.

But she only had herself to blame.

Head down, with the missive from her father still in hand, she headed out to the road as he watched her go. No more conversation between them because there was no point. By the time Christelle hit the road that led into Hull, she was sobbing uncontrollably.

What she didn't see was that Leonidas was weeping, too.

CHAPTER TWENTY

"TALAN?"

Talan had been bent over an old spear that had been dragged out of the armory by Zander. In fact, Dayne and Zander were in the old armory, which was full of de Cottingham relics from the past, grumbling and complaining because they'd not been included in the meeting going on in the solar with the king and queen and Earl of Carlisle. It seemed that only the senior knights were permitted in that gathering, and given the three junior knights didn't have that kind of seniority, they had been relegated to managing the castle.

Just like always.

No excitement in their lives.

Talan had been thinking the same thing, only with him, it was a little different. He had woman troubles these days. He'd walked away from Catherine after their most recent spat and hadn't spoken to her since, but that didn't mean she wasn't on his mind every moment of every day. He couldn't remember why he was so opposed to marriage right now because whatever the reason was seemed foolish. He loved her. He would always love her. He wanted her to be the mother of his children, but he was asking her to wait until he was damn good and ready. *She* was ready, but he wasn't.

Was that fair to her?

There were probably a hundred men in England who would be ready at that very moment to marry Catherine. Maybe he was one of them, but the more she pushed, the more stubborn he became. Now, it was simply his stubbornness against hers, and he was determined to win. Or at least he had been until he woke up this morning and realized he wasn't willing to fight with her any longer. If she wanted him to speak with Leonidas, then he would. After the man was done with the king and queen. That had been his decision, in fact, before that soft voice he knew so well suddenly rang out in the armory.

Catherine was standing in the doorway.

"Zander and Dayne are nearby," he said quietly. "Be cautious of what you say."

She smiled timidly. "They are outside breaking spears in half and declaring their anger at Leo," she said. "Why are they so angry?"

Talan came over to the door where she stood and stuck his head out. As Catherine had told him, Zander and Dayne were violently breaking up old spears and grumbling. Shaking his head at their antics, he returned to his work.

"Edward arrived not long ago with the Earl of Carlisle and Stephen of Pembury," he said. "He had business with Leo and Kenneth, I suppose, and the younger knights were not invited to partake of the conclave, so they are offended."

"I heard they had come," Catherine said. "In fact, I've just come from the kitchen to ensure we have a proper meal for them tonight."

"Do we?"

"We do," she said. "And are you angry?"

"For what?"

"For the same thing that has angered Zander and Dayne?"

He paused and thought about that. "Probably," he said. He went back to work. "Why are you here? Do you require something?"

Catherine came inside the door, watching him work over the tip of an old spear to break it free from the brittle staff it was attached to.

"I do not require anything," she said quietly. "But I wanted to apologize for my behavior the other day. I was mean and nasty and I am very sorry for it. I do not want to fight with you, Talan. Please forgive me."

He stood up from the spear and looked at her. "There is nothing to forgive," he said. "I know I can be stubborn and difficult. I know I am not the easiest person to speak with sometimes. Whatever happened, I'm sure I drove you to it, so I think I need your forgiveness, too."

Her timid smile turned genuine and she rushed him, throwing her arms around his neck and hugging him tightly. He responded, for a brief moment, before kissing her soundly and then pushing her away so there was a safe distance between them.

"Stay there," he cautioned. "The last thing we need is Zander or Dayne coming in here and seeing us in an amorous embrace. I do not want rumors reaching Leo's ears before I've had a chance to speak with him."

"You can do it when you are ready," Catherine said. "I should not have pushed you so hard when you were only trying to do what was right. I understand everything now."

"Understand what?"

"That I must let you keep your pride."

He shrugged. "Pride is one thing," he said. "Self-respect is another. And if I lost you, I would lose all that and more. I do not want to lose you, Catie."

She shook her head. "You will not," she said. "I will wait for you, Talan. When you are ready to speak with Leo, I am ready to be your wife."

He cocked his head. "Why the change of heart?"

She averted her gaze. "I am not sure," she said. "But I think it has everything to do with what is important in life. Is it important that I be married? Or is it more important that I be married to you? I think it's more important that I am married to you, so I will wait. For as long as it takes, I will wait."

He smiled faintly. "If you mean that, then I am very glad," he said. "Because I have been thinking that I am simply being stubborn. Of course I want us to be married, Catie. I'm sorry if I implied otherwise. I cannot imagine my life without you."

In spite of his telling her that she needed to remain a respectful distance away, she rushed to him and grasped his hand, joyfully. "Nor I, you," she said. "All is forgiven?"

"All is forgiven."

"Good," she said, kissing him quickly before darting away. "Then I shall see you at sup."

"You will."

She flashed him a toothy smile as she turned for the door, but he stopped her before she could leave.

"Catie?"

She paused, looking at him. "Aye?"

"You may be Lady de Shera sooner than you think."

Her grin broadened, but she didn't push him. She was going to have to learn not to. Just because she didn't get what she wanted, when she wanted it, didn't mean she wasn't going to get it at all.

She had to have a little faith

With a giggle, she fled the armory, leaving Talan feeling better than he had in days.

Everything was going to be all right.

CHAPTER TWENTY-ONE

Hull

The Flying Fish

THE WALK FROM the castle shouldn't have taken so long, but it had.

It was the longest walk Christelle had ever made in her life.

The road leading up through Hull went straight to the castle before veering off to the northwest, and it was along that road that Christelle made her final journey. It seemed like she'd been at Ashendon for years. Maybe even her entire life. She couldn't remember when she hadn't lived here, yet she remembered the moment of arrival with unusual clarity. She remembered the entire experience with unusual clarity. From the moment Leonidas approached her on the deck of that rolling cog as she stood at the side and tried not to become ill, it was a moment she would remember for the rest of her life. The moment when she realized there was something between them.

Even if he didn't kill the captain for cooking onions and fish.

But it was more than that. Making their way to the castle

had been a moment when she knew that she belonged to something bigger than herself. She and Leonidas and Kenneth had accompanied Phillipa in their quest to protect her. Truthfully, it had always been Christelle's intention to protect the woman. Even though she was on a mission from her father, she would have never let anything awful happen to Phillipa. She would have laid down her life for the woman. A woman who had been a friend and a mentor to her.

And a woman who knew she was being spied upon.

Was that the most shocking revelation out of this entire situation? The fact that Phillipa knew Christelle, her own personal guard, was a spy? Christelle had thought long and hard about that very thing on her walk into Hull, and perhaps that was why it had taken so long. At one point, she stopped and sat on the side of the road, pondering the course her life had taken. She thought about Phillipa and how sweet and innocent the woman came across sometimes when the truth was that she was a royal, born and bred, and she wasn't naïve. She had a mind like a steel trap. She had done the right thing and suspected Christelle from the beginning. That being the case, Christelle wasn't really surprised that Phillipa was onto her.

Perhaps she would have been disappointed had she not been.

Still, Phillipa had allowed her to remain at her side. She remembered well that Phillipa was always asking about her father and whether she'd heard from him. Christelle had always thought it was simply because Phillipa was trying to be polite and interested, but the truth was that it was much more than that. Even as Christelle was spying on Phillipa, Phillipa was spying on Christelle. She had to smile when she realized just how astute the queen was.

Her lady wasn't so naïve, after all.

Christelle was proud of her. Proud of the young queen for growing into a seasoned, smart queen. Christelle liked to think that she had a hand in that because Phillipa was so young, but the truth was that she was probably a very hard lesson for Phillipa to learn. A lesson that taught her that not everybody was who they seemed.

Not everybody was who you wanted them to be.

Therefore, Christelle sat on the side of the road for quite some time pondering that very real fact. The truth was that she wasn't who *she* wanted to be. Her father had tried to mold her into what he wanted her to be, and, before she met Phillipa and Leonidas, Christelle was content with what her father wanted. But after living in their world for the past couple of years, she knew that her father's world was not where she wanted to be.

And she was going to tell him so.

As the sun began to set, she cast a final glance to the castle on the rise, fighting off tears as she knew the glance would be her last. She was going to have to start a new life now, a life without Leonidas. In a sense, she would have done better had she been the one to drown in that cold river instead of Georgiana, because her life was ending in precisely the same manner. She was to be cut off from everybody and everything she had grown to love. For someone who had experienced those feelings for the first time in her life, feelings of acceptance and love, that was a fate worse than death.

By the time Christelle reached the town, the sun was nearly down. Along the river's edge, fishing boats had laid out their nets for the night. The town itself was closing up for the day as she made her way to the waterfront and finally to The Flying Fish, the last establishment in a line of various business along the river's edge. Already, at this early evening hour, it was quite busy.

The common room was packed with fisherman who had just put in a hard day's work. Some kind of fish stew was clearly being eaten because she could smell it. It reminded her of those three weeks on the cog, and she immediately became nauseated. Grabbing the nearest serving wench, she asked for her father, but the woman didn't know who Bernard de Lorrain was. As the wench darted off to serve some of the loud and hungry fishermen, Christelle wandered deeper into the tavern and came across another young wench, round and buxom, and told that lass whom she was looking for. This time, however, she described him rather than state his name, and that brought about the desired results. The serving wench directed her to two chambers on the ground floor, facing the street.

The chambers were located under the stairs that led to the second floor. It was dark and quiet back here, away from the common room, and Christelle went to the first door and rapped softly on it. There was no answer, so she went to the second door and did the same thing.

That drew a response.

"Who comes?"

Christelle knew that voice. God help her, she did, and her stomach sank as she responded.

"Your daughter."

The door flew open, and the first thing she saw was her father standing in the doorway. He had an expression full of glee until he realized she was alone.

"Where is the guest I asked you to bring?" he demanded.

That was so typically her father. No warmth, no pleasantness. Simply business. That was all she'd ever been to him—

business.

"May I at least come in before I tell you?" she asked. "Or do you wish for everyone in Hull to know our business?"

He looked at her, greatly displeased. "Come in."

He opened the door wider so she could slip in. Once she was inside the chamber and he shut the door, he swiftly turned to her.

"Well?" he said. "Where is she?"

Christelle was looking around the chamber. She recognized her father's ally, Gautier de Leon, but didn't recognize the third man. He was big and brooding and heavily armed from what she could see. She could only imagine that he would be the muscle to take Phillipa back to the Continent, which didn't sit well with her. Phillipa didn't need a barbarian to contain her. She needed a gentle hand.

But her father didn't care about that. He'd come ready to do business.

"Greetings to you also, Bernard," she said, calling him by his given name because she'd never addressed him as Father or even Papa. "We've not seen each other in at least two years, but instead of a word of salutation, you simply make demands as if I am another one of your vassals and you only saw me yesterday. You could have at least been civil."

Bernard faced off against his daughter. "As you wish," he said sharply. "Greetings, Christelle. Where is Phillipa?"

"She is not here."

"I can see that," he said. "Where is she?"

"At Ashendon Castle, surrounded by heavily armed men," she said. "I could not bring her with me."

Bernard frowned. "Why not?"

"Because they discovered who I am."

That wasn't something Bernard had expected to hear. At first, he looked at her with confusion, then disbelief.

"What?" he spat. "That is impossible!"

Christelle eyed the men in the room, particularly Gautier, whom she knew to be hot tempered. The man had always concerned her.

He wasn't going to take this news well.

"I am afraid is it very possible," she said. "It seems that I was discovered early in my mission by Phillipa herself. Though I've not spoken with her directly about it, that is what I was told. She had been reading every missive I sent you and every missive you sent me, including the most recent one. They know what you want. Rather than executing me as a spy, they simply sent me on my way with nothing but the clothes on my back. I suppose I am more fortunate than most spies in that regard, but here I am. Your mission has ended."

She said it all so casually that it drove Bernard to despair. He rolled his eyes and put his head in his hands, possibly a dramatic response, but not overly dramatic considering he'd been working on this scheme with his daughter for almost half her life. Ten years of training and connections. Ten years of hard work.

Clearly, the man was not pleased.

"But the queen has said nothing to you?" Bernard said incredulously. "Not a word?"

Christelle shook her head. "She said nothing," she said. "If she has read everything that passed between us, even though no names were ever mentioned, then she knows I was sending you information. I think she could deduce solely by the clues what we were speaking of and what we were potentially planning. The woman is not stupid."

"And what did you do to convince her that you were not a spy?" Gautier finally spoke up, eyes as cold as ice. "Did you try to convince her that she misread the missives? Better still, did you stress that her actions were wrong?"

"Her actions were not wrong," Christelle said, eyeing the man she had a genuine dislike for. "As I told you, she did not speak directly to me about this. I was told by one of her knights. He is the one who banished me rather than execute me. A man who taught me the important things in life, like honesty and loyalty. In truth, I owe him everything."

The fact that she had survived spying on the royal couple didn't seem to matter to Gautier or to her father. All they could see was their ruined plans.

Being grateful for her life never entered into it.

"And you did nothing to try to salvage this?" Gautier persisted. "Nothing to convince them that they were mistaken?"

Christelle knew they didn't care about her, personally, but it was never more obvious than it was at this very moment. "And how am I to do that when they have irrefutable evidence?" she said. "I am not going to deny the obvious. These people are not stupid. They are strong and brilliant and loyal. Even you should appreciate that kind of loyalty, Gautier, as my father's faithful dog."

Gautier laughed low, but it was without humor. "I see that spending two years with Phillipa has not made you more charming," he said. "You still behave as lowborn as ever."

Christelle smiled thinly. "Be careful what you say to me," she said. "It may not reflect well on my father."

"It already does not reflect well on me," Bernard said. "*You* do not reflect well on me. You had a mission, Christelle. Now you are telling me that you have failed? That our hard work is at an end?"

Christelle sighed sharply and faced her father. "I am telling you that Phillipa knows of my mission," she said. "She has from the start, but still, she kept me on, though I do not know why. Mayhap she thought somehow you would divulge useful information from the French, but in any case, she knows. Even if she did not, your arrival in town is fortuitous because I was going to send you a missive telling you that I refuse to spy on Phillipa any longer. Now I can tell you face to face."

Another thing Bernard was not expecting to hear. He scowled. "What's this you say?" he said, aghast. "What is the matter with you? Have you gone daft?"

Christelle was feeling strong. From the bottom of her devastated heart, she was nonetheless drawing strength. Strength that had never been there before. It was the strength of righteousness, the strength acquired from knowing what path she wanted to take in life.

It was the strength taught to her by people she loved.

And one in particular.

"If being daft means I understand how wrongly you have used and treated me, then I am most assuredly daft," she said. "If being daft means that I understand the difference between right and wrong, then I am quite daft. If it means I will no longer live the way you want me to live, like a snake slithering around on its belly, then I am most happily daft. All of it!"

She had spoken rather strongly, which made both Bernard and Gautier look at her as if, indeed, she had jumped off into the abyss of madness.

"What has *happened* to you?" Bernard demanded.

Christelle pondered the question. "Truth happened," she said. "In fact, I have something to tell you. When I first came to

England, it was at your direction. You sent me to Blackchurch. Do you recall?"

"Of course I recall," Bernard snapped. "It was the one thing you did in your life to make me proud."

Christelle gave a grin, one of true humor. "Then I am happy to tell you that I lied to you about Blackchurch," she said. "I never finished the training. I failed at a particular test when I was three years into the training and they banished me from the program, as is their rule. Knowing what it meant to you, I knew I could not return home, so I spent a year—an entire year— working as a serving wench at a tavern in London. I enjoyed it, in fact. When the year was over, I came home and told you I had finished Blackchurch. Now that you know the truth and I am a complete failure in your eyes, how proud are you?"

Bernard's eyes were wide with horror. "Nay," he said. "Nay… it is not true!"

"It is."

Bernard's eyes were still wide, now joined by a gaping mouth. "How could you shame me so?"

Christelle's smile faded. "At one time, a question like that would have been like a dagger to my heart," she said. "I tried for years to please a man who would never be pleased. But now… now, it is my mark of greatness. You think I have shamed you, and I am happy you think so. Bernard, I do not want to follow you into the dark underbelly of politics any longer. Before, I had no choice, but now I do. I realize now that I want to live in the light, with people who are good and decent. Decent like Phillipa, who is the kindest, most genuinely caring person I have ever met. *She* lives in the light. I want to be more like her. That was a side of life that you never introduced me to."

Bernard looked at her as if she'd lost her mind. He started

to reply but couldn't seem to find the words. He was so shocked, so infuriated, that he had to find an outlet other than words. Therefore he resorted to a method he'd resorted to before—he lashed out and hit Christelle in the chin with the back of his hand. Her head snapped back and she lost her balance, falling to her knees as Bernard loomed over her.

"Two years with the English has made you weak and mad," he said. "I will not listen to this, Christelle. Do you hear me? You are going to tell me everything about the situation and we are going to determine a way to fix it."

Hand on her stinging jaw, Christelle eyed him as she slowly rose to her feet. "Do not do that again," she growled. "I may not have completed Blackchurch, but I was still trained there. I can, and I will, fight back."

By this time, Gautier was standing over near Bernard and the hulking figure in the shadows had moved. He was lingering behind Christelle, which she sensed, so she moved to the side, trying to get away from an armed man coming up behind her. That put her over by the window, her back against the wall next to it. The dynamics of the chamber were changing and she didn't like it. If she had to bail from the window in order to save her life, then she wanted to be prepared.

"Answer me," Bernard said, ignoring her threat to fight back. "Tell me who told you about Phillipa's awareness and relay the conversation to me. Do not leave out anything."

Christelle sighed as she leaned back against the wall, getting a good look at the brute with the sword. In fact, she found herself fixed on the man.

"I do not know you," she said. "Who are you?"

"He goes by Le Mort," Gautier answered for him. "He is my swordsman. Answer your father."

Le Mort. That meant Death. She eyed the warrior, mildly concerned that he'd come out of the shadows. He was waiting for a command to attack her, especially after her father had struck her. Given how she intended to answer her father, she was going to have to be on her guard.

Her warrior training was kicking in.

"There is no use in telling you anything because I am not going back," she said frankly. "I am not going to try to salvage the situation. I am going to leave this town and start my life somewhere new. Mayhap I'll find a kind man and we'll have children and I will raise them to be loved and cherished, which was certainly not how I was raised. You tried to teach me how to be deceitful and underhanded, and for a time, I was. But, as I said earlier, that is not the life I want for myself. I want to live like a decent person."

Bernard was gazing steadily at her with rage in his features, when suddenly they rippled into something incredulous. As if a thought had just occurred to him. He lifted a finger, wagging it at her.

"I understand now," he said. "I do not know why it did not occur to me before."

"What has occurred to you?"

Bernard looked at Gautier. "It is perfectly obvious."

Gautier wasn't any less confused than Christelle was. "What is obvious?" he asked.

Bernard was still looking at him. "Don't you see?" he said. "She serves Phillipa now. She is here on behalf of the queen to glean information from us. She is spying on *us!*"

Christelle shook her head. "I am not here on behalf of the queen," she said. "I am here of my own accord to tell you that I will no longer be your spy. After I am done with you, I am leaving Hull and you will never see me again. And I, thankfully, will never see you again, either."

"You are not leaving," Bernard said. "At least, you are not leaving alive. You should never have betrayed me, Christelle. You are a positively inept spy if you permitted Phillipa to know of your mission. How stupid of you. How ridiculous."

Unfortunately, Christelle wasn't armed. She'd left her sword with Leonidas when she fled Ashendon. When she'd begged him to execute her and he couldn't bring himself to do it. It was the first time since entering the chamber that she'd thought of Leonidas in a conversation where she'd tried desperately not to think of him at all. She'd kept the focus on her father and on Phillipa, because to think of anything else would divert her attention.

It would make her want to crumple and die.

But she couldn't give in to such emotion, not now when her entire life was on the line. She could see that, very quickly, this was going to become deadly.

Concentrate!

"I do not know what you expect of me," she said. "I cannot return. My ruse has been exposed. There is nothing I can do."

"You can tell us of Phillipa's future plans," Bernard said. "Mayhap we can salvage what you have so badly damaged."

"She does not have any future plans," she said. "The woman is going to have a child. She has not made any plans for the future other than delivering a healthy infant."

Bernard cocked his head in a gesture that suggested he didn't believe a word she had said. "You sent word to me that Phillipa was being separated from Edward and moved to Hull," he said. "This is not where she is to remain for the rest of her life. There are more plans. What are they?"

"There are no more plans until she delivers the child."

"When will that be?"

"I am not certain. Soon."

"How soon?"

"I told you that I am not certain."

Bernard snorted rudely. "You have spent every day with her for the past two years," he said. "Of course you know when the child is coming. Tell me."

"I am not a midwife, Bernard. All I know is that it will be soon."

"And then what?"

"Then she will raise the child."

Bernard was at his limit of patience. He turned to Mort and gestured. "Make her tell us what we wish to know," he said.

Mort immediately moved in Christelle's direction. Seeing this, she reacted with equal swiftness, grabbing the nearest chair and swinging it at the man's head. He managed to get an arm up and deflect most of the blow, but not entirely. Some of it connected with his head and shoulder. Infuriated, he lunged at Christelle and, as she was unable to move away fast enough because her father was blocking her path, was able to grab her by the hair. He yanked as hard as he could, which had Christelle hurling across the chamber and flying headfirst into a wall.

Unfortunately, it didn't knock her out, but it did wound her. Blood poured from a gash over her eye and, dazed and seeing stars, Christelle struggled to crawl away from Mort, who was coming in for another blow. He was a big man, and she was injured, so it was a simple thing for him to catch her and toss her onto her back. Once she was sprawled out, he pounced on her, grabbing her by the front of her bloodied hair. When she tried to fight him off, he slammed her head back onto the floor to stop her struggles.

"Now," Bernard said as he bent over Mort's shoulder, "I will ask you again. What are Phillipa's future plans?"

Christelle was closely approaching unconsciousness. In fact, she was praying for it, because then they'd leave her alone until she came around again. But until that time, she had to draw on what Blackchurch had taught her, and that was resistance.

She would resist to the end.

"Go to hell," she snapped at her father, blowing blood off her lips. "And take your bastard friends with you."

Mort slammed her head into the floor again, which mercifully knocked her out completely. But that was a tragedy for Christelle.

She would have very much liked to have seen what came next.

And it wasn't long in coming.

CHAPTER TWENTY-TWO

Ashendon

"GOD," TATE GROANED. "I should have known something was amiss when we discussed Christelle. You could see it all over Leo's face."

Seated in the solar after Leonidas had departed to send Christelle along her way, Phillipa confessed the entire situation to Tate and Edward and the rest of the men. The only one who didn't seem surprised by it was Kenneth, because he had seen Leonidas and Christelle on their travels to Hull. He had seen what was transpiring, though he hadn't realized how far it had gone.

"I know," Phillipa said with sorrow. "That is why I thought I should tell you once he was out of the chamber. Sending Christelle away is going to be devastating for him. I hope you realize that."

Tate looked at her with some doubt. "How serious is this, your grace?"

Phillipa could only shrug. "Truthfully, I have never seen either of them so happy," she said. "All of us have that one person meant for us in this world and it's a miracle if we find them. I have been fortunate enough to find my person, as have you."

"Indeed, I have."

"Can you imagine what your life would be like without Toby?"

Tate shook his head, closing his eyes tightly. "I cannot," he said. "It makes me ill to think on it."

"Then you can imagine how Leo feels right now," Phillipa said softly. "I do believe he found his person in Christelle, and she with him. As much as I hated to tell him the truth, I had to. I had no choice."

Tate's gaze lingered on the young queen, so full of heart. He could see that she was genuinely broken up about the situation.

"You are not to blame," he said. "It is not your fault. The only person at blame here is Christelle."

Phillipa looked away. "Mayhap," she said. "Mayhap not. I allowed her to remain even after I knew who, and what, she was. That is my fault for letting her remain so long."

Tate shook his head. "Your reasoning was sound," he said. "There is an old saying—keep your friends close and your enemies closer. You were watching her as much as she was watching you. I applaud your logic."

"Then we should be more like the queen," Kenneth said, moving out of the shadows where he had been lingering. "We should be logical about this situation and leave the emotion out of it. I feel that we have a great opportunity now that we must not let slip away."

Everyone turned to him, king and queen included. "What is it, Ken?" Edward wanted to know. "What do you have in mind?"

Kenneth looked at the young monarch, a lad he'd watched grow up. Literally. Edward was now nearly taller than he was, which was saying something. The young man had grown considerably over the past couple of years, very much a man these days. He looked like one and thought like one. It was no longer a matter of telling the young king what to do because, these days, he was giving the orders.

Therefore, Kenneth addressed him accordingly.

"Let us assume a few things, your grace," he said. "Leo is, at this very moment, telling Christelle to leave Ashendon. When she does, the assumption is that she will go to her father in the town. Does that seem logical?"

Everyone nodded, Edward most of all. "And?" he said.

"And when she goes to her father, it would also be logical that they discuss the situation," Kenneth continued. "Not only will they discuss what has happened, but they will probably make additional plans. Mayhap to even get Christelle back into Phillipa's good graces. Do you not think we should know those plans as well?"

Edward had to think about what he was suggesting. "Of course we should," he said. "But how?"

"Do to her what she did to us," Stephen spoke up. He knew exactly what Kenneth was leading to. "We spy."

Edward's eyes widened with realization. "We go to the tavern where her father is?"

Kenneth and Stephen nodded. "Doesn't the missive say where he will be?" Kenneth said.

"It did," Phillipa said helpfully. "He will be at The Flying Fish."

"Then two of us must go to the tavern and conceal our identities," Kenneth said. "Find a place in the common room and observe. The remaining two will follow Christelle to make sure she arrives. Once she and her father converge, we must decide how to listen to the conversation."

Tate nodded with approval. "It may help us to know what the French are planning," he said. "You are correct, Ken. This could be a grand opportunity for us. But you mentioned four men—are we taking Edward with us?"

"Leo."

Tate almost hesitated, but quickly thought better of it. "He is a knight above all things," he said. "This situation may be painful for him, but it cannot be helped. We cannot waste this opportunity. Ken, find him and inform him of our decision. And I am putting you personally in charge of keeping track of Christelle. If Leo has already dismissed her, then find her. Quickly. I do not want to lose sight of her."

Kenneth was already on his feet, heading for the door. "Right away, Tate."

"If she is on the move, then you and Leo can follow her into town," Tate called after him. "Stephen and I will figure out a way into The Flying Fish without her seeing us. We'll meet you there."

Kenneth was on the move. He headed out to the bailey, where he saw Catherine and Gabriel coming in through the gatehouse, arms full of chickens. They were very proud to show Kenneth, who wasn't compassionate enough to return real interest in a pet chicken. But he patted Gabriel on the top of his bushy red head and the lad ran toward the keep, but Kenneth stopped Catherine long enough to ask her where Leonidas was. She pointed outside of the walls and he thanked her.

As Catherine continued toward the keep, Kenneth went to the gatehouse and sent a couple of soldiers running for his and

Leonidas' weapons. He wasn't sure the man was already armed, but he didn't think so, and he continued outside the walls. Since the castle was on a rise, the road, as it moved around the castle, was below him by about twenty feet. He could look down the slope and see that there wasn't anything other than the usual traffic on the roadway. Rounding the side of the castle walls, he immediately spied Leonidas and Christelle as they stood several feet apart and spoke to one another. Leonidas had his back to him, but he saw quite clearly when Christelle suddenly tossed her sword along the ground in Leonidas' direction and plunged to her knees.

That brought Kenneth's concern and curiosity.

He was close enough to the wall and its defensive buttresses that he could have ducked behind one and they wouldn't see him, but they weren't looking at anything other than each other. He saw Leonidas pick up Christelle's sword and charge at her with it lifted, and it occurred to him that he was about to watch the woman get her head cut off. Shocked, he watched it play out because he couldn't really believe Leonidas would kill Christelle. At least, he hoped not, for the man's sake, and he was thankful to be right. Leonidas eventually tossed the sword away.

Kenneth had to admit that he breathed a sigh of relief.

But that wasn't the end of it. There was some conversation going on between them and Leonidas was quite animated about it. Kenneth saw clearly when Leonidas turned his back on Christelle and she stood up, making her way down the slope to the road beyond. She had her hands on her face, and Kenneth could only assume that she was weeping. Indeed, it didn't take a genius to figure out what had just happened.

A very sad scene, indeed.

Kenneth watched Christelle head down the road before

returning his attention to Leonidas. The man was still standing where she had left him, and as he watched, he wiped at his face. That told Kenneth that Leonidas, too, was suffering through a few tears, so he gave the man some space. He went over to the edge of the rise to watch Christelle as she made it about halfway to the town before sitting down on the side of the road.

And there she remained.

When Kenneth was fairly certain she wasn't going to jump up and start running, he made the decision to interrupt Leonidas, because a plan was in the works and he needed to be part of it.

He'd given the man enough time to compose himself.

"Leo?" Kenneth called to him when he was still a good distance away. "I bear news."

He wanted to give Leonidas enough time to wipe away any emotional residue, but Leonidas turned to him with a wet face and red eyes. It wasn't like Kenneth could ignore it.

He had no choice but to acknowledge the obvious.

"Phillipa told us what has happened," he said, his voice quiet. "If there is anything I can do to help, I hope you will tell me."

Leonidas sniffled, wiping at both eyes with the back of right hand. "There is nothing," he said. "Although I know you mean well, I would prefer not to discuss it."

"Of course, Leo," Kenneth said in a surprising show of compassion. "But I'm afraid the news I bear might make that difficult."

Leonidas took a deep breath, a final attempt to compose himself, and looked at him. "What news?"

"We are to follow Christelle into town," Kenneth said. "Tate and Stephen are joining us. Undoubtedly, the lady is going to go to see her father. Tate believes we should use the situation to our advantage to see if we can listen in on any conversation and find what the French are planning."

Leonidas stared at him a moment, perhaps in horror, before letting out a long, heavy sigh. "Of course," he said. "That makes perfect sense."

Kenneth couldn't let him linger on the situation, not when time was of the essence. "Then come with me," he said. "The lady is on foot and so shall we be, but I've sent soldiers for our weapons."

"Good thinking," Leonidas said, but he sounded dull and weary. "Ken… I apologize that you have seen me like this. I am not a weak man by nature."

Kenneth looked at him sharply. "You are one of the strongest men I know," he said. "There is no need to apologize. I'm simply sorry that you have had to endure so much tragedy lately. I truly am."

Leonidas nodded, a silent acknowledgement of Kenneth's sympathy, and they began to head in the direction of the road. Kenneth could see that Christelle was still sitting on the side of the dirt avenue, which was a good thing. She hadn't moved. He stood there, watching, turning to say something to Leonidas, only to see that the man was looking at his feet. He couldn't even look down the road, to see the woman he loved in such agony and knowing there was nothing he was willing to do about it. Nothing he *could* do about it.

And now he was expected to use that agony like a weapon.

Soldiers spilled forth from the gatehouse, carrying broadswords with them. Kenneth hadn't asked for more than that, no mail or armor, although both he and Leonidas were wearing mail breeches and heavy, padded tunics. Just no mail coat, which was only donned when they traveled or went into battle. He hoped there wouldn't be a confrontation, but it couldn't be helped. He strapped on his broadsword as Leonidas strapped on his. Kenneth took another look down the road to see Christelle still sitting there.

They settled in for the wait.

As the day began to wane, Tate and Stephen emerged from the castle and joined the vigil. That gave Kenneth and Leonidas the opportunity to return to their cottages and don the rest of their mail. They were almost finished when a soldier came running all the way from the gatehouse to tell them that Tate and Stephen had departed for the town, meaning Christelle must have moved and they followed. That bit of news had Leonidas and Kenneth running for the stables to collect their horses. They were to be the forward team that was already in place when Christelle reached The Flying Fish.

They were going to have to hurry.

Just north of the castle, the road that ran alongside it branched out. A smaller road headed west, and from that road, they were able to take a path that led to the western side of town. Tethering their horses at the back of the tavern, they entered the establishment through the rear and took a table in one of the corners, facing the main entry, and they saw quite plainly, about an hour later, when Christelle entered.

By that time, it was completely dark outside and the place was full of fishermen and patrons wanting to eat and drink away a hard day's work. The smell of fish and onions was heavy on the air, which only made Leonidas relive the memories of the two weeks they'd spent aboard the cog. Cloaks on, hoods down, they watched Christelle ask a couple of serving wenches a question. The first one didn't seem to have an answer, but the second one did. She pointed to the east side of the common room where the sleeping chambers were.

Christelle headed into the darkened corridor.

"Go," Kenneth whispered.

They were up, moving through the crowd, coming to the edge of the corridor in time to see Christelle being admitted into the chamber that was closest to the common room. When she went inside and shut the door, Leonidas turned to Kenneth.

"Get as close as you can to that door," he whispered. "I'll find Tate and we'll figure out which chamber window faces the street."

Kenneth waggled his blond eyebrows. "Thank the saints that it is on the ground floor, eh?"

"That makes our task far easier."

Kenneth headed into the shadowed corridor while Leonidas went outside, quickly spying Tate and Stephen in the livery two doors down. With his face camouflaged by his hood, Leonidas headed down the street, ducking into the livery once he reached it.

"She's gone inside a chamber with a window that faces the street," he told them. "The windowsill is about five feet off the road, so we should be able to get underneath it."

Tate nodded. "That's a stroke of good luck," he said. "At least they aren't in a chamber over our heads."

"That is exactly what Ken and I were saying to one another."

"Where *is* Ken?"

"Trying to get near the interior door so he can listen in."

Tate turned to Stephen. "Join him," he said, watching the tall knight rush off. Then he turned back to Leonidas. "You and I can listen from the street."

Leonidas nodded. "Quickly," he said. "She has just been admitted."

He seemed to be in professional mode. At least, that was what Tate thought. Leonidas seemed very much in control of himself, and the truth was that Tate expected nothing less. He didn't want to say anything to him about Christelle, not when they were in the heat of a mission like they were right now. Somehow, it didn't seem appropriate. But later, in private, he would. However, given what Phillipa had told them, he found it hard to believe that there was ever a love affair between Leonidas and Christelle. From the way Leonidas was acting, he would have never known.

Perhaps it hadn't been that serious after all.

Leonidas was in the lead as they made their way down to the tavern with its wattle and daub walls and exposed, painted beams. Silently, Leonidas indicated which window it was and they got up underneath the sill, listening to what was a rather loud conversation in parts.

Someone was very unhappy.

"And what did you do to convince her that you were not a spy? Did you try to convince her that she misread the missives? Better still, did you stress that her actions were wrong?"

Leonidas had no idea who was speaking. The voice sounded thin and full of angst. But he heard, very clearly, when Christelle responded in her soft, steady tone.

"Her actions were not wrong. As I told you, she did not speak directly to me about this. I was told by one of her knights. He is the one who banished me rather than execute me. A man who taught me the important things in life, like honesty and loyalty. I owe him everything."

Hearing those words were like daggers. Tiny little daggers

being flung out of the window and into his body, where the pain was unbearable. He realized that he was more than likely going to hear everything she wanted to tell him but he hadn't let her. He had shut her up because there was nothing she could say that could prompt him to believe her or even forgive her. But it further occurred to him that everything he was hearing wasn't for his benefit.

These were Christelle's own words, unrehearsed.

Painfully honest.

He lowered his head, closing his eyes as he listened to the conversation, which was shockingly clear. No muffled voices, no whispers. He heard Christelle speak of Phillipa's discovery, how she knew Christelle was a spy, and he heard at least two men badgering her on why she hadn't tried to lie her way out of it. Christelle remained firm about it, giving them the honorable answer Leonidas had so believed she was capable of. That sounded more like the Christelle he'd fallen in love with. Fearless in the face of adversity.

That was the young woman who had risked her life to save a drowning child.

Christy.

The pain he'd been trying to fight off was now embedding itself in him, like the talons of a falcon into its prey. He was feeling the physical pain now, something he was struggling not to surrender to. Hearing the words of truth from a young woman he'd believed in, once. Perhaps the truth was that he had always believed in her, even when Phillipa had told him the truth. There was a huge part of him that hadn't wanted to believe any of it because that wasn't the Christelle he knew. But he couldn't refute the evidence. That terrible, confusing evidence.

But then he heard something that caused him to open his eyes.

"Your arrival in town is fortuitous because I was going to send you a missive telling you that I refuse to spy on Phillipa any longer. Now I can tell you face to face."

Leonidas lifted his head, locking gazes with Tate as he did so. The two of them stared at one another as they both heard the same thing—a declaration from Christelle of her true intentions. Words that weren't spoken in desperation, only honesty.

But those honest words weren't well met by those she was speaking to.

There was a good deal of back and forth after that, with a man who was obviously Christelle's father and also another man she had called her father's dog. There was also the mention of someone else, someone named Mort, but if he was in the chamber, he had yet to make a sound.

Then the Blackchurch confession came out.

After that, the argument began to grow more intense. The more Leonidas listened, the more he began to transform from betrayed lover to the man who could only see that the woman he loved was in a difficult position. Repeatedly, he'd heard her tell her father that all she wanted to do was live a true and decent life, and repeatedly, he scorned her for it. She spoke of finding a decent man and having children, something that sang to Leonidas' heart, because up until earlier that day, he had also been having visions of his future with her. He was a true and decent man. He was *her* man.

Do you love me enough to forgive me?

She'd asked him that question, once, and his answer had been unkind. But after the unsolicited confession he'd just heard from her as part of this conversation, he was more than willing to change his answer to the affirmative.

Yes, he did love her enough to forgive her.

Everyone made mistakes.

She clearly wanted to learn from hers.

But then came the biggest confession of all.

"I tried for years to please a man who would never be pleased. But now… now, it is my mark of greatness. You think I have shamed you, and I am happy you think so. Bernard, I do not want to follow you into the dark underbelly of politics any longer. Before, I had no choice, but now I do. I realize now that I want to live in the light, with people who are good and decent. Decent like Phillipa, who is the kindest, most genuinely caring person I have ever met. She lives in the light. I want to be more like her. That was a side of life that you never introduced me to."

Leonidas had to smile when heard that. It sounded so much like the Christelle he knew.

The one he loved.

In fact, he was losing himself in the relief of forgiveness when they heard a slapping sound and something hit the floor. Startled, both he and Tate tried to listen a little closer to what was going on. Fortunately, the sun had gone down and the street was mostly barren, so their activity wasn't terribly obvious, but that wouldn't last forever.

They had to figure out what was happening before their cover was blown.

More conversation, this time about Phillipa and the child that she carried. It took very little time for them to realize there was a fight going on inside the chamber, and Leonidas instinctively put his hand to the hilt of his sword, preparing to go to battle. Christelle was in that chamber and he knew she wasn't armed. Her sword was still lying in the field north of the castle. But the moment he put his hand on his sword, Tate reached out to stop him.

The Earl of Carlisle had other ideas.

Silently, Tate motioned his intentions—that he was going to try to catch a peek at what was going on inside the chamber. Leonidas kept an eye out on their surroundings as Tate stood up and peered into the chamber through the slats in the window shutters. It took him all of a few seconds to see what was going on, and when he did, he grabbed Leonidas by the arm.

"Inside, now, or she dies," he whispered. "Leo, *go!*"

Leonidas didn't hesitate. He launched himself through the wooden shutters, through the window, and burst into the chamber just as a big knight twice the size of Christelle smashed her head against the floor. As she lay there, limp and bleeding, the Wolfe on the hunt went to work. Sword in an offensive position, Leonidas flashed his fangs before attacking the man who had injured Christelle. The knight didn't have time to unsheathe his sword, but he lifted an arm to protect himself and Leonidas sliced right through it. As the man bellowed in pain and his left hand fell to the floor, severed, the chamber door burst open.

Kenneth and Stephen barreled in.

There were swords flying all over the place, and in the middle of it, men were screaming. Bernard, who was armed, was the first to be cut down by Kenneth, who only saw what Leonidas saw—Christelle on the floor with blood on her head. Gautier proved to be a little more difficult for Stephen because he managed to unsheathe his weapon, but he was no match for the tall, powerful knight. That left Leonidas going after the warrior who had attacked Christelle as Tate launched himself through the window with the sole intention of removing the wounded woman from the chamber.

With Kenneth and Stephen dragging Bernard and Gautier out of the chamber, Tate followed with a limp Christelle. Leonidas, however, had his hands full with a man whose missing hand only seemed to enrage him. He wasn't as big as Leonidas was, or as skilled, but he had a beastly fury that fed his survival instinct.

He was formidable.

A kick to Leonidas' thigh had sent him stumbling back enough that his opponent could unsheathe his broadsword. He was right-handed, so the missing left hand didn't matter. All it did was spray blood all over the walls, the ceiling, the floor, and Leonidas. The warrior was crazed with pain and fury, and Leonidas found himself fighting off a serious offensive. But the truth was that no one was a match for a de Wolfe in battle, and after several hard strikes and chops, Leonidas charged forward, slammed an elbow into his opponent's nose, and then used his sword to spill the man's guts all over the chamber floor.

And that was the end of it.

Without hesitation, Leonidas vaulted back out through the window in time to catch sight of Kenneth and Stephen dumping bodies in the river. He shouted and they turned to see him, pointing toward the livery two doors down.

Leonidas raced into the livery.

Tate had just laid Christelle down on some clean straw. It was dark in the livery, but there was enough light from the torches out on the street outside to cast a small bit of illumination inside. Leonidas dropped to his knees beside her as Tate examined her skull.

"How bad?" Leonidas said anxiously.

Tate looked at the man, covered in blood from his fight. "Is any of that blood yours?"

Leonidas hadn't even realized how much gore was on him. He looked down at himself. "None of it," he said. "It is all from my opponent."

Tate's focus returned to Christelle. "Tell Ken and Stephen to get the body of the man you killed out of that chamber and dump him in the river with the others," he said. "I hear that Hull is a man who stands for justice, and he might not like what we've done."

Leonidas waggled his eyebrows. "Under normal circumstances, you would be correct," he said. "But in this case, justice was served as far as I'm concerned. Those who would harm Christelle have been found guilty and the sentence was carried out. But your point is taken. I will go back to the tavern and give them some coin to compensate for the mess they're faced with."

"Lord Hull is not only fair, but he is generous, too."

Leonidas would have smiled at the comment had he the strength to do so, but he didn't. His focus was on Christelle's bloodied face as Tate finished examining her head.

"I do not feel any breaks," Tate finally said. "But she is wounded. Leo, I'd like to take her back to the castle where she can be properly cared for, but I also know what has transpired between you two. I do not want to create any trouble for you, so I will let you decide. If you'd rather not take her back to the castle, then I am certain we can find another tavern and let a room for her where a physic can attend her."

Leonidas was shaking his head before the man was even

finished. "We will take her back to Ashendon," he said. "Phillipa is an excellent nurse, and I am certain she will want to help."

"But what about you?"

"What *about* me?"

"Are you going to force me to be plain about it?"

Leonidas knew what he meant. He looked at the man, sighing heavily. "You needn't worry about my feelings," he said softly. "I just want her to be well again, truly. Let's focus on her, please."

Tate fought off a smile. "Spoken like a man who is truly in love," he said quietly. "Knowing the little of this situation that I do, I would say that she did say several things that would vindicate her in my eyes."

"I know."

"I believe they were honest words, of her honest intentions."

"I agree."

"Sometimes people, women in particular, are forced to—"

"*Nay!*"

Christelle suddenly came around, remembering her last moments of a fight, and began to kick and swing her arms. She clipped Tate in the mouth with a fist before Leonidas managed to grab her flailing arms.

"Christy, stop," he said firmly but gently. "You're safe, sweetheart. Look who is here with you—Tate is here. I am here. You are safe, I promise. No one is going to hurt you."

Christelle couldn't see very well because of the blood that had trickled down to seal her left eye shut, but she heard Leonidas' voice and that calmed her down considerably. It also greatly confused her.

"Leo?" she said, sounding incredulous. "What... what are

you doing here?"

The sound of her voice nearly undid him. All he could think of was how cruel and unforgiving he had been—and how brave she had been in standing up to her father the way she had. All she'd ever been was brave, and God help him, he loved her for it. He forced a smile as a lone tear popped out of his left eye.

"We came to help," he said simply, collecting her hand and bringing it to his lips. "Christy, I am so sorry for what I said to you. Sorry for being harsh. You asked me if I loved you enough to forgive you, and you must forgive me for giving you the wrong answer. Of course I love you enough. I think I always have."

She just looked at him, watching him as he kissed the palm of her hand again, before answering.

"Am I dead?" she asked.

Leonidas chuckled softly. "Nay, sweetheart, you are not," he said. "Why do you ask?"

"Because only in heaven would you be saying such things to me."

He nodded, weakly, his gaze fixed on her, and more tears began popping out of his eyes, which he struggled to control. "You are not dead," he said. "And we are not in heaven. We are in Hull, where you were meeting with your father. Do you remember?"

She began to struggle to sit up, and no matter how much Leonidas and Tate tried to hold her down, she fought to go in the other direction, so they gently pulled her into a sitting position. Her hand went to her head, where it was bloodied, and her eye.

"What is on my face?" she said. "Why can't I see?"

Tate stood up, looking around for water to clean her eye off with, as Leonidas tried to keep her calm. "There was a fight," he said steadily. "You were wounded. Do you not recall?"

She was still trying to pull gunk off her left eye so she could see something. "I remember… my father!"

She looked at him in horror, and he put his arm around her shoulders to steady her because she was weaving around, unbalanced and dazed. "Your father was here," he said evenly. "But there was a fight and he was killed. He and his comrades."

Memories began tumbling down on her, disjointed, and she grabbed hold of him. "He wanted Phillipa," she said. "I swear to you, I was not going to give her over to him. I would never do that!"

He nodded soothingly, kissing her on her non-bloodied forehead. "I know, sweetheart," he said gently. "I know. You needn't worry. I know everything."

Things were becoming a little clearer to her, and she paused in her panic, but still looked at him most anxiously. "I am sorry, Leo," she said, her lower lip trembling now. "I am so sorry for what I have done. You trusted me and—"

He kissed her to quiet her. "Listen to me," he murmured. "I know everything. I know who you are and what you are. I know the depth of your honor and your quest for truth. I've always known that about you, Christy. You are a woman of astounding bravery and compassion, a rare and precious jewel that I shall spend my life trying to be worthy of."

Hardly able to believe what she was hearing, Christelle put her free hand on his cheek tenderly. "You… you said I ruined everything with my deceit."

He closed his eyes at the sound of his own words. "I ruined it with my lack of understanding," he said. "You are not that woman who first came into Phillipa's service. You have changed and you have grown. You still need to run a comb through your hair every so often, and there are times when you make me daft, but please let that be something I must endure for the rest of my life."

"But…"

He shushed her softly. "What has happened over the past few hours does not define who we are," he murmured. "It is done and over with. We are strong together, you and I. And I cannot wait to share my life with you, if you'll still have me."

Realizing that the anguish they had experienced so recently was something he was willing to put behind them brought about a smile that was brighter than the sun. Bruised chin and all, she put both her hands on his face and kissed him with more love and adoration than she'd ever thought possible. By the time Tate returned with some water to clean off her face, she was holding Leonidas so tightly that it took both Tate and Leonidas to loosen her grip so they could tend to her wounds. Even then, she kept a grip on Leonidas as if to never let him go.

And she wouldn't.

Ever.

For the woman who had been used as a pawn most of her life and the Wolfe who had struggled to find his way in life, the advent of a red cross stitched on a forehead was a catalyst for greater things to come. A love that was as unbreakable as the honor of the people who shared it.

We are strong together, you and I.

And they were.

EPILOGUE

Ashendon
Eight months later

"A RIDER, CHRISTY!"

Christelle had been staring morosely at a garment she'd been trying to sew for the better part of a month. She had never had serious training when it came to creative sewing, and although Phillipa had tried to teach her, it seemed that she really didn't have any talent for it. Stitching up a man's wound, yes. Stitching together a tunic, no. Her garment looked like a blind man had put it together. However, Catherine's excited words had her leaping up from her chair.

"Where?" she demanded. "And if you go running down those stairs again, Catherine de Cottingham de Shera, I will personally tie you to your bed until your husband returns. Do you hear me?"

Catherine grinned. At almost nine months pregnant with her first child, she was round and rosy and happier than anyone had ever seen her, in sharp contrast to Christelle, who was almost seven months pregnant and feeling every twitch, every pain.

Well, almost.

Their husbands had gone off with Edward to subdue Roger Mortimer once and for all, but that had been six months ago. Six months of waiting for word, of trying to keep busy, and of enduring what had been a rather harsh winter so far. Lots of rain and storms, and Christelle was ready to sell her soul to the devil for a bit of sunshine. On this very day, in fact, they'd had a little, and now Catherine was declaring that a messenger was on the approach. It was a good day, indeed.

Perhaps it was what they had been waiting for.

News.

News of their husbands, of Mortimer, and of England in general. Perhaps it was even news from Phillipa, who had delivered a healthy son during the summer months, and his name was Edward. That was the same name Christelle was considering for her firstborn because it was Leonidas' father's name and she rather liked it. Not that Leonidas even knew he had a child coming, because she'd been reluctant to tell him, fearful that it would distract him from the very serious task of subduing Roger Mortimer. But she knew she couldn't wait much longer to tell him or the child would be his own introduction.

Hopefully the messenger was coming with news that her husband was on his way home.

She could only hope.

"I will not run down the stairs," Catherine said, breaking into her train of thought. "And the messenger could just as easily be about Gabriel."

Christelle moved over to the window that overlooked the gatehouse, spying a tiny speck, a rider, on the road beyond.

"Why would Castle Questing be sending news about Gabriel?" she said. "He has only been there for a few months."

Catherine's smile faded. "I still think he was a little young to go," she said. "It seems cruel to send him away."

Christelle turned toward her. "I know," she said, coming to the door. "But Leo explained that he would be well taken care of, surrounded by other pages, and it would give him something to focus on other than the loss of his sister. The last missive we did receive about him said that he was settling in nicely."

"Do you think he'll even remember me?"

Christelle put her arm around the young woman's shoulders and led her toward the stairwell. "I think he'll remember you and love you," she said. "Come along—let us go and meet the messenger."

With renewed vigor, Catherine went down the stairs, a little too fast for Christelle's liking, and the two of them headed out of the keep. By the time they crossed the muddy bailey to the gatehouse, the messenger had arrived and Zander was there to greet them. He was the only knight that had been left behind when Leonidas took his army to Nottingham, a gentle knight who did very well in a command position. When he saw the ladies, he handed the missive right over to Christelle.

"Lady de Wolfe," he said, smiling. "From your husband."

Christelle couldn't help but let out a little squeal of delight. "I pray that it is news they are coming home," she said as she quickly popped the wax seal and carefully unfolded it. Whereas most warlords had clerks or scribes who wrote their correspondence, Leonidas preferred to write his own. That was great comfort for Christelle, who ran her fingers lovingly over the careful letters before she began to read. Realizing she had an audience standing around, waiting for the news, she read aloud.

My dearest wife,

I hope this message finds you well. I miss you more than all the poets in all the world can describe, but I take comfort in knowing we will soon be together. I am sorry we could not make it home for Christmas mass, but our task against Mortimer was successful. Isabelle was true to her word. We captured them both in October and Mortimer was tried and hanged on 29 November. Edward is now king, by God and by right, and Parliament is convening. I shall remain until it is disbanded, at which time I will rush home faster than is probably safe or necessary, but my want to see you is so great that if I had wings, I would fly to you this very moment.

Talan wishes to tell Catie that he will see her soon and to not have his son before he returns home. I would also ask the same of you, seeing as you have not seen fit to mention something that Catie told Talan. I will continue to pretend I do not know about my son, but know that I would like to name him after my father if you are agreeable. A lad that will go on to do great, courageous things. I could not be prouder of him or of you. You are my world, Lady de Wolfe, and I love you more with each breath I take.

Faithfully yours,
L

Christelle was wiping away tears by the time she was finished, but they were tears of joy. She was, however, greatly perturbed with Catherine, and when she looked up from the letter, Catherine put her hands up in surrender.

"It is Talan's fault," she insisted. "I told him *not* to tell."

Christelle rolled her eyes. "Of course it is his fault," she said. "You had nothing to do with it."

Catherine didn't have an answer for her. She shrugged sheepishly, and Christelle was angry for a few seconds more before she simply gave up and put her arm around the young woman's shoulders again. She handed the missive off to Zander so he could read it for himself, but not before telling the young knight that she wanted it back. It would be something she read, and reread, until her husband was safe in her arms once more.

A man who helped shape the direction of a nation.

These were days of solace and hope, days in which a new future was promised with a strong, young king to guide them. A king shaped by men who were forged by honor and driven by steel, who helped make a fine country for their children and their children's children.

Men like Leonidas de Wolfe.

Tate de Lara.

Kenneth St. Hever.

Stephen of Pembury.

That generation of men who lived by the sword in the hopes of something greater.

Christelle had been honored enough to know those men and deeply humbled to have married one of them. The man they called *Le Morsure*, the Bite, was the man who had become her everything and then some.

Stitching that red cross on his forehead was the best thing she'd ever done.

La protecteur de la reine had found her true calling in love...

The best calling of all.

❦ THE END ❧

De Wolfe Pack Generations:

WolfeHeart

WolfeStrike

WolfeSword

WolfeBlade

WolfeLord

WolfeShield

Nevermore

WolfeAx

WolfeBorn

WolfeBite

Leonidas and Christelle's children

Edward "Ward"

William

Matthias

Lance

Lucien

Henry

Caspian

James

Georgiana

Sophia

AFTERWORD

ROGER MORTIMER REALLY was captured in Nottingham in October 1330, followed by his execution in November. Isabella was exiled to one of her properties. Of course, this tale told just one small part of a very complex situation involving Edward III and Roger Mortimer, but it was fun to weave the actual events into Leonidas and Christelle's story. Edward III never gave up his quest for the French throne, by the way. His determination to press his claim is what started the Hundred Years' War.

Also, I have to tell you about the whole "fish and onions" thing. Those are probably two of the things I hate most on this earth, and many years ago, while I was dating a VERY handsome man (who is not my husband), we went to Hawaii and took a catamaran out to the east side of Maui to snorkel. Well, I have a problem with seasickness, anyway, but I didn't want to disappoint this guy, so I popped a Dramamine and went on this boat. And it was a rocky day on the ocean (though beautiful) and the Dramamine couldn't really compete with the extreme seasickness that I was feeling. The captain of the catamaran prepared lunch for his passengers and—what do you know—it was fish and onions cooked in foil. Well, he opened up that foil, I took one whiff, and over the side I went. Literally. I jumped over the side of the boat. We were about a half-mile from shore and I started swimming for it like crazy. Anything to get away from that rocking boat and fish and onions. My date had to jump in and bring me back to the boat, where I suffered until that horrible adventure was over. So—my experience is Christelle's experience with that damn fish and onions (which was a dish in Medieval times!).

Sadly, I will always make a terrible pirate…

Hugs,

Kathryn

The Parents, Children, and Grandchildren of de Wolfe

(Note: Don't be intimidated by these family trees—refer to them if you need clarification on a relationship)

<u>William (deceased 1296 A.D.) and Jordan Scott de Wolfe</u>
Total children: 10
Total grandchildren: 75+ (including 4 deceased, 7 adopted, 3 step grandchildren)

Scott (Troy's twin)—(Wife #1 Lady Athena de Norville, has issue. Wife #2 Lady Avrielle Huntley du Rennic, has issue)

With Athena
- William "Will"
- Thomas "Tor"
- Andrew (deceased)
- Beatrice (deceased)

With Avrielle
- Sophia (with Nathaniel du Rennic)
- Stephen (with Nathaniel du Rennic)
- Sorcha (with Nathaniel du Rennic)
- Jeremy
- Nathaniel
- Alexander

- Seraphina
- Jordan

Troy (Scott's twin)—(Wife #1 Lady Helene de Norville, has issue. Wife #2 Lady Rhoswyn Kerr, has issue)

With Helene
- Andreas
- Acacia (deceased)
- Arista (deceased)

With Rhoswyn
- Gareth
- Corey
- Reed
- Tavin
- Tristan
- Elsbeth
- Madeleine

Patrick—(Married to Lady Brighton de Favereux, has issue)
- Markus
- Cassius
- Magnus
- Titus
- Thora
- Kristiana

James—(Wife #1 Lady Rose Hage, has issue. Wife #2 Asmara ferch Cader, has issue)

With Rose

- Ronan
- Isabella

With Asmara (as Blayth)

- Maddoc
- Bowen
- Caius
- Garreth (known as Garr)

Katheryn (James' twin)—(Married to Sir Alec Hage, has issue)

- Edward
- Axel
- Christoph
- Kieran
- Christian

Evelyn—(Married to Sir Hector de Norville, has issue)

- Atreus
- Hermes
- Lisbet
- Adele
- Aline
- Lesander (goes by Zander)

Baby de Wolfe—(Died same day. Christened Madeleine)

Edward—(Married to Lady Cassiopeia de Norville, has issue)

- Helene 1281

- Phoebe 1283
- Hestia 1286
- Asteria 1289
- Leonidas 1291
- Dorian 1294
- Dayne 1297
- Stephan 1299
- Pallas 1306

Thomas—(Married to Lady Maitland "Mae" de Ryes Bowlin, has issue)

- Artus (adopted)
- Nora (adopted)
- Phin (adopted)
- Marybelle (adopted)
- Renard & Roland (adopted)
- Dyana (adopted)
- Alexander
- Cabot
- Matthew
- Wade
- Tacey
- Morgan

Penelope—(Married to Bhrodi de Shera, Earl of Coventry, hereditary King of Anglesey, has issue)

- William
- Perri

- Bowen
- Dai
- Catrin
- Morgana
- Maddock
- Anthea
- Talan 1305

Kieran and Jemma Scott Hage

- Mary Alys (adopted)—(married, has issue)
- Baby Hage, died same day. Christened Bridget
- Alec (married to Lady Katheryn de Wolfe, has issue)
- Christian (died in the Holy Land 1269 A.D., no issue)
- Moira (married to Sir Apollo de Norville, has issue)
- Kevin (married to Lady Annavieve de Ferrers, has issue)
- Rose (widow of Sir James de Wolfe, has issue)
- Nathaniel

Paris and Caladora Scott de Norville

- Hector (married to Lady Evelyn de Wolfe, has issue)
- Apollo (married to Lady Moira Hage, has issue)
- Helene (married to Sir Troy de Wolfe, has issue)
- Athena (married to Sir Scott de Wolfe, has issue)
- Adonis
- Cassiopeia (married to Sir Edward de Wolfe, has issue)

Holdings and Titles of the House of de Wolfe and close allies as of 1293 A.D.

Scott de Wolfe—Baron Kilham, heir to the Earldom of Warenton (Heir: William "Will" de Wolfe)

Troy de Wolfe—Lord Braemoor (Heir: Andreas de Wolfe)

Patrick de Wolfe—Earl of Berwick (Heir: Markus de Wolfe, Lord Ravensdowne.)

Blayth (James) de Wolfe—Baron Sydenham (Heir: Ronan de Wolfe)

Edward de Wolfe—Baron Kentmere (Heir: Leonidas de Wolfe)

Thomas de Wolfe—Earl of Northumbria (Heir: Alexander de Wolfe, Lord Easington)

Wark Castle (Wolfe's Eye):
Larger outpost for the Earl of Warenton. Literally sits on the border between England and Scotland.

- Titus de Wolfe (son of Patrick de Wolfe), commander (moved to Jedburgh as of 1312)

Berwick Castle (Wolfe's Teeth):
Massive border castle, strategically important, de Wolfe holding and seat of the Earl of Berwick, Patrick de Wolfe.

- Alec Hage, commander
- Edward "Eddie" Hage, commander

Castle Questing (Wolfe's Heart):

Massive fortress, seat of the Earl of Warenton, Scott de Wolfe.

- Apollo de Norville, second
- Nathaniel Hage
- Owen le Mon

Rule Water Castle (Wolfe's Lair):

The largest outpost in the de Wolfe empire, known as The Lair. At this time, commanded by Thomas "Tor" de Wolfe.

- Magnus de Wolfe, second
- Adonis de Norville, second
- Perri de Shera, son of the Earl of Coventry and Penelope de Wolfe de Shera (squire)

Monteviot Tower (Wolfe's Shield):

Smaller outpost in Scotland, strategic. Holding of Troy de Wolfe.

- Brodie de Reyne, commander

Kale Water Castle (Wolfe's Den):

Larger outpost on the England side of the border, strategic.

- Troy de Wolfe, Lord Braemoor, commander
- Troy also commands Sibbald's Hold, former home of Red Keith Kerr (his wife's father). A minor property commanded by son, Gareth de Wolfe.

Kyloe Castle (Wolfe's Howl):

Seat of the Earl of Northumbria, Thomas de Wolfe.

- Christoph Hage, second

Roxburgh Castle (Wolfe's Claw—unofficially) *

Large royal-held castle near Kelso, formerly manned by knights from Northwood, but awarded to the House of de Wolfe by royal decree for meritorious service to the crown. Volatile location, often attacked by Scots, and is manned by both royal and de Wolfe troops.

- Blayth (James) de Wolfe, Lord Sydenham, commander
- Axel Hage, second

*Note: Because of the extreme volatile location and nature of this garrison, Blayth (James) de Wolfe was given the title Lord Sydenham and the Sydenham Barony, a small but strategic barony between Wark Castle and the town of Kelso.

Carlisle Castle (Wolfe's Fangs):

Massive and large royal-held castle, perhaps one of the largest castles in the north. Awarded to the House of de Wolfe by royal decree. Very volatile location, often attacked by Scots, and has changed hands many times in its history. The castle is manned by both royal and de Wolfe troops.

- Will de Wolfe, Lord Irthington, commander
- Hermes de Norville

Northwood Castle:

Massive border castle, very important and strategic. Belonging to the Earls of Teviot. Not part of the de Wolfe empire, but strongly allied to de Wolfe by marriage and blood. The Earl of Teviot is John Adrian de Longley, Adam de Longley's eldest son. John's mother is Cayetana Fernanda Teresita Silva y Fausto de Longley, Princess of Aragon.

- Hector de Norville, captain of the guard (also Lord Bowmont)
- Atreus de Norville, second
- Tobias de Bocage, second

Castle Canaan (Wolfe's Bite):

The Earl of Warenton's southernmost holding in Kendal, not directly related to the Scottish border but a source of additional troops if needed. Inherited the property when he married the widow of Castle Canaan.

- Stephan du Rennic, commander

Seven Gates Castle:

Seat of Edward de Wolfe's Barony—Kentmere in Kendal that adjoins brother Scott's lands at Castle Canaan.

- Isleworth House, Surrey

Hell's Guardhouse (The Hermitage):

- Andreas de Wolfe, commander
- Theodis de Velt, second

Ravenscar (fortified manse near Scarborough):

- Ronan de Wolfe
- Christian Hage

Jedburgh Castle (1312)

- Titus de Wolfe, Commander
- Peter Summerlin
- Reynard and Roland de Wolfe

Ashendon Castle, East Yorkshire (1330)

Belongs to Leonidas de Wolfe, Earl of Hull

- Dayne de Wolfe
- Zander de Norville
- Talan de Shera

KATHRYN LE VEQUE NOVELS

Medieval Romance:

De Wolfe Pack Series:
Warwolfe
The Wolfe
Nighthawk
ShadowWolfe
DarkWolfe
A Joyous de Wolfe Christmas
BlackWolfe
Serpent
A Wolfe Among Dragons
Scorpion
StormWolfe
Dark Destroyer
The Lion of the North
Walls of Babylon
The Best Is Yet To Be
BattleWolfe
Castle of Bones

De Wolfe Pack Generations:
WolfeHeart
WolfeStrike
WolfeSword
WolfeBlade
WolfeLord
WolfeShield
Nevermore
WolfeAx
WolfeBorn
WolfeBite

The Executioner Knights:
By the Unholy Hand
The Mountain Dark
Starless
A Time of End
Winter of Solace
Lord of the Sky
The Splendid Hour
The Whispering Night
Netherworld
Lord of the Shadows
Of Mortal Fury
'Twas the Executioner Knight
Before Christmas
Crimson Shield
The Black Dragon

The de Russe Legacy:
The Falls of Erith
Lord of War: Black Angel
The Iron Knight
Beast
The Dark One: Dark Knight
The White Lord of Wellesbourne
Dark Moon
Dark Steel
A de Russe Christmas Miracle
Dark Warrior

The de Lohr Dynasty:
While Angels Slept
Rise of the Defender
Steelheart

Shadowmoor
Silversword
Spectre of the Sword
Unending Love
Archangel
A Blessed de Lohr Christmas
Lion of Twilight
Lion of War
Lion of Hearts
Lion of Steel

The Brothers de Lohr:
The Earl in Winter

Lords of East Anglia:
While Angels Slept
Godspeed
Age of Gods and Mortals

Great Lords of le Bec:
Great Protector

House of de Royans:
Lord of Winter
To the Lady Born
The Centurion

Lords of Eire:
Echoes of Ancient Dreams
Lord of Black Castle
The Darkland

Ancient Kings of Anglecynn:
The Whispering Night
Netherworld

Battle Lords of de Velt:
The Dark Lord
Devil's Dominion
Bay of Fear
The Dark Lord's First Christmas

The Dark Spawn
The Dark Conqueror
The Dark Angel

Reign of the House of de Winter:
Lespada
Swords and Shields

De Reyne Domination:
Guardian of Darkness
The Black Storm
A Cold Wynter's Knight
With Dreams
Master of the Dawn
One Wylde Knight

House of d'Vant:
Tender is the Knight (House of
d'Vant)
The Red Fury (House of d'Vant)

The Dragonblade Series:
Fragments of Grace
Dragonblade
Island of Glass
The Savage Curtain
The Fallen One
The Phantom Bride

Great Marcher Lords of de Lara
Lord of the Shadows
Dragonblade

House of St. Hever
Fragments of Grace
Island of Glass
Queen of Lost Stars

Lords of Pembury:
The Savage Curtain

**Lords of Thunder: The de Shera
Brotherhood Trilogy**
The Thunder Lord
The Thunder Warrior
The Thunder Knight

The Great Knights of de Moray:
Shield of Kronos
The Gorgon

The House of De Nerra:
The Promise
The Falls of Erith
Vestiges of Valor
Realm of Angels

Highland Legion:
Highland Born
Highland Destroyer

Highland Warriors of Munro:
The Red Lion
Deep Into Darkness

The House of de Garr:
Lord of Light
Realm of Angels

Saxon Lords of Hage:
The Crusader
Kingdom Come

High Warriors of Rohan:
High Warrior
High King

The House of Ashbourne:
Upon a Midnight Dream

The House of D'Aurilliac:
Valiant Chaos

The House of De Dere:
Of Love and Legend

St. John and de Gare Clans:
The Warrior Poet

The House of de Bretagne:
The Questing

The House of Summerlin:
The Legend

The Kingdom of Hendocia:
Kingdom by the Sea

**The BlackChurch Guild: Shadow
Knights:**
The Leviathan
The Protector
The Swordsman

Guard of Six:
Absolution

Regency Historical Romance:
Sin Like Flynn: A Regency
Historical Romance Duet
The Sin Commandments
Georgina and the Red Charger

Gothic Regency Romance:
Emma

Historical Fiction:
The Girl Made Of Stars

Contemporary Romance:

**Kathlyn Trent/Marcus Burton
Series:**
Valley of the Shadow
The Eden Factor

Canyon of the Sphinx

Sons of Poseidon:
The Immortal Sea

The Eagle Brotherhood (under the pen name Kat Le Veque):
The Sunset Hour
The Killing Hour
The Secret Hour
The Unholy Hour
The Burning Hour
The Ancient Hour
The Devil's Hour

Pirates of Britannia Series (with Eliza Knight):
Savage of the Sea by Eliza Knight
Leader of Titans by Kathryn Le Veque
The Sea Devil by Eliza Knight
Sea Wolfe by Kathryn Le Veque

Note: All Kathryn's novels are designed to be read as stand-alones, although many have cross-over characters or cross-over family groups. Novels that are grouped together have related characters or family groups. You will notice that some series have the same books; that is because they are cross-overs. A hero in one book may be the secondary character in another.

There is NO reading order except by chronology, but even in that case, you can still read the books as stand-alones. No novel is connected to another by a cliff hanger, and every book has an HEA.

Series are clearly marked. All series contain the same characters or family groups except the American Heroes Series, which is an anthology with unrelated characters.

For more information, find it in **A Reader's Guide to the Medieval World of Le Veque**.

ABOUT KATHRYN LE VEQUE

Bringing the Medieval to Romance

KATHRYN LE VEQUE is a critically acclaimed, multiple USA TODAY Bestselling author, an Indie Reader bestseller, a charter Amazon All-Star author, and a #1 bestselling, award-winning, multi-published author in Medieval Historical Romance with over 100 published novels.

Kathryn is a multiple award nominee and winner, including the winner of Uncaged Book Reviews Magazine 2017 and 2018 "Raven Award" for Favorite Medieval Romance. Kathryn is also a multiple RONE nominee (InD'Tale Magazine), holding a record for the number of nominations. In 2018, her novel WARWOLFE was the winner in the Romance category of the Book Excellence Award and in 2019, her novel A WOLFE AMONG DRAGONS won the prestigious RONE award for best pre-16th century romance.

Kathryn is considered one of the top Indie authors in the world with over 2M copies in circulation, and her novels have been translated into several languages. Kathryn recently signed with Sourcebooks Casablanca for a Medieval Fight Club series, first published in 2020.

In addition to her own published works, Kathryn is also the President/CEO of Dragonblade Publishing, a boutique publishing house specializing in Historical Romance. Dragonblade's success has seen it rise in the ranks to become Amazon's #1 e-book publisher of Historical Romance (K-Lytics report July 2020).

Kathryn loves to hear from her readers. Please find Kathryn on Facebook at Kathryn Le Veque, Author, or join her on Twitter @kathrynleveque. Sign up for Kathryn's blog at www.kathrynleveque.com for the latest news and sales.